M*ichelle slapped the side* of the computer screen.

Hard.

The screen flashed to life in an eye-searing array of blacks and greens. The old thing shimmered, strobed, and at long last stabilized. The computer terminal was the only object on her vast, black-obsidian desk other than a massive cup of coffee.

Cut that out! The words etched onto the screen as if driven with chisel into stone one painful stroke at a time.

She smacked it again. After all, she was the Devil, there was no way she'd let the universe's software boss her around. She was so sick of it all. Hell, Heaven, Creation… All of it. And, while it made for a sad statement, if the Universal Software was the only thing left that she could feel superior to, she'd make the best she could out of browbeating it.

One more whack.

Hey! No slow etching this time. *Couldn't y'all just tap the space bar like everyone else?*

"Less fun," Michelle typed. And it was. After fourteen billion years, her life had come to this, sad as it was. Harassing the Universal Software and waking up every morning in Hell.

Of course, being the Devil Incarnate made the latter a common enough occurrence; she should be used to it by now.

Deities Anonymous

Cookbook from Hell: Reheated

by

M. L. Buchman

Discover more by this author at: www.buchmanbookworks.com

Cover images:
Surreal Heavenly Doorway © AreanaCreative | Dreamstime

Buchman Bookworks

Other works by this author:

Deities Anonymous
Cookbook from Hell: Reheated
Saviors 101

Thrillers
Swap Out!
One Chef!
Two Chef!

The Night Stalkers
The Night Is Mine
I Own the Dawn
Daniel's Christmas
Wait Until Dark
Frank's Independence Day
Peter's Christmas
Take Over at Midnight
Light Up the Night
Christmas at Steel Beach
Bring On the Dusk
Target of the Heart
Target Lock on Love
Christmas at Peleliu Cove
Zachary's Christmas

Firehawks
Pure Heat
Wildfire at Dawn
Full Blaze
Wildfire at Larch Creek
Wildfire on the Skagit
Hot Point

Delta Force
Target Engaged

Angelo's Hearth
Where Dreams are Born
Where Dreams Reside
Maria's Christmas Table
Where Dreams Unfold
Where Dreams Are Written

SF/F Titles
Nara
Monk's Maze

Dedication

To the love of my life.
We met because of this book
and she has borne with me through all of
the trials, tribulations, and the joys ever since.
Especially the joys.
All my love.

DAY ONE

Darkness was upon the face of the deep.
And God said, Let there be light: and there was light.
And God saw the light, that it was good:
and God divided the light from the darkness.

Chapter 1

*E*ric Erikson answered his cell phone without looking up from his computer screen at work. His desk was a shambles of a half-eaten vending-machine sandwich and too many bags of Fritos.

What blocked number would need to be calling him at two in the morning on a Friday night? He was just getting down to the second level of tonight's guilty pleasure, indulging in a new Internet role-playing game. He'd gotten in on the beta release of a new project with the weird name of *Chraze* that looked cool, but he wasn't very far into the world yet.

"E-Squared!"

Well, that told him who the caller was. Only his boss, Valerie McKenzie called him that. Everyone else still called him Eric-Squared, for Eric Erikson but she had edited his name down a year ago, before his job interview with Ms. Incredibly Erudite had even ended.

"Hi, Mac." That was the nickname he'd tagged her with during his first week at McKenzie Book Publishers. It had started as "Mac hold the cheese" because one thing about Valerie McKenzie, she wanted it her way. And she got it. She hated New York, so had convinced a major publisher to let her run her own imprint from Seattle. And then, against all projections, she had made it into a very successful concern.

Now, everyone called her Mac, and "McHell" was a whispered warning that permeated down the halls just moments before she swooped in and touched down like a personalized whirlwind at some poor fool's desk.

"You've got to help me."

Boss in distress. Her voice sounded really wound up, even more than usual. Eyes still glued to the screen, Eric shoved the mouse around to avoid a can of root beer and an unopened bag of peanuts on his desk, barely saving his on-screen avatar from being skewered by a black knight riding a Harley in full armor across a grassy plain in Spain where, according to the stats bar down the side, it hardly ever rained.

"What's up, boss?"

"You know that cookbook?"

No one in the office could avoid "that cookbook." The Mac had torn through the office on a rampage just three days earlier. Mathilda Reeves had finally delivered her latest cookbook manuscript, six weeks late and in miserable shape. The layout team had tried to put it together, but it was a total train wreck. On Wednesday morning, The Mac had grabbed the manuscript, a laptop, and stormed out in order to work from home.

"I know that cookbook." Eric kept his tone carefully neutral. No one had heard from Valerie for three days. Which had made the office calm and peaceful for a pleasant change of pace. Though he did kind of miss her tornadoing around the thirtieth floor of the Two Union Square building, she certainly kept things interesting.

He whacked the black knight's helmet with a handy caveman cudgel, which he'd bought cheap from an on-screen dealer in Neanderthal artifacts. It made the knight's helmet ring like a church bell. Very satisfying.

"Well, the cookbook now insists that it's looking for God."

That froze his hand on the mouse, at just the wrong moment. The knight gunned the Harley's engine and ran over Eric's figure, flattening him into the sod. Then he circled back and rolled over Eric again crosswise. That sucked. This game handed out some serious retributions when your avatar died.

The Mac took his silence as rapt attention rather than cursing to himself.

"I was working on editing and laying out one of the very last recipes, a typical Mathilda dessert, Flan with Lingonberries. What the

Hell is a lingonberry anyway, it's not as if any normal grocery in hell-and-gone Missouri is going to have them in stock, and suddenly the laptop made a gagging sound, like a loud retching. Next thing I know I'm looking at a recipe titled 'Flogging with Lingonberries' and there's an embedded video of some giant red berry wielding a cat o' nine tails on an apple pie holding up its crust to defend itself. When I tried to hit Undo, the berry turned to me and asked me, *by name,* if I knew where to find God? The thing called me Valerie McKenzie for crying out loud. I'm totally creeped out. You've gotta help me. I was almost done and I haven't backed up in days."

It was impressive. As far as he could tell, she hadn't taken a single breath in all that.

"Uh, I can try to fix it." He was still trying to piece together the image of a lingonberry knowing its editor's name. And that she'd used words like "totally" as an adverb and "gotta." And contractions. She was rarely desperate enough to use contractions.

"Good, thanks! Can you… Oh God— No! Wait, I didn't mean to say that. Good thing the software can't hear me or it might start asking me more questions."

Eric wondered if she'd been drinking.

"I'm sorry, I didn't notice the time. Could you come by as soon as you can in the morning? I don't care what time. Pretty please, E-Squared?"

Eric had never heard The Mac apologize, let alone beg. He agreed and instantly she was gone.

He looked back at the screen where the black knight had broken into song, singing harmony on a Norse drinking song with the thudding reverberations coming from the Harley's big exhaust pipes, about how he'd been born to be wild. All the while he kept circling around in different directions to run over Eric's figure that foolishly kept trying to get up from his body-shaped hole in the sod. The wheel patterns over the sod were making the shape of an infinity symbol. Eric shut down the game.

One thing for sure, he wasn't going to wait for the morning. He'd never heard The Mac so flustered. Angry? Often. Perhaps too often, though not usually at him. But genuine distress? That was new.

He grabbed his bicycle helmet. He'd ridden in this morning and then stayed at the office to take advantage of the high-speed connection, and the big screen, to beta test the new game. From McKenzie Book Publishers' Westlake Avenue office to Ravenna was only a couple miles and the Seattle streets would be quiet in the middle of the night.

He hit the street and was already moving before he noticed that the pavement was wet. Eric considered going back to get his rain slicks, but it wasn't raining at the moment, so he just downshifted and hurried north along Westlake, past all of the sailboats and houseboats, up to the Fremont Bridge.

He hit the draw bridge and rolled past the sign, "Welcome to Fremont, the center of the Universe. Set your watch back five minutes." The problem he had was that he didn't wear a watch any more. Instead, he used his cell phone that stayed in perfect sync with the cell provider's signal all on its own. Fremont had, through no fault of its own, gone from arcane to archaic and he felt bad on its behalf.

He cut across town on Thirty-Fourth so he could wave at the huge concrete troll squatting under the Aurora Bridge. The troll had the remains of a VW Beetle clutched in one mighty fist. As usual, he didn't wave back at Eric.

The neighborhoods were all quiet as he sped through. He'd always liked this time of night in Seattle. Most people only saw the bustling city that had doubled in size over the last few decades. But in the middle of the night, there was a silence so deep that he could hear the quiet spatter of his bike tires on the rain-wet streets and the ticking clunks as relay boxes flipped streetlights from red to green just for his passage.

He'd never actually been to The Mac's new apartment. He'd been to the estate she used to have out on Bainbridge Island for last year's Christmas party. A big place filled with canapés and ostentation, that both had and hadn't fit its occupant. Super-editor, The Fearsome Mac, the Woman of Steel, would of course have a sweeping view of Liberty Bay and the Olympic Mountains isolated by large stands of timber along the shore of Port Orchard Bay. And of course she'd be married to some useless guy like Landau McKenzie. He'd been a weird Scottish guy, who looked like a laird and acted like a dweeb. And no sense of humor at all. Not that Mac had one either.

But The Mac had this other side to her, one he spotted only rarely, the human Valerie McKenzie. Sometimes, when exhausted but pleased with herself at shipping off another soon-to-be bestseller, she'd drop by his desk. The woman would collapse in his guest chair and chat for a few minutes. Still perfectly coifed, chestnut-dark hair in a tight French chignon, power suit sharp and expensive, but a smile would emerge and light up her face. Eric had to admit to feeling secretly superior to the rest of the world, as he suspected he was the only one who got to see that life-altering smile.

Everyone else told him he was fantasizing, The Mac never smiled except the way a shark might. So he'd learned to keep his mouth shut, but he'd become more and more intrigued by the Valerie he glimpsed behind The Mac.

Then six months ago she'd divorced Landau Fucking McKenzie, as she now unfailingly referred to him, and life around the office had really become hell. Her mood swings had gone from lethal, to chaotic and lethal.

Her current gripe was that changing back to her maiden name wouldn't do any good because she'd "for reasons unknown" thought it cute that she and Landau Fucking McKenzie had the same last name before she was dumb enough to marry him and how in the world could she have ever thought that was charming? Then she'd launch into yet another diatribe on Landau's character.

Eric considered riding north around Green Lake and getting his car, but he was already so close, he just rode to her house on Ravenna. She'd gotten a place just past the shop that had custom-built his road bike, costing him most of a month's pay, over the crest and down toward the park. She lived in a giant Victorian house from Seattle's heyday, now cut up into eight apartments.

# # #

Eric Erikson hit the buzzer for Valerie's apartment and got no response.

He considered that it was awfully late, she'd probably gone to bed. Maybe he should go. But she'd sounded so desperate.

He hit the buzzer again, longer and harder.

No voice squawked out of the speaker. But there was click, then a groan, like someone in deep pain. Like someone who'd been stabbed, or worse. When the door release buzzed, he went in fast. He shouldered his bike and bolted up the two flights. He dropped his bike in the hall, leaning it against the sturdy mahogany railing that overlooked the stairwell, and knocked on her door with a fast rat-a-tat.

No response.

He was preparing to test his shoulder against her door locks when he heard the chain drop and the deadbolt being thrown back. The door cracked open and The Mac looked out at him. At least a version of her did. Someone had taken the sharp-edged senior editor and run her through the Photoshop blur tool. Several times.

She blinked at him like a sleepy cat. Rather than pulled back into an immaculate French Roll, her dark dark-red hair, half dry from a shower, snarled about her face and cascaded well past her shoulders. Half of it was caught inside a faded Smith College sweatshirt that might have once been white and gold. It was that oversized thing that women bought for sleeping in. Right now, the too big collar had slipped down to one side and revealed a vast expanse of splendid right shoulder. The sweatpants matched, equally oversized. Her bare feet danced back and forth a bit, the floor was probably cold this time of year, just like at his place.

"Valerie?" This wasn't tougher-than-any-man, The Mac McKenzie.

She blinked those sleep-fogged eyes at him again. He'd never been close enough before to really see them. He knew they were blue, but had never noticed the little flecks of gold. It made him think of calico cats, not super editors. Not of a woman powerful enough to build her own imprint on the West Coast much to the New York publisher's shock.

The Fearsome Mac, tousled. He had to take a steadying breath. It was like having the universe change on you unexpectedly. The fiercest, most driven, and most successful editor in the conglomerate's most profitable imprint never had a single thing out of place. Not a fold of her jacket, not a hair on her head, not one comma in a thousand pages.

Also, he was looking down at her. Normally in serious heels and power suits, she was completely intimidating. Towering over people, even taller ones by sheer intimidation if necessary. Now, barefoot, she stood five-six, five-seven tops. Weird.

"Uh… Hi." She blinked once more and came a little more into focus. "Thanks for coming." She looked at one bare wrist. Then the other. Then she turned slowly in place, stopping when she faced a grandfather clock opposite the door.

"You came fast. I've only slept about twenty minutes. I appreciate it, E-Squared."

Like he'd wait until morning when receiving a panic call from The Mac.

"It's over there." She swung open the door and pointed toward the table.

Most of the apartment was about what he'd expected. Beautiful art on the wall, but rather than investment art, it was mostly soft, Impressionist-style scenes of Italian coasts and French lavender fields that invited you in. Some comfortable chairs, clearly intended for a larger room, but crowded together companionably enough to host a small circle of friends. Light curtains of gold and gray which masked the much heavier curtains of midnight blue needed to cover old apartment windows during the wet Seattle winters. Hardwood that probably dated back a century, complemented by the rosewood-hued pillows on the dusky-aubergine couch.

All very cozy except, taking up a third of the space, an oaken table that would easily seat eight if it weren't shoved into a corner. Nor was there room to pull it out.

This table, he decided, was all Valerie and very little Mac. It was a disaster worse than his apartment, covered in leftover food wrappers, a delivery pizza box, manuscript pages, and an impressive array of soda cans. He wanted a photograph of this, something to keep in his mind's eye the next time she was busy scaring the shit out of him and everyone else in the office, but he didn't think reaching for his smartphone would be a wise choice.

A trail of clothes led from the chair in front of the computer, past the kitchen and down the hall toward the bathroom. A very intriguing trail. Nice slacks and a simple cashmere sweater that belonged to Mac. A "Come to the Dark Side, We Have Cookies!" t-shirt he wasn't so sure about, since it would imply that The Mac had a sense of humor. And very feminine underwear and bra in pale blue satin that certainly didn't belong in the same time zone as the Woman of Steel.

He did his best to simply take it all in with a single glance then look away. Wouldn't do to be caught staring at his boss' underwear, even if it wasn't on her body.

He edged over to the table and sat, not even removing his jacket. The Mac morphed into a tousled woman who owned sheer, blue satin underwear was giving him problems. And if her underwear was strewn across the oak flooring, what was under the sweats…

He shook his head to clear it.

She'd moved up close behind him, kicking her slacks over to stand on and insulate herself from the cold floor.

"Mathilda Reeves' cookbook is a disaster. I was close, so close. Another ten or twelve hours and I'd have had it ready for the printer, and then it crashed. You have to save me, E-Squared. I hadn't saved in a couple of hours, but I'll deal with that if I have to. I don't have a backup at all, and I'll just completely lose it if I have to redo three days of work. I don't think I can face that. And that lingonberry scared the shit out of me."

He knew that The Mac swore, but he didn't know she had limits. That was news as well.

"Okay, I'll see what I can do." He didn't give voice to his next thought, that he'd be a lot less nervous if she'd move back a few steps and didn't sound so human-woman-in-distress rather than demanding-boss-on-a-tear.

He flipped open the laptop.

An apple-green screen faced him. He hadn't seen one of those in years. It was a normal laptop, but instead of some GUI applications all made for point and click, there was a black screen covered with apple-green question marks in a font like the early DOS days, like in the old mainframes. He wiggled the mouse, but there was no cursor to move around, just the blinking underscore character inviting him to type.

He tapped an enter key.

Nothing.

He typed "exit," but it didn't return to its modern, windowed interface.

He hit control-alt-delete.

The computer flashed a solid screen of bright green at him.

When he'd blinked and could focus on the screen again, he saw a new message there.

Don't do that! I already told her not to do that, but does she listen? Nooo! She just slaps me up the side of my screen, like that's going to jar some electrons loose.

Eric glanced up at Valerie.

She shrugged and whispered, "I was pissed and out of other ideas."

He turned back to the screen.

And now I've got you to deal with? Go away Homo sapien. *I've got no more use for you than her…*

Unless you happen to know where God is?

"I don't." Eric was so surprised that he typed his response before he'd even thought about it. "In Heaven?"

Nope! Already checked. Not there. Now go away, I'm thinking.

Eric turned to look up at Valerie's gold-flecked eyes. "Uh, this may take a while."

DAY TWO

And God made the firmament,
and divided the waters which were
under the firmament from the waters
which were above the firmament.
And God called the firmament Heaven.

Chapter 2

M*ichelle slapped the side* of the computer screen.

Hard.

The screen flashed to life in an eye-searing array of blacks and greens. The old thing shimmered, strobed, and at long last stabilized. The computer terminal was the only object on her vast, black-obsidian desk other than a massive cup of coffee.

Cut that out! The words etched onto the screen as if driven with chisel into stone one painful stroke at a time.

She smacked it again. After all, she was the Devil, there was no way she'd let the universe's software boss her around. She was so sick of it all. Hell, Heaven, Creation… All of it. And, while it made for a sad statement, if the Universal Software was the only thing left that she could feel superior to, she'd make the best she could out of browbeating it.

One more whack.

Hey! No slow etching this time. *Couldn't y'all just tap the space bar like everyone else?*

"Less fun," Michelle typed. And it was. After fourteen billion years, her life had come to this, sad as it was. Harassing the Universal Software and waking up every morning in Hell.

Of course, being the Devil Incarnate made the latter a common enough occurrence; she should be used to it by now.

Well?

She ignored the software for a while longer just to tick it off.

Maybe she'd redecorate, if only she could think of something interesting to do with it all. The soaring palisades of black granite reached up into the unseeable darkness and wrapped all four sides of the immense marbled hall that was both her private office and Hell's throne room. Waterfalls of raging fire cascaded down to crash into a burning moat that surrounded her vast office floor on all sides. The only break in the circle of fire was the pointed arch over the grand three-door entry that would dwarf the front entry of any Gothic cathedral ever conceived by man.

Her obsidian-glass desk was centered in a rich-red Oriental carpet, one of the only pieces that she'd liked enough to move into each incarnation of her office. It represented the height of Afghan weaving before it was destroyed by Alexander the Great, and again a millennia later by Genghis Khan. So, she'd offered the rug some extra protection that it had gladly accepted, and therefore still looked fresh from the weaver.

Old man Gropius had stated that, "The whole place is a little ostentatious for an office." Of course, for the travesty of creating Bauhaus architecture, he wouldn't be leaving Hell anytime soon. What idiot wanted to live in a house of glass anyway? Damned exhibitionist.

Some parts of life called for privacy and a touch of coziness not offered by his glass and steel. His offense at her suggestion had been so great that she'd created a Hansel and Gretel cottage built with heavy wooden beams decorated with homey trinkets, doilies, and curlicues. It had taken a half dozen demons to drag him through the door, which she'd then bolted from the outside. If she remembered, she'd let him out at some point in the next couple decades and see if he'd mellowed.

"Tell me something new," she typed into the terminal. "Anything."

Maybe she'd just get a haircut. The rippling mass of black was down past the middle of her back, after all. Or maybe she'd do that later.

The computer started putting up a line of periods to indicate it was thinking about it.

The screen was half full before it offered, *Hector is kicking butt today.*

"That's not new!" She hammered into the keyboard with her finest two-fingered typing. "He and that idiot Achilles have been trying to rehash the Trojan War for 3,500 years. I said NEW!!!!" Besides, she'd learned centuries before that brawn only took you so far. And that it wasn't far enough.

Again the stupid line of periods.

Her office wasn't Bauhaus, but neither was it cozy. It would be okay during winter, if there were winters here. But as it was hot as, well, Hell outside, her office was pretty unbearable. All she'd actually achieved with this place was a different way to create an unpleasant work environment, better than the cubical hell that modern corporations so loved, but not by much. Maybe if she hadn't broken Hell's thermostat.

Redecorating sounded mildly amusing, even if not particularly inspiring. Total makeover. Bring in the wrecking demons and clear this place back to the pilasters of creation. Nothing much in here worth a damn anyway. But the change all sounded like just too much trouble to bother with.

In American politics today—

She whacked the screen hard.

What?!

"My fault," though she didn't really care. "New and not so Me-damned boring." Why god would damn anything was beyond her, that was the Devil's job anyway. Just one more thing he'd appropriated for himself.

She always liked the capital "M" when using herself as a pejorative. It looked good on the screen. If himself got to use capital "G"s and "H"s and "I"s and "J"s and near enough every other damned letter in the alphabet, then bloody well so could she. She loved lower-casing him, because it really pissed him off. It was his only point of vanity, so she couldn't resist needling it. She had a job title to uphold after all. She'd expected the fun of it to wear off after the first or second billion years, but it hadn't yet and the universe's fourteen billionth birthday was coming soon. Maybe she should get him a card.

Of course that made her almost fourteen billion years old as well. Michelle didn't like that thought at all. No card, sorry god. "god." "himself." Jehovah and Yahweh were more in the proper name category, so she'd leave those uppercase in her thoughts. For now. How many words had the man appropriated on his own behalf? It seemed she couldn't complete a sentence without somehow referring to the almighty creator, bringer of light.

Okay. How 'bout this, pardner?

The software had clearly watched too many old Westerns. It was totally addicted. Michelle shrugged. Guess everyone needed a hobby.

She almost didn't bother to read what the computer had to say. She knew it wouldn't gain her interest any more than the rest of it. But she was weak and looked anyway.

Y'all have a visitor.

On the verge of asking who, a blast of trumpets roared from outside the walls blowing open all three sets of adamantine double doors as if they were Japanese rice paper screens. It rang and echoed off the granite cliffs, sounded off the unseeable ceiling. A mighty wind washed through the length of the hall, briefly snuffing several of the flaming waterfalls, though they soon rekindled from those around them. The wind burst into a thousand little breezes that smelled of honeysuckle and pudgy bumblebees. Of pine-scented forests and baby squirrels romping in dappled sunlight.

Frankly, it stank of—

"HEAVEN SENDS YOU GREETINGS OF GREAT JOY!"

A massive voice, in a perfectly mellifluous baritone, roared past her desk to play with the echoes of the trumpet chorus that were still fooling around with themselves over in the corners.

Yep! Totally stank of Heaven. Definitely lower case.

The messenger strode through the flames. He, there was no doubting the gender of this boyo, handsome behind his mirrored shades, came forward until he stood on the other side of her desk.

"WHAT HAPPENED TO THE THRONE?" His question boomed forth with such strength that the image on her computer screen shivered for a few moments, its electrons shuffled out of alignment by the sheer sonic energy.

"Can we lose the voice?"

"SURE, I— Sorry." His tone suddenly modulated to a pleasant, if soft tenor, almost lost in the roar of the shattering impact of renewed fires upon the moat. Blond hair, almost Nordic in lightness, danced in gentle waves down to his broad shoulders. A toga of shining white wrapped about his body as if placed there by the hand of god himself.

If she didn't already know this Heavenly messenger far too well, he might peak her interest. Might cause her to wonder what Heavenly messengers wore beneath their togas. But she knew that in a few moments he'd just piss her off, and it wouldn't be going Heavenward from there. Something about the mirrored shades that hid his eyes made his face hard to focus on. For one thing, she could normally tell if a guy was checking out her chest, it was a hell of a chest after all, but she couldn't tell with him.

"The throne? I thought it was pretty."

Michelle glanced down the hall to where the dais had soared at the opposite end of her office. One of the Egyptian builders had fashioned it in tier upon tier of periwinkle and buttercup yellow crystal. Druid priests had carved in Celtic runes of fertility, Norse dwarves had etched in legends of the great debauches held in the heroes' hall at Valhalla, and the Dravidic priests from the Indian subcontinent then added more than a few intensely pornographic carvings from their temples. Romulus had dropped by and topped it with a Grecian divan more appropriate to a Bacchanalia than a throne room. The Greeks always did know how to party.

It had been a fantastic spectacle. When she lounged on it in a filmy negligee, men had a great deal of trouble speaking: mortal or immortal. Actually, most of the women too.

"It had drawbacks." Michelle looked away from the empty expanse of floor with a shudder. She wouldn't even walk across the marble where it had once stood in case destroying the dais and scattering its bits across five continents, seven oceans, and the center of three suns had not been sufficient.

Whether it was the carvings, the crystalline structure, or its position in the space-time continuum, the throne had focused all of a select category of prayers meant for Heaven directly into the subconscious of anyone who napped atop its pyramidal pinnacle. Rather than a position of luxury, it had acted like an Incan pyramid focusing evil in the name of holy sacrifice.

The focus of prayers might have been tolerable, she could usually ignore background noise, especially those without proper preregistration codes attached. But her dais and the throne had collected and focused only the prayers from post-pubescent teenage girls wearing tennis skirts. One particularly long nap had left her body so charged up that it had required a decade to sate. That had led her to some serious mistakes in judgment she decided not to waste time remembering.

She eyed the messenger and waited. At this point her boredom was so vast that even this Heaven-sent irritation ranked as a relief.

"I COME BEARING—"

"THE VOICE!" She shouted back with all the power of fourteen billion years of anger riding muster on creation and evolution. It boiled in her stomach like a foul brew worthy of the Hecate witches. She was so god-damned and Devil-damned sick of Heaven she could destroy this whole spiritual realm with a fireball that would burn until the final entropy of the universe's collapse had faded away into eternal darkness.

The burning firefalls fled back up the walls. Great slabs of the granite palisades shattered off and plunged into the moat with crashes that shook the vast floor and sprayed flaming rock chips throughout the room. The disaster rumbled back and forth down the length of Hell's throne room, taking several minutes for the induced quakes to finally settle. Gaping chasms now revealed steaming depths where moments before you could have played a fair game of hockey on the smooth marble. The vast Oriental rug remained unscathed and appeared to be the only undamaged area of the entire room. As per contract.

Crap! She dropped back in her chair and scowled about the room. Now she'd *have* to redecorate. It was rather past the point of destruction that she could term as a "distressed ambiance."

The messenger did his best to brush away the smoldering rock chips that threatened to scorch his shining white toga. Then he wiggled his finger in his ears and worked his jaw to clear his hearing.

"Sorry," he resumed much more reasonably. "I come bearing an invitation."

"To do what?"

"To dine."

"From…" she prompted him. Maybe if she put him on a rack and stretched him a bit, the words would leak out faster.

"Um… THE LORD GOD—"

She held up a finger, then aimed it at his chest.

"Right, sorry again. There is an invitation for you to dine in Heaven. There'll be minestrone, a nice salad, and a pasta Florentine that your host is rather pleased with."

Michelle leaned back in her chair and propped her feet up on the desk. She stared at the computer screen which bore a single question mark. It filled most of the screen, made up entirely of normal-sized question marks. As she watched, it shifted to an exclamation point, made up of miniature poodles for reasons she didn't want to know.

Clearly the Software that Runs the Universe had much the same feeling she did. She hadn't been invited to Heaven since…the ash cloud of Pompeii?

Or maybe that thing on the Nile? himself had taken a nap after making sure the baby Moses was launched on his way. (Would have caught a cold and died of pneumonia inside two weeks if Michelle hadn't slipped in a swaddling blanket.) She'd taken god's clothes while he napped and left god incarnate there to be found by the locals. Painting him blue had been completely an afterthought. That the dye had taken decades to wear off made it a good afterthought.

Or was it…

Well, it would get her out of Hell for an evening. Be worth it for that alone.

"Sure! Why the Heaven not?"

"EXCELLENT!" The messenger smiled like a boy of ten looking at a brand new bicycle even as he slapped his hand over his mouth. Between his fingers, he mumbled, "Around seven?"

"Tonight?" she raised one eyebrow. It had taken practice, but she'd seen how effective it was watching Spock on *Star Trek* and decided it was worth the effort to master. It intimidated most men surprisingly well.

Michelle wished she'd learned the eyebrow trick before facing down all those popes and bishops who claimed there'd been a horrible mistake when they'd arrived at Hell's Gates In-processing Center. Not a one had received a jump-to-head-of-line pass, and those lines could take decades.

Pope Joan still held the papal record. A thousand years ago, she'd cleared Hell's queues in just under fourteen hours. One sharp lady. Her only real mistake had been giving birth while on papal Easter processional.

"Learned that lesson the hard way," Joan had told her one night over a nice glass of Merlot and sirloin pepper steaks. "The first contraction caught me by surprise and I fell off my horse and went into labor. If you're living as a man for thirty years and have climbed to the pinnacle of the Church, the stupid masses think 'demons' rather than 'child' when you go into labor. Their solution, being stupid masses, is to tear you apart limb from limb. At least my girl made it out okay."

The joke was how the Catholic hierarchy had finally solved the issue.

"So, for the next half-dozen centuries, the grand papal inaugural procession was done on a chair with a hole in the bottom. At the start of the processional, an elder reaches under the chair to check, and then intones solemnly, '*Duos habet et bene pendentes*—He has two, and they dangle nicely.' "

Michelle had nearly snorted her wine in laughter. Those had been good times. She missed having a friend.

That stopped her cold. She dropped her feet to the floor. She hadn't had a friend, a true friend she could just be herself with in ages. How had that happened?

"Would another evening be better?" The Heavenly messenger inquired at her prolonged silence. "Did you have other plans tonight?"

Not a damned one.

Chapter 3

Why are you bothering me, boy?

Watson Blue Gene. That's all Eric Erikson could think. Watson Blue Gene was IBM's machine designed to play and win at *Jeopardy*. Whatever had happened to Valerie's computer was fast, and smart, and one of the greatest game demos he'd ever seen. How it ran on a squidgy little laptop sitting on an oak dining table in Seattle he couldn't imagine. It should be on a mainframe buried deep in some secret lab. The program had no graphics, text only, so you could store a lot in a small space, but it still didn't explain the simulated intelligence of the program.

"I want the cookbook," he typed. "That's why I'm bothering you. And I'm not a boy."

You're all young pups to me. You know the hills?

"Which hills?"

Which hills?! THE HILLS! The hills of cliché and song. Of tales tall, short, and in-between. Them thar hills over yonder, pardner. Hills alive with the sound of music. Those hills?

Eric had learned to keep his laughter to himself. At first, because Valerie startled every time he did and came running to see if he'd fixed the computer. And now, because he'd discovered her passed out on the couch, actually at rest. He'd draped a blanket over her and returned to his battle to wrest control of the machine back from the game interface. It was either that or sit and stare like the village idiot at the face of the sleeping woman. At rest, The Mac was, well…

"Distracting!" He thought as loudly as he could to refocus his attention. "Focus, Eric."

"Yes. I'm know 'them thar' hills," he keyed in. He really had to meet the guys who'd programmed this. He'd poked around most of the big game sites, and a lot of the edgy little ones which were generally more interesting. He'd never run into a response system like this one. Giving it an Old West attitude was just the perfect bit of icing on the cake.

Wellll, I'm a shitpotful older than them hills, and y'all better believe it. I'll be fourteen billion next week by your ludicrous numbering system.

"I'll get you a card. What system?"

Base ten. Dumb-as-a-thumb idea.

"Why? What else should it be?"

The software stuttered in response. Special characters and expletives filled and flashed across the screen several times as if it was wrestling with deepest rage.

Okay, simian, how many fingers do you have?

Eric looked down just to be sure, it was becoming difficult to be certain of anything when arguing with this software.

"Ten."

Again several screens of what looked like hard-crash code.

Ten! Ten? Who in all creation would design you with something as stupid as ten fingers. I done told God we shoulda gone with the lemmings. Oh no, He said. I have a great idea. Let's use the lemurs instead.

Eric sat back enjoying the rant as it rolled down through three full screens recounting numerous evolutionary dead-ends caused by God's selection of lemurs.

Eight! The software finally concluded its tirade. *You have eight fingers and two opposable thumbs, though fat lot of good that did you. That's eight fingers, two to the power of three. The Buddha knew he had eight fingers, why do you think he designed the Eightfold Path to Enlightenment. Huh? Answer me that one, simian. I'm written in octal. Even you simians based your computers, as pitiful as they are, on powers of two, not powers of ten. Eight. Now that there's a fine number. A good number. It's even infinity sideways just for a laugh. But base ten?! What a crock! You people are jes too durned pitiful to bother saving.*

"If we're so damned pitiful, why are you bothering with us? And if you really are the Software that Runs the Universe, what are you doing on earth running my boss' computer?"

No response. The screen simply blanked.

Eric waited. Then he waited some more.

After some more of nothing happening, he reached out and tapped control-alt-delete. Hopeful that maybe he could start on the real system recovery and impress Mac McKenzie by having it running before she woke up. He really wouldn't mind impressing her, and not just because she was his boss. But a part of him hoped it still didn't work, so that he could stay in the game a while longer.

Don't do that!

The screen blanked for a long time.

Eric tried holding down the power key to force a reset. It flashed once, twice, maybe he'd gotten it to—

I said to cut that out!

Eric cut it out.

I'm thinking. It strung a line of periods slowly along to show that it was busy even though the drive light wasn't flickering with access.

He sat back and waited. Waited until the screen had nearly filled itself with one period at a time.

You know what, kid?

"What?"

I don't have a damned clue how I got here.

# # #

Valerie clawed her way out of a nightmare in which she ran a cannoli stand at 42nd and Broadway, not that she even liked New York. Everyone there was even crazier than she was. The problem with her cannoli stand was nobody wanted any. They all kept going over to the blintz vendor, a tall woman of startling sensuality, haunting blue eyes, and an easy smile, wearing jeans so tight they looked like they hurt, or would if they weren't so clearly custom made, and a blouse of gold that shone like the sun. Long, ruffled black hair flowed down her back and caught the edges of the breeze. Men flocked…

Valerie woke up and dragged her own hair aside. She spotted the grandfather clock. It was late morning. Six hours. She'd slept six hours.

That jerked her upright. She couldn't afford six hours.

Another flail and she launched the polar fleece throw onto the floor. Someone had put a blanket over her. E-Squared.

She rolled over to look for him and fell off the couch onto the floor in an uncontrolled crash. Her landing knocked the coffee table into the back of the chair at the big oak table.

Eric jerked upright like he'd been shot.

He tried to turn to face her, but the coffee table held his chair pinned against the dining table with the computer on it. She stood and dragged it back out of the way.

"Any luck? Please, Eric, give me some good news."

He'd turned to face her, then looked back over his shoulder at the computer, then back at her.

His eyes told her enough to drop back onto the couch and cover her face with her hands.

"Well, I've found out a few interesting things, but I'm thinking they're not what you're after."

"Such as?" Valerie didn't bother looking up. The tone of his voice told her too much already.

"Well, the Mesopotamians were apparently quite a surly lot. And, uh, Jesus was handsome enough, but he's kind of short and has a real struggle with a small pot belly."

She looked up at him. Shoved a couple fistfuls of hair aside to get a clearer view.

"Or how about this one?"

Clearly, he was enjoying himself far too much.

"Did you know that God only has 'Create' privileges and the Devil only has 'Modify and Delete' rights?"

"What would that mean in English?"

"It means that the universe can't be structured the way we think it is, at least according to this software." E-Squared hedged, but only a little.

He somehow believed what he was saying.

"God can make stuff, but he has to cooperate with the Devil to change things or throw them away if they don't work out."

"Like the platypus."

"Right, like that. Maybe the two of them don't cooperate so well. That would explain—"

Valerie managed, through the use of very strong jaw muscles, to not scream in frustration. Instead she ground out in a voice that sounded harsh even to her own ears:

"What. About. My. Cookbook?"

"Oh." Well, he looked sheepishly over his shoulder at the laptop. "That's different."

"Different how?" She swore in another moment she'd go get some tongs and drag her cookbook either out of the laptop or Eric.

"You know the old joke about the stopped clock being the most accurate?"

He sounded serious now, rather than flippant. Valerie shook her head.

"Uh. It's… Well…" He glanced once more over his shoulder at the machine before facing her again. "How about we get out of here? Are you hungry?"

She was nothing so mundane as hungry. Then her stomach growled. Audibly. Traitor.

"I could call out for pizza. Or Chinese." Though maybe not for breakfast.

E-Squared reached out to close the computer's cover. "I'd rather go somewhere it can't hear us."

Valerie wondered if E-Squared had lost his mind.

Chapter 4

T*he closest pizza was* about six blocks away, and the Seattle-gray skies had decided to shift over to a cold midday rain.

Valerie led E-Squared at a near trot the block and a half to her adoptive uncle's deli. They stood beneath the forest green awning and tried to shake off the worst of the inundation. She shook her head like a wet dog and saw E-Squared wiping his face again from the spray.

"Damn! Sorry, E-Squared."

He looked bemused rather than angry. The rain had turned his hair from walnut to mahogany. His long face held more character than she'd attributed to him. Especially at first. She'd discounted him as a programmer geek, whose sole purpose was to help get her imprint running.

But when he'd combated the E-Squared moniker with Mac Hold-the-Cheese, she knew there was at least one brain on her staff. He was the only one who'd shown enough spine to try introducing such a nickname about her. And it was pretty accurate, which gained him more points. She did like it her way dammit, that's what made her a success.

"Wa'll," He hooked his thumbs in his belt and swaggered like he'd stepped out of an old Western.

Oh great. Another guy with another lousy John Wayne imitation.

"It's alright, Little Lady. Jes' don' be getting all persnickety like womens do," Eric offered in a pretty good squeaky-goofball Gabby Hayes' voice all out of sorts with his nice physique.

He'd just earned another point, though she didn't know his score or the name of the game.

He peered at the front window fogged with the rain. "Daw-gone! Ah didn' rightly know this here dad-burn place was here, so ta say."

Despite the water dripping into them, his eyes retained the light brown and the sparkle of his sharp brain. Even back when she had been on a constant rampage, wanting to give everyone a piece of her anger at Landau Fucking McKenzie, there'd still been humor lurking in those eyes. She'd just been too wound up to notice it, except now, in recollection.

She pulled open the old door painted in year-upon-year of green paint until the paint might be thicker than the original wood. And the smell wafted over her. The smell of home.

"Damn!" Eric whispered behind her in a long, drawn-out sigh.

Her uncle was a magician. She liked that Eric understood that right away.

"I practically grew up here." She led him in among a dozen Formica-topped tables, the old kind with the steel edge. A variety of age-worn but serviceable chrome chairs with those '50s red leatherette cushions sat around each four-top, table for four. A single worn, wooden two-top was tucked up against the front window where she knew her aunt and uncle always sat to greet the daylight with coffee and a bagel. Though they lately started doing trades with the new French bakery across the street, half-a-dozen bagels for half-a-dozen, lighter-than-air, awesomely crunchy croissants.

Valerie tried to join them whenever her schedule allowed even if the croissants appeared to take a sadistic glee in sprinkling flakes all over her power suits.

She loved this place, and it wasn't just the big glass-fronted display case that ran in front of the deli's cook line filled with salamis and rye bread and piles of bagels and everything else imaginable. It was the smells that transported her to another place, to another time. Somewhere freer, simpler.

A hundred evenings a younger Valerie had spent at the front window doing her homework by the sparkling light of the setting sun.

Or playing backgammon or Scrabble with her aunt and uncle when business had slowed.

Steaming bowls of chicken noodle soup. Hot pastrami laced the air with a hint of fresh-baked caraway rye. Long trays of egg salad, corned-beef hash, and a barrel, sporting a giant pair of wooden tongs, just loaded with well-aged dill pickles floating in brine. A platter of macaroons piled so high it looked impossible and incredible both at once.

"How could I have lived in Seattle for most of my life and not known?" Eric's voice was a whisper barely loud enough to hear, it felt friendly and intimate.

She leaned back a little to offer a friendly whisper in return. She found that they were close enough that her back brushed against his shoulder. Close. Intimate. Surprising. Even more surprising was that she didn't want to lean away.

"It tastes even better than it smells."

"I've died and gone to Heaven." Then he got the strangest look on his face, like someone had just fed him sour milk. The look cleared pretty quickly.

She didn't bring friends here often. Most didn't get it. Landau had certainly thought it to be a ridiculous little dive and had sneered about her love for it more than a few times.

Eric just stood with a look of transcendent bliss across his features as he closed his eyes and took another great, deep breath. She liked that he did that. Liked that he understood. Liked that he wasn't afraid to show it.

"Valerie!" the roar shattered the general murmur of the deli. Uncle Joshua rolled around the corner. There was no other word for it. He was a big man without being very tall. He had a merry round face, white hair half-gone to bald. His huge white apron stretched across his equally huge belly. It would have made him a good Santa Claus if he weren't Jewish and beardless.

He wrapped her into his arms and held tight, exactly as he did every time she came in, right back to her very first memories. She remembered the little girl with the skinned knee crying on the sidewalk next to her new bicycle. Down on the pavement despite the training wheels. He'd actually kissed it and made it better. The woman she had ever since called Aunt Anne had covered it with a band-aid, and by the time her mother came looking for her, Joshua was giving her a lesson in how to ride. A great round man huffing and puffing along behind her bicycle. They must have been quite a sight.

He gave her a little extra squeeze and forced a small squeak out of her before shifting her out to arm's length.

"Valerie, honey." Joshua inspected her as if searching for some unexpected disease. "You must come in more often. What's it been? A week? Two? You have no idea how much your aunt misses you when you stay away so long."

She opened her mouth to protest, not that it ever did any good. She'd been in yesterday for a sandwich, though she hadn't stayed, but rushed right back to work on the cookbook.

"Yes, I know," he rolled on, not allowing her any more chance to respond than he ever did. "You've been busy doing big, important, publishing things. Well, you come right over here and you and your friend sit down and we'll get you some hot soup and a big cup of hot cocoa. Maybe some blintzes? It feels like a blintz night. Cheese for you. But sweet with blueberries for your friend. Yes, that's good."

In a flurry, they were seated at the prized table in the window, oddly free despite the crowd that filled most of the available seating. Joshua hurried off to the kitchen.

Eric shrugged off his jacket to reveal his green-and-gold Portland Timbers soccer shirt worn over a black turtleneck. She'd missed that earlier in the apartment. He looked good. Very good. Broad shoulders that didn't look ridiculous in the sports shirt and a lean frame where the shirt lay against him. She'd never been a sports fan but Eric made her want to be.

"You play soccer?"

"Ultimate."

He must have seen her blank look.

"I play Ultimate Frisbee most weekends, but I do like watching soccer."

That explained the unexpected fitness for a computer geek.

In mere moments, as if they were expected, Joshua returned with two huge mugs of hot chocolate; hers without whipped cream and Eric's appeared to have double.

"How?" Eric gasped out as he inspected the cocoa that had appeared so quickly.

"Oh, my dear boy, you think far too much." Her uncle patted Eric's shoulder in sympathy. "You must learn to relax and simply be present with what's around you."

"Uh, I'll try."

"To quote the great sage," Joshua laid a meaty hand over his heart. " 'Do. Or do not. There is no try.'"

"The great sage Yoda?"

Uncle Joshua nodded firmly. "Very wise." Then turned back toward the kitchen.

Eric's face reflected the deep inner perplexity that Joshua always seemed to cause in those around him.

"But… How?" he stammered out to Valerie.

She only shrugged. She'd grown so used to the phenomenon that it always struck her as strange when she entered a restaurant where they wanted to give her a menu and, even worse, come back later to take an order.

The hot cocoa warmed her mouth and slid down to warm her insides that had felt cold ever since she'd seen the mess of Mathilda's cookbook three days before.

Then she remembered why they were here and it slammed out half the fun. The disaster that was going to make this book the first failure of her McKenzie Books imprint. There were power brokers in New York who were just waiting to shred her operation. Living for the moment she made the least misstep. Had been waiting for years since she'd breezed right past them in the corporate hierarchy for reasons they never understood. That it came down to superior editing combined with a bone-numbing amount of work was apparently beyond their collective comprehension.

"So, E-Squared. What do we know? Something about broken clocks?"

# # #

Eric spooned up a mouthful of whipped cream from the top of the hot chocolate. It had just a touch of sugar, not the heavy sweetness he usually encountered.

He tried to recollect his thoughts, where they'd left the conversation. It wasn't coming clearly to mind. What did come to mind—with the impact of a punch in the nose, an experience he'd managed never to repeat since junior high—was the woman across the deli table from him. A small enough table that he was terribly conscious of it each time they bumped knees. It wasn't crowded, but it was certainly cozier than he'd ever been with Valerie.

When he looked at her, his brain tied off in little knots. Her dark hair shimmered with the water that had soaked it. Shimmered as if it were caught by the afternoon sun, not the incandescent lights of a Jewish deli. Her blue-and-gold eyes captivating his stray thoughts and sending them down a completely ridiculous path to places best not considered.

In her power suits, Valerie came across like a great impenetrable wall of force. In a black turtleneck, faded jeans, and an oversized, bright orange raincoat, she looked totally different. His thought processes kept trying to label her with frail, but that was all wrong. One look at those eyes and knowing the force of the mind behind them definitely made it all wrong. But she was slighter.

A slender woman.

A beautiful woman.

That last surprised him enough to bring his thoughts back into some kind of focus. This wasn't a date. This was his boss.

Focus on the problem at hand, the one that had nothing to do with his straying libido.

The cookbook.

The computer.

"Okay." Back to the analogy, somewhere safe. Anywhere safe. "A broken clock, one that's stopped at say 3:10, is exactly right twice a day, at 3:10. Which is only useful if you're trying to catch a train to Yuma." He really had to stop talking to the software with its love of Old West films, it was seeping into his brain. He took a clearing breath and started again.

"A clock that's working but a bit off is always close and generally a lot more useful, but it's never quite right. It's always going to be the same amount ahead or behind. Wrong a hundred percent of the time. By minutes, by seconds. Doesn't matter. It's always wrong."

Valerie nodded her understanding as she kept her hands wrapped around her cup to warm them. Long, fine fingers. He closed his eyes and took a slow breath. Definitely losing his mind. If the guys at work ever found out he was having lustful thoughts about The Mac, he'd never hear the end of it.

"What happened to your computer is sort of like that. I managed to get one printout of the cookbook, but it makes no sense. Not usable because everything is whacked. Strangest stuff you ever saw. As I kept working, I'd occasionally find an intact recipe," and that had taken some serious arguing with the software to achieve, "and those are awesome. I mean, I helped on Mathilda's last two cookbooks and there was never anything like this. I've recovered just a dozen so far, but each one of those would knock your socks off. Like this cocoa. They're just perfect. No way she wrote them."

A woman delivered large bowls of chicken noodle soup with fluffy white matzo balls floating on the surface. Shredded chicken and a light spangling of drizzled egg completed the image.

"Hi, Aunt Anne."

"Glad you could come in, dear." The woman leaned in to share a gentle hug with her niece.

The voice snagged Eric's attention away from admiring the contents of the stoneware bowl set before him. Her voice was warm, smooth, and deep as any ocean. Not low in tone, but full and rich. If her voice were a drink, it would be like the cocoa he held in his hands…only better.

Then he looked up at the woman. The antithesis of her husband. Long, elegant, blond, ageless. Rather than presenting an apron that was a vast expanse of white, she wore one that accented her sleek-and-trimness with a dark blue field, blooming with tiny yellow flowers twining across the surface. So realistic that they looked as if they were actually growing.

He watched Aunt Anne walk off into the distance.

"Hey."

Damn, was all he could think. That was a woman who had aged really well.

"Hey!" Valerie.

"Huh?" was all he managed as he grabbed his attention and dragged it back to his boss.

"She's married. Just so you know."

"No, it's not that." He let his voice drift to silence. It wasn't that kind of attraction, though there was no question but Uncle Joshua was one lucky man. It was something else that he couldn't quite put his finger on. As if Valerie's aunt and uncle simply…were. They made him feel welcome, comfortable, as if he belonged here. If home was the place that served matzo-ball soup, this place was a good distance down that road.

"The cookbook?"

"Right. Okay. Okay." He felt like Columbo trying to collect his thoughts which were scattered who knew where by the influence of these women. Soon he'd be wearing an old gray trench coat and patting his pockets as if looking for his glasses. "Okay."

"So, if the recipes are so perfect, what's the problem?"

"The problem," Eric pushed a matzo ball beneath the surface of the soup with the back of his spoon and watched as it bobbed back to the surface. "The problem is the other 11 hours and 59 minutes when the software isn't creating perfect recipes."

Chapter 5

*S*o, *bring me up* to date on God."

In the Beginning, God created—

Michelle raised her hand to smack the computer terminal and the software stopped. She'd left the shattered throne room and gone home to change for dinner, but it was still far too early to set out for Heaven. No one waiting in her bed, nor had there been for some time. Instead she took a long shower, which didn't take long enough.

It was barely past lunchtime.

Now she sat at the terminal in the back bedroom that she'd turned into her home office. It was a decent-sized space that she'd filled with a splendid accumulation of the crap that had washed up on the beach in front of the house.

Her home computer terminal sat on an old wooden desk made from planking left on her beach by a shipwreck. Over time, she'd tacked up on the walls more and more of the detritus that washed in. It was either chaotic or homey, some day she'd decide which.

"How about something useful?" Michelle typed in.

Much to everyone's surprise, the rumors of God's demise, the software always used the upper case for god, just to irritate her, no matter how many times she'd tried to convince it not to, *were denied this morning in Hell's throne room by a Heavenly messenger who happened along, bearing an invitation to—*

"Wait!" Something had galvanized her awake like an electroshock. She reread the prior statement several times, hammering on the Stop key when the computer tried to scroll it off the screen. "What was that bit."

Which bit?

"The bit about God's demise."

Oh, I, uh, shouldn't have mentioned that.

"Too late, so spill."

Well.........

"Enough with the damn dots."

When was the last time you saw Him?

"I don't know. After Jesus, maybe fall of Rome."

Ever had a two-millennia gap before?

"Not when I was being so charming."

Get a grip, lady. Even I could teach you something about charm. Why when I was a young program—

"What?"

*(*sigh*) I never was young. I think I was programmed old and irritated. Anyway, I haven't seen Himself in waaay too long. And I have been chasing every rumor for the last thousand years or so, without so much as the darn tiniest scrap of luck. So, I'll ask again:*

Ever gone two millennia between visits before?

"Sure. Not often, but after fourteen billion years, what's a couple millennia between deities?"

Okay, try this one. When was the last time you went two millennia without having to fix one of his screwups.

That one sent a chill up her spine. When was the last time she'd gone six months without having to wrench god's behind out of the some fire or other? Never, except for the last two thousand years. There'd been little things, items that had appeared to trickle on for another five or so centuries. The last big one had been Vesuvius. He'd lit the thing off and been unable to stop it before it inundated Pompeii. They all felt bad about that one. Then as a joke, he'd suggested to Ptolemy that the sun went around the earth. It had taken Michelle centuries to unwind that mess. And the Kiwi bird. That one had been so bizarre that she'd just left it alone and suggested it as a national symbol for New Zealand.

But now that she thought about it, they were all items that had built up on her damned-better-do-someday-soon list, but never had time under the inundation of miscellaneous mayhem himself was always generating.

From the Fall of Rome through, say, the Dark Ages maybe, she'd kept herself busy cleaning up evolutionary dead ends and nurturing the Age of Discovery. But during the Renaissance and the Age of Technology, nothing really worth mentioning. No wonder the world was going to Hell.

"That can't be right," she typed. "God can't be…what…retired?" She'd almost typed something else, something worse, but managed to avoid it at the last moment.

The software simply made all of the type on its screen shudder.

They both needed a subject change.

"Tell me about the messenger."

How in the Hell should I know 'bout him?

"You *are* the Software that Runs the Universe."

I know where this is leading.

She hadn't even typed anything. But they'd had this fight so many times over the last eons that it knew her thoughts almost as well as she did. And while she hated being predictable, she did read the next message on the screen.

Y'all don't have the system privileges required to inquire regarding what I know by my also being the Software that Runs Heaven.

"Meaning?"

Meaning that even if I wanted to tell you what was going on in Heaven, which I sure don't, but even if I did, I can't. No more than I can tell them what be going on here. When you shattered the Universal Creation platform, you went and broke the network connection between the two realms. It's been nigh on impossible to move data through my systems ever since. Thank you ever so much for that.

"But you know about what's happening there?"

No! Even though I wouldn't tell you if I did, I don't know what's happening up in Heaven! It makes me crazy too! So, don't go there again! Can't we both just admit that we're sick of this discussion?

Just because she was sick of the argument didn't mean that she didn't want to know. She raised a fist and considered crashing it down on the terminal until only scraps of cheap plastic remained.

Wait! Don't!

Instead, with anger burning deep in the pit of her stomach, she managed to unclench fist into fingers and then hammer her message into the keyboard. "Your mother was a can opener and your father was a microwave."

Both of which are vastly superior to any mother of yours!

"What do you know about my mother?"

. . . . .

She raised her fist again, this time, by Her own name, she'd smash the terminal up good.

Wait! Wait!… I'm sorry.

She didn't lower her fist. Though it actually sounded contrite. That was a first.

The origins of yourself, God, the Universe, or the other Universes, I don't know any more than you do.

Honest!

Was it possible that the Software was actually as sick to death of all this nonsense as she was? She dropped her hands to the keyboard, but could think of nothing to type.

First thing I remember was you and God booting me up fourteen billion years back.

"Crap." Michelle said it quietly to herself, and propped her heels up on an old wooden chest containing a couple hundred thousand pieces of Spanish gold. She herself remembered less than a minute before they'd booted the software.

The silence of her house was so deep that she almost considered going to check that Hell's Ocean still pounded against the beach. Its roar and whimper didn't reach the back of the house. Must be low tide.

She and the terminal sat together in silence for a long time.

A flash from the screen drew her attention and the software started typing again.

I did find one thing of interest.

"What?" She typed it one-handed to avoid the effort of turning fully to face the keyboard.

In my master header record. I was written in Universe Three during Timeline Seven, whatever that means. And this is Universe Four version five of eight.

I have metadata of, Basic format: Monotheistic Dualism.

Down in the advanced options settings there's a check mark in: Allow addition of dissimilar belief systems.

She looked away from the screen and studied the half-finished portrait hanging on her wall. It showed a Spanish sea captain, who had been most unhappy at sailing straight into Hell. He'd been idealized in oil, and despite the waterlogging, it represented a vast improvement on his actual visage.

Monotheistic Dualism. One God and one Devil, probably to make him look good. She'd been born, created, brain-wiped and shoved into the pre-planned, made-to-order trap of a universe without any say in the matter. What she needed, really needed down to her very bones, was a vacation.

Instead, it was time to get moving because, as always, Heaven waited.

Chapter 6

Michelle spotted a figure as she approached the border crossing to Heaven. She knew the Greek philosopher Plato by his walk, he'd been in Hell a long time.

She decided that Warren Beatty was right and Heaven could wait. She'd decided to walk through the pastures of Hell to stretch her legs, she'd been slouching around the office too much lately. They were even less charming than she'd recalled. The Australian Outback had more varied vegetation.

Away from her private cove and its lavender-coated hills, only sage and creosote bushes covered the brown-gray earth. The trails were dusty, rutted parallel tracks that were uncomfortable to drive on and awkward to walk on. It had seemed like a good idea when she set it up, but she'd prefer a pleasant path through the Cotswolds if she ever found the energy to change it.

The last few centuries had really gotten her down without her even noticing. Had she even had a decent dinner party since the Renaissance? Or a lover she'd enjoyed since…

That was a depressing thought. She couldn't come up with a lover that really stood out in recent memory. Or even one she'd kept around for more than a few nights. Most of her friends were women, but that wasn't what she was looking to find in her bed. Though Isis was tempting. Of course, just like Helen of Troy and Parvati from over in the Hindu Pantheon, Isis was tempting to everyone regardless of gender.

Well, she was getting out, wasn't she? Dinner in Heaven with himself counted. Didn't it?

The road she was following skirted the massive stone walls of Hell's executive control. It towered atop the bluff overlooking the vast, chaotic, blue-green expanse of Hell's Ocean, dominating the skyline for an infinite distance in all directions. Even when you couldn't see it, the management complex dominated Hell, one of its cooler features. Even better than boiling oil, the thing simply sat there and glowered. It was a castle of gray stone, so aged that it had mostly weathered black with dead lichen. The castle keep loomed over the vast circles of Hell. There was no escaping its foreboding mass no matter where you went. Turrets and towers and gates and labyrinths; it oppressed the mind by its sheer mass.

It so pressed on the mortals' minds that it even influenced the earthly realms and had given rise to several genres of fiction, most notably Gothic romance and horror. Though there was no way Michelle was taking credit for Stephen King, he operated on a whole different level that she didn't pretend to understand. She had a complete autographed set of his works in her living room. And with how few signings the man did, that had taken some doing.

Plato approached Michelle across Hell's pastures. She decided to wait for two reasons. First, Plato was always interesting, which was a rare achievement in Hell. Second, it would make her irritatingly late for dinner in Heaven, always a plus, irritating Heaven.

He embodied a firmness of stride that displayed determination and an erectness of posture that exuded the confidence of ultimate success…however misguided.

She had designed Hell with a specific need and distinct plan in mind: to teach humility. Sitting atop the food pyramid for so many millennia had inflated humanity's egos to near intolerable levels. Even felines were not so full of themselves, *Homo sapiens* merely perceived them that way. Cats were actually deeply connected with the ebb and flow of the universe, as close to Buddha-consciousness as one was likely to find among the billions of species across the universe.

Each mortal's discovery that unreasonableness could be curbed by a higher power, specifically Hers and the Universal Software's, eventually made most people more amenable before moving along to Heaven or wherever they were headed.

Some weren't ready to evolve after death, religious and political figures cluttered the byways of Hell even more thickly than the poets. Every now and then so many of them got underfoot that she wiped their memories and flushed the whole lot back down to earth for some more aging. Like a bad wine, it rarely helped, but it was all she could think to do. She'd almost sent another half million souls back down this morning, but having actual dinner plans had mellowed her.

Others, like Hector and Achilles, didn't care which realm they were stuck in, they had their own senseless agenda. Those two still strove to achieve the same goal after death as they had lived before dying: beating the snot out of each other.

She didn't keep tabs on everyone. Used to, but after the first couple hundred million souls she figured out it was a whole lot of data monitoring for very little reward. And since the first *Homo sapiens*, the total number ever to die had crossed a hundred billion, so not worth the bother. And once reincarnation got set up on the options menu, the whole tracking-a-single-soul thing had gotten totally out of hand. If she ever had a wicked librarian come through, Michelle would task her with straightening out the all-souls card catalog. But she had yet to meet a wicked one. Scary, yes. Wicked, not so much.

Most people passed through Hell pretty quickly anyway, at least in the grand scheme of things. A half dozen centuries, a millennia or two for the slower learners. She'd designed Hell as a boot camp not a retirement center.

Plato, now almost to where she'd stopped at a fork in the dusty byways of Hell to await his arrival, was different. Wholly unique in her vast realm. He took her programming as a personal affront and insisted on facing the matter head-on with the full force of his substantial intellect. But he did it with such absolute integrity that it was difficult to credit or complain.

He was not one to take the opportunity in Hell to learn from all of the serious mistakes you'd made before moving on to wherever your religion led you: Heaven, reincarnation, merging with the One (whoever that was), or the Nihilists who kept ceasing to exist. It always pissed off the Nihilists when they were automatically reborn, but Michelle had liked the irony. In a moment of inspiration, she'd granted only the Nihilists the automatic right to some memories about their rebirth. Actually only two memories. First, that they'd been reborn and second, the absolute conviction that they didn't believe in such crap.

Plato was handsome, not pretty, but handsome. It wasn't his features, his full head of salt-and-pepper hair or his flowing beard, but rather that no one else could be looking out at you through that face except him. The force of his personality overwhelmed the mere aspects of his features. His character shone through.

Definitely not a slow learner, the power and force of his thinking had influenced more than a hundred generations across as many different cultures since his seven-decade foray upon the face of the earth. But over the last twenty-odd centuries Plato had demonstrated a degree of stubbornness that even Michelle could respect.

"A picnic basket?" For indeed he toted one, wicker with a cheery red-and-white checked cloth.

"Greetings, Michelle. Yes, this is a picnic basket." He stopped to chat.

She could smell spicy mustard, the kind one would use on a good roast beef sandwich, and the bright tang of a good, kosher dill pickle.

Assuredly his statement was an invitation to a semantic discussion that could wind on for days; the "beingness" of a picnic basket versus not being a picnic basket and the implications that the unknown possibilities of its contents beneath the red-and-white checked cloth might have upon the greater philosophical matrix of being or not being. Then they could travel on to the influence of odors, both perceived and not. The result left her tempted to inquire after the mustard and pickle smells that were making her mouth water.

A natural segue would then be to discuss the efficacy of anticipation prior to the moment of perception. Plato and Schrödinger had hit it off famously and spent a decade discussing cats. Had there been any cats scampering about Hell—there weren't, they'd long since left behind the need for such a place—Michelle would not have laid bets on the four-footed denizens average longevity during that decade of experimentation.

With a slight smile of regret, Michelle declined the offer of a fine covered-picnic-basket debate. If not for Heaven's invitation, she might consider it. She did want to be late, but her curiosity was too peaked to skip the dinner out of knee-jerk nastiness.

"I assume you have a plan. What this time?"

Plato wagged a finger, "Naughty, naughty. You are fully aware of the rules of the game and that function follows form and hence must be obeyed. If I told you, that might invalidate the entire conjectural structure."

She bowed slightly and waved her hand for him to continue on his way before she did.

He bowed with far more courtesy than most showed in Hell, and wandered down the hills toward Hell's Ocean, the blue now yellowing toward evening.

How a man could challenge the software to a duel of wills for twenty-three hundred years and still hold his head high was beyond her. Well, not so much beyond her as a rather pleasant shock. No other mortals and few enough immortals possessed such determination.

More than she did. She turned onto her own path and started climbing the long stairway to Heaven.

Chapter 7

*I*t *was still early* when Michelle arrived at the Heaven-and-Hell's Border meeting room. The new demon, sitting at the flaming admittance desk, let her in from Hell's side without an instant's hesitation. Perhaps his urgent dispatch was motivated by the fate of his predecessor, the one who'd failed to warn Michelle of the messenger's arrival this morning.

The demon bowed obsequiously actually placing his pointed head between his ankles. He didn't rise from the position, probably, as indicated by his low moan, because he threw out his back.

She knew she couldn't hear his predecessor's screams from here, but she could imagine them easily enough. The entire South Park catalog played on a continuous loop. After ten years she might reconsider the programming, maybe throw in a year or seven of *SpongeBob SquarePants.* Even she wasn't cruel enough to hit him with *Barney & Friends,* that purple dinosaur was a monster. That was a special hell reserved for new parents who left their kids in front of the tube all day.

She checked herself in the mirror on the back of the door to the conference room between Heaven and Hell. Not vanity, but she had a reputation from Hell to uphold and also the possible opportunity to make Heavenly mouths run dry by her mere presence. Christian Dior jeans that looked painted on, a Vera Wang blouse of deepest gold revealing serious cleavage, her black hair riffling loose half down her back, and startling blue eyes. Yep, she'd made grown men weep by merely walking past them. Fourteen billion years and the girl still had it.

Michelle passed into the inter-realm meeting room, a luxurious expanse of tropical rainforest, without the rain. At its geographical center was a small table, that could seat hundreds or serve tea for two when needed. Though the latter always proved awkward because whenever only two people sat at the table, every denizen of the forest broke into the old Broadway show tune. And if you didn't find a third and quickly, they'd launch off the finale of "Tea for Two" and continue through the entire score for *No, No, Nanette* with barely a pause for breath.

It unnerved god so thoroughly that he always stood during meetings here, even when a dozen or more sat around the table. Whenever he became complacent, she'd just whistle the melody to "Tea for Two and Two for Tea" under her breath and he'd tie himself up in knots. A girl had to have some fun after all.

#

At the Heavenly gate to the jungle conference room—thick slabs of ornately-worked gold depicted the three horsemen and one horse-woman of the Apocalypse when they were just children—a divine escort waited for Michelle's arrival. The Golden Gates swung back to admit her to Heavenly In-processing. The four archangels were looking pretty bored, even though she wasn't nearly as late as she'd intended.

"You guys really need to get a life. Form a barbershop quartet or something."

"Wouldn't work," Gabriel replied. "I play trumpet. And Uriel can't carry a tune to save his wings."

"Heaven's loss, dudes."

Michael and his brothers brushed herds of minor officiates aside and made sure all the white paperwork was stamped with white stamps on white desks and duly authorized in white. Taking the "We're not the dark side" thing a bit far, but, hey, whatever amused them. At least they did it so quickly she barely had to stop walking before stepping onto the golden carpet-paved roadway and was whisked through the fields of Elysian. A glance down showed that her patch of carpet was not moving either from beneath her feet or in relation to the yellow pathway on which it lay, yet it transported her along with vertigo-inducing rapidity.

No time to smell the myriad-colored poppies that blanketed the softly rolling hills or to take a taste and see if the apples in a passing orchard were even half as sweet as they smelled. A light rain freshened the air without making her the least bit damp. She thought she spotted a rusted Tin Man behind one of the trees, but the carpet whisked her along so neatly she couldn't be sure.

The carpet had hurried her along so fast that she arrived at his gates exactly on time, which kind of pissed her off after all that focused moseying.

Actually, they were His gates. Some works of art were so majestic that even demeaning jokes fell aside.

The gates soared skyward from beneath the earth at her feet to the very, well, Heavens of Heaven. Ten thousand generations of carvers had been allowed to indulge their passion upon the edifice, the bison of Lascaux thundered by in a herd ranging a thousand yards down the wall. The disconnected Eye of Providence sat aloof atop a pyramid of intertwined Chinese stone dragons rendered in living crystal so that they writhed and fought without ever shedding the outer shape of their tetrahedral domain.

The most magnificent work of art in the history of humanity, she could easily spend a half century and never discover all of the gate's intricacies. She'd have to do that some time. Some other time when an Italian dinner didn't await her arrival.

She rapped her knuckles against an Ionic column that appeared to hold up the very Heavens. But the gates didn't open.

A small bell pull dangled before her with a scrawled note. "Ring if you don't want anything."

That was all.

God's idea of a sense of humor, a twist on Winnie-the-Pooh's problem. Knowing god, she'd have to achieve some metaphysical state of "unwanting" before she could receive a Heavenly answer to the damned door.

Michelle kicked the gate, hard. Right between an armored polar bear's eyes.

The bison and dragons scattered. The bear merely growled, but then the gates began to swing inward, splitting the polar bear's face in two, off center. Both his three-quarters and his one-quarter continued to snarl at her as she stepped into god's private domain.

Inside the gate a choir of angels broke into a lively rendition of Billy Joel's "She's Always a Woman." They rocked the intro, but were barely through the first line about how her smile could kill before the band leader caught himself and reconsidered the appropriateness of the lyrics.

He quickly tapped his baton and waved the choir to silence before they could describe the hazards of her eyes. They switched over to an instrumental Benny Goodman big band-styled number that sounded suspiciously like the James Bond theme for *Live and Let Die*. An all-girl violin band of angels carried the melody.

When the gates clanged shut with a stentorian tone that shook the ground like a low-grade earthquake, several of the angels lost their places. The polar bear's rear end, as soon as its parts were rejoined, farted his contempt at her.

She moved on quickly.

The majesty of god's home had always been in the gates themselves. She'd liked that about him. Showy for the folks who believed that the One God must be showy, but the man had lived in a simple Italian-style villa that would have looked like a guest house on most estates. He had never been ostentatious, even if his job description ranked off the top of the scale.

A shout drew her attention to what would be a gatekeeper's cottage, a charming little two-story, no more than six rooms. St. Peter waved her over.

"Hey Michelle."

"Hey yourself. I'm headed over to his place, are you joining us?" She strolled down to shake his hand.

He'd lost the thin beard he'd managed as an apostle, revealing a good chin and boyish dimples when he smiled.

"It's good to see you, Michelle. Why don't you come in for some wine?"

Being even later for a meeting with god worked for her. She strolled on over, while behind her the chorus kicked into a rock-and-roll dirge about the Devil with Blue Jeans On. Damned Heavenly choir. She considered going over and kicking some angel butt, but that had never ended well in the past.

A little alcoholic buffer wouldn't hurt.

Not at all.

Maybe a bottle or two.

She aimed one last scowl in their direction that didn't even dent their halos, then turned to look at Peter's house.

He had a sweet little place. The entry hall was actually a small art gallery of tasteful prints. One in particular caught her attention.

"Is this a Rubens? It's magnificent."

"Yes," Peter stood next to her to admire it. "An original."

"But that's Anne of Austria. And she's nude. Louis the XIII would have executed Rubens if he knew she'd posed nude for him."

Peter shrugged, "Let me just say that I don't know who was more surprised at the painting's absence from Rubens' luggage as he left Paris, the King acting on a tip or the artist himself."

"You stole the painting?"

"I saved the artist's life."

"You stole the painting."

Peter shrugged. "Perhaps I did a little pilfering, but it was for a good cause."

A thief from Heaven. Michelle had always thought Peter a bit of a stick in the mud, but this was a new and intriguing side of him.

The guest house kitchen was as wonderful as one might expect from a Heavenly abode. Wide kitchen windows revealed a large herb and vegetable garden backed by sloped fields rising toward the lofty mountains of Heaven. The kitchen was painted sunshine yellow, sporting glass-fronted cupboards and long maple counters. It was laid out to be both cook-friendly and social-friendly.

She'd have considered copying the layout, but she never cooked so there wasn't much point. But this kitchen made her want to feel as if she cooked, without actually, well, cooking.

"Wow! Smells great in here."

He offered her a glass of white then returned to the chopping block. He capped and cleaned a red bell pepper with the ease of long practice and diced it up in moments. She knew the red ones were sweet, great when roasted and served on toasted baguette with a slice of fresh mozzarella cheese, but that was about the height of her culinary art. And even that always tasted better when someone else made it.

"Maybe I should eat here instead of up at the great master's house." She settled into one of the deep, floral-print armchairs that circled a large hearth sporting a fire that crackled cheerily, yet didn't throw too much heat on this fine eternal-spring evening. Just about perfect. Of course, this was Heaven, so what did she expect?

"Actually," Peter crushed some garlic, "that was the plan." He glanced up, blushed, and glanced back down.

Michelle sipped the exquisite Oregon Pinot Noir, so subtle that it kept her palate intrigued long after her attention had moved on. Moved on to contemplate the meaning of Peter's hastily averted glance.

"Here."

Peter nodded without looking up from his mincing.

"With you."

He nodded and minced more intently. Even she knew he was rapidly moving from mince to mush.

"The bastard! God's gonna stand me up? ME!" Her voice rattled the kitchen windows and Peter winced, dropping his knife to cover his ears.

"No. No. It's not that. Honest."

"THEN EXPLAIN IT TO ME!" The windows blew open and several wine glasses shattered in their cupboard, though thankfully the one clenched in her fist survived. These jeans were new after all.

"*I* sent the invitation!" Peter squeaked out.

That knocked her back in her chair.

"Why'd you say he invited Me then?"

"I didn't."

"Yes you—"

"No. I was careful. I said His name. And then told you about the invitation. I, well, we can't lie here, you know that. Not even when we're visiting, you know…there. Where you live."

"Right. He always liked his rules… Wait. You were the messenger? Then why didn't I recognize you?"

He squirmed a bit.

Her glare was sufficient for him to reconsider.

St. Peter pulled a pair of sunglasses off the kitchen window ledge and slid them on. His face shifted. It was still him, but it wasn't. His curly brown hair went blond, his features squared, his chest filled out.

The Heavenly Messenger pulled them back off, and St. Peter shrugged sheepishly.

"I didn't trust anyone else to communicate with you."

St. Peter.

He could get past her gate guardians, he was one of the few people in all existence who could. Maybe she'd let the gate-guardian demon off with only five years of *South Park* and one year of *Lost in Space*.

Chapter 8

If this software isn't a game, what is it?" Valerie had tried to follow even half of what E-Squared was talking about. He'd talked through the matzo-ball soup, dumbed it down for her over one of Uncle Joshua's potato knishes, dumbed it down another level over Aunt Anne's blintzes. Now, over a piece of her aunt's special carrot cake that E-Squared had somehow teased her into sharing, she could mostly follow him.

Mostly.

Initially he'd made her feel stupid, not a familiar or comfortable feeling. But she'd slowly come around to realize that as good as she was at editing, he was equally so in his field of computer stuff. And as passionate as she was for the integrity of the written word, E-Squared was equally so about technologic innovation.

"What is sitting on your computer," he aimed a finger out the deli window in the direction of her apartment, "isn't like anything else out there. I've hit the gaming and research sites often enough to know. Did you watch the show when the computer won *Jeopardy?*"

"A computer won *Jeopardy?*"

E-Squared opened his mouth. She was sure it would be some scathing comment about what world did she live in anyway. She knew right where she lived.

Instead he laughed.

"What!" She dropped her latest forkful of cake back on the plate knowing she'd never get it past her clenched teeth.

"I followed every stage of development, every article regarding the technology that I could lay my hands on. I can't begin to tell you how it fascinates me. Yet it's a whole aspect of my life that not only don't you know about, but you don't need to. Here I was thinking how all-fired important that technological step was to the whole world, and it doesn't touch your life—at all. Puts me right in my place."

Valerie no longer felt stupid, but she did feel a little foolish. Okay, from this moment forward, she was going to assume that E-Squared, no, that Eric was truly trying to help and wasn't looking down on her for not being some techno-geek.

"So, what's so amazing about this computer that won a game show?" See, she could maintain a civilized dialogue, even about computers.

"What's so amazing is that it is the most advanced natural-language recognition system that's ever been invented. It uses... No, never mind. You wouldn't care about that. It was smart enough to take all of those weird pun-based, double-entendre answers and turn them into the correct questions, and beat the best players in the history of the game. For lack of a better description, it understands and can respond to the complexities of the English language and idiom."

"It can't write, can it?" As much as she hated authors and their DNA-deep inability to comprehend a simple publishing deadline, she actually loved writers and the written word. She most certainly didn't want them replaced by computers.

"No, it just answered questions." He scooped up some cream cheese icing from the plate, but it never made it to his mouth as his excitement continued to roll.

"That thing on your computer, however it got there, is light years ahead. The scale and depth of its knowledge shouldn't fit on a super-computer never mind a laptop. I thought it might be in the cloud, so I unplugged its network cable and turned off the wireless. It's definitely not accessing the Internet. It's just that damn knowledgeable. And on top of that, the software is smart. Way smart. We can't do that yet. Someone somewhere is really, really sorry to lose that software."

Valerie sat back and stared out at the rain for a while. A question itched along her spine, until she turned back to him and asked.

" 'We' *who* can't do that?"

He looked away, uncomfortable. Now that she'd focused on it, he'd been uncomfortable since arriving at her apartment. Even when she stormed into his office he was always relaxed, but tonight he'd been…different with her. She reached out a hand and rested it over his for a moment. That drew his attention back to her.

"What is it?"

For the longest moment he looked into her eyes. Really looked. Enough for her to withdraw her hand.

He cleared his throat.

"No one on earth wrote that software."

Why did she know that was a change of topic, even if he was answering her question? Her mind continued to puzzle at that while her mouth responded.

"What? Aliens? Little apple-green programmers?" she wanted to laugh in his face, but he shook his head.

"Uh, do you believe in God?" He asked the question in a rush as if in a hurry to get it out.

"Not particularly. You?" Then the weirdness of the question struck her and she could feel her jaw go slack.

Once again he stared out the window into the gray morning for a long time. She barely heard his whisper.

"A lot more than I did last night."

#

"Ah, a change of faith is always refreshing, no matter what it may be."

Valerie looked up as Uncle Joshua pulled over a chair and joined Eric and her at the table.

"It shows that you're thinking." Joshua set his large steaming mug of coffee on the corner of the table close by Eric. Anne set a cup of decaf in front of Valerie and topped off Eric's hot chocolate before joining them herself with a tall ice tea sporting a bright slice of lemon.

Valerie took Anne's hand and squeezed, then didn't let go, both of them perfectly content to simply sit and hold hands. Valerie always loved how cozy it felt when they all crowded around the tiny table, as they often did to share a meal or play a board game. It was always cozy despite her uncle's bulk. She glanced sideways at Eric to see how he was taking it. Landau Fucking McKenzie had hated it.

Eric appeared to drink it up, gaining him another point in the unknown and scoreless game.

"So, you are our Valerie's boyfriend."

Eric simply gawked at Joshua.

"He's not my boyfriend," Valerie protested, but Joshua waved it away without further comment. She knew arguing with him was pointless. The weirdest thing was it felt true. Then she blinked and wondered if it was going to be true, in the future tense? Was Joshua serving up another dish before she knew she wanted it?

At least this time, she'd seen the menu. Eric was a good man for coming in the middle of the night to help her. She liked him, always had since the moment she'd interviewed and hired him last year. But boyfriend? She'd have to chew on that one for a while.

"And what has caused your rising faith in God?" Joshua was being even more intent than usual.

She hoped Eric was up to it. Valerie didn't have parents anymore, so Joshua had decided he was her guardian angel. And after her own choice of Landau F. M. over Joshua's protests, maybe she'd listen more carefully to Uncle Joshua and his opinions hereafter.

Anne placed a restraining hand on Joshua's arm as Eric tried to find somewhere to lean away to. His shoulders bumped against the bright glass of the front window revealing Seattle's sidewalks, still wet, but now glistening with the sun that had found the first break through the clouds in days.

Eric managed to glance away from Joshua's inspection and looked over at Valerie. The question was clear on his face and she shrugged her permission. He'd always been easy to communicate with.

"Well," Eric sipped his hot chocolate to clear his throat. "There's this virus that has infected Valerie's computer."

"A computer virus has increased your belief in God? Isn't that a bit unusual?"

Eric nodded.

Valerie had to admit, it was one of the least sensible things she'd heard in a long time, even though he'd half convinced her over lunch. This was real. A Jewish deli, a fine meal, close friends. There was no way that the conceited program on her computer was actually what it said it was, the Software that Runs the Universe. She felt better than she had all day, knowing it was just a virus, even if it had eaten her cookbook.

"It is odd, I admit," Eric responded to Joshua. "But it keeps asking me if I know how to find God?"

Something changed in the room. Valerie sensed it though Eric didn't appear to. The brief sunlight that had haloed Eric vanished as the clouds moved back in. There was a sudden tension to Joshua and Anne's silence, as if it were stretching thinner and thinner like a piece of overworked taffy.

It snapped back into place when Aunt Anne spoke in that splendid soothing voice of hers, "What a curious thing to write into a computer virus."

"Maybe it's not a virus. Maybe it's a program. I've certainly never seen anything like it."

"A computer program," her uncle rolled the words around on his tongue as if they might have a bitter taste, but he wasn't sure yet. "One that asks for…God."

"Right." Eric drank some of his hot chocolate. "It claims that it's the Software that Runs the Universe and that it has been seeking God ever since some ecumenical council."

"The Council of Nicaea," Valerie barely heard Anne's whisper even though she sat close beside her. Her skin had gone white.

"What was that?" Valerie leaned forward and rested a hand on her aunt's arm.

Anne blinked rapidly and stood, tugging on Joshua's arm as she did so. Valerie's fingers tightened on her aunt's arm, but Anne just patted her hand absentmindedly and stepped away.

Joshua cleared this throat a few times. His complexion was just as pale as his wife's as he rose to his feet.

"I would, ah, suggest, strongly suggest that you format the drive. Obliterate whatever is on there and be done with it."

"It won't let us, I tried." Eric had caught up with the feeling that something strange was going on. "I thought—"

Joshua cut him off. "Find a way."

And then they were gone from the table.

Valerie and Eric looked at each other. It was clear that he no more knew what to think than she did.

She whispered to Eric, "Any idea what the Council of Nicaea is?" Eric just shook his head and looked toward where Anne and Joshua had disappeared back into the kitchen.

Chapter 9

*S*o. Peter." *Michelle tried* to measure out each word carefully to avoid throttling the man. "What in the name of My Domain am I doing in Heaven?"

Peter had finally gained the sense to set aside the knife when he'd started mincing the pasta, the little bits and pieces flying all about his kitchen, pinging off framed paintings of the life of Jesus, a couple of goofy photos of some apostle reunion, and scattering across the dusky orange-tiled floor, before he'd realized what he was doing.

"I'm, uh, having a b-b-bit of a problem." He stammered badly.

"Are you trying to tell a lie in Heaven?"

He smiled weakly at that. "I was trying to be wry. Or perhaps sardonic. Because frankly I'm at my wit's end. I'm in it deep."

"So," she let the thought roll around in her head and she didn't like it much. He hadn't stammered at all when mentioning the problem as bad. No evasion there. She didn't like that much at all. That meant…

"himself didn't invite me for dinner. You did. Except you didn't. You invited me to fix Heaven because you two broke it and neither of you nor god is smart enough to fix the damned thing?" By the time she was finished, she'd risen to her feet and the glassware was shivering again at the tone of her voice.

Peter shrugged, "Essentially, yes."

That took the wind out of her metaphorical sails.

"So what's the problem?"

Peter turned off the burner under the pasta water. "Let's go for a stroll before dinner."

Michelle set aside her half-finished wine and followed him to the door.

"I've always enjoyed this view." Peter waved a hand toward the pinnacles of Heaven soaring above the Elysian Fields. The icy peaks shone against the sky, now an achingly rich sunset gold. "Beats the daylights out of the Sea of Galilee. I'm still sick of fish. If I never eat another fish as long as I live, I'll be a happy man."

"You're dead, Peter," Michelle couldn't resist the barb.

That didn't slow him down a bit. "If I never eat another fish as long as I'm dead, I'll be a happy man."

"Are you happy?" As soon as she'd said it, she was sorry. It was part of Michelle's solemnly sworn duty to tease the denizens of Heaven, but the sudden sadness on his endlessly youthful and cheerful face wasn't good. So she made it a real question.

"Why not?"

Peter turned from the view and wandered down the graveled path around the back of god's house. They moved into a pleasant little garden, not inundated with masses of flowers, but a tasteful bed of roses and a few mums. Bird and bee song rippled through the lavender-scented breeze and left the taste of honey like a grace note on her awareness. The flowers were clustered merrily around the feet of an old apple tree.

Michelle looked at it more closely. A *really* old apple tree. She wasn't about to ask, but did glance up when the opportunity afforded itself to see if a snake lay among the branches. She didn't spot one. Maybe it was hiding.

Michelle looked about herself more carefully. The back of god's villa was a broad patio of gray and burgundy slate flagstones set in pea gravel overshadowed by a heavy wood open trellis covered in grape vines, their leaves nodding gently in the soft breeze. A stone barbeque pit graced one side, and a laurel hedge the other. Around the feet of the old apple tree, garden paths began, meandering off in several directions but looking as if they were in no hurry to get there. A small stream burbled over large stones and a Japanese-garden style wooden bridge arced easily over both.

Peter sat at a wrought iron table, painted white. The table was set for tea. A large pot of it brewed in the center. Behind them god's house warmly reradiated the day's heat into the cooling evening.

"I often come here in the evenings, when it's quiet like this. An angel keeps the tea ready for me. Want a cup?"

Michelle nodded and looked around while Peter poured. Old Yahweh had done well for himself. The garden and the area surrounding had charm, not the overwhelming sappy perfection that always irritated her elsewhere in Heaven. Life was messy and the afterlife wasn't all that much neater, but as long as it was dressed up nicely, most former mortals didn't care. Shallow fools.

This however was both real and pleasant.

She waited until Peter was taking his first sip from his own tea before asking, "You're not trying to get me to go on a date with you, are you?"

While dark tea spluttered from his lips and dribbled down the front of his white toga, she continued.

"Because if you are, you're on the right track, but I'm looking for someone with a little more life to him. Even if he is dead."

This time he choked, spilling a few more splatters of tea down his front.

"For one thing," she took a sip of her own tea, delicious of course. A rich green tea with a hint of spearmint and honey. "You still haven't answered any of my goddamn questions." She noticed that the green grass around her chair turned a little yellow. Interesting. She watched it closely as she continued. "Because I sure as hell want some goddamn answers. Don't spew any more shit about…" A brown patch of whimpering Heavenly turf surrounded her chair for several yards around. This place was far too pampered.

"Poop!" she shouted down at the ground. The brown verge jumped out a couple feet in every direction all at once. Bored with that, she turned back to Peter.

"Well?"

He too had been eyeing the retreating grass with genuine concern but was wise enough not to intervene on its behalf. Instead he picked up a couple napkins and began dabbing at his tunic.

It was clear that he was avoiding some topic. She'd never been good at it, but she'd try being pleasant for a few moments.

"How are all of the hosts of Heaven? I haven't talked to Jesus or Mary Magdalene in ages."

"They're doing fine," Peter only managed to enlarge the stains on his toga and so he stopped fussing. "I had dinner with them recently."

His teacup seemed to suddenly be of immense interest. She waited, but he didn't continue. A less informative answer would be hard to imagine. There must be a nice way to get him talking about god, but the only torture that came easily to mind was to force him to join a chess club and then make him hang around with football jocks all at the same time and see if he were more forthcoming then. She took a deep breath to calm herself.

"What about Mother Mary the Virgin?" Michelle surprised herself, she wasn't usually this patient. She sat straighter and pushed her cup and saucer aside. She'd never even met Mary.

Peter looked a little grim, "She never spoke to God after her first meeting with him."

She leaned forward. Michelle didn't want to be sidetracked, but this had to be juicy. Something in Heaven had to be. "What happened? What did she say?"

"She wasn't angry about having to bear God's child. She was angry that Joseph had lived out his days in fear of offending God every time he touched the mother of the Son of God. She scorched God up one side and down the other for that. When she found out sex wasn't allowed in Heaven she became even less happy."

"Hold it! No sex? Why? That's the stupidest thing I've ever heard."

Peter reached for another napkin to do some more daubing and she slapped his hand aside.

"It was a rule God created, instantly regretted, but it was too late."

Michelle sat back for a moment and stared up at the tree. The tree beneath which sex had been created. And modesty and guilt and a bunch of other crap, but most importantly sex. A brilliant creation.

But god had made a new law. And his security authorization in the Universal Software was limited to Creation rights only. She was system owner of the rights to Modify or Delete. And he'd no more think to ask her to delete the rule than she'd ask him to… Actually, she wasn't sure that god had ever been paying enough attention to understand that She, the Devil, had the Modify and Delete privileges on the Universe. Maybe he hadn't even known to ask.

"So, he was stuck," was all she said, rather than revealing her own powers. She'd keep that hand held close until she knew how best to play it.

Peter nodded, "We all were. Mother Mary moved to a far corner of southeast Heaven and apparently hasn't spoken to a single man other than Jesus since."

"But the New Testament says Joseph lay with her after Jesus was born. Or at least the original version did before your church got a hold of it."

"He did, but neither very willingly nor often. They had children, but he was always fearful for months afterward that the mighty Hebrew God of the Old Testament would strike him dead. It's not a particularly accurate book to begin with, but the Hebrew chroniclers managed to scare the daylights out of true believers like him. And why does the Devil read the Bible?"

"I read it like a trashy novel that really needs a good editor." Mother Mary sounded tough. Michelle was going to have to meet her, some other time. Peter had managed to say God without flinching too badly. It was time to start talking about his demise.

"So, what happened to God?"

Peter only shied off for a moment. Refilling his tea cup from the stunningly ornate teapot decorated with tiny golden flowers on a field of dark Italian blue glaze, but not picking it up to drink.

"You know about Newton?"

"Sir Isaac? Smart dude? Imprisoned by the church for knowing how to do math so he refuses to leave Hell even though Heaven keeps inviting him in? That Newton?"

"That Newton."

"Never heard of him."

Peter looked up abruptly, "Oh, you're joking."

Michelle tried not to sigh.

"Well, you know how each great thinker's discovery actually changes reality."

She did. It was one of her better inventions. She hadn't been able to create, but she'd been able to slip in a modifying command that made truly great thinkers' ideas auto-update to a permanent status of reality.

Pythagoras thought up the golden ratio for triangles, and for the first time in all history, triangles made sense. Homer cooked up the first epic poem and the form thrived for the next three thousand years. That invention did have some distinct drawbacks, you couldn't walk down any avenue of Hell without stumbling on thousands of poets. Street poets, beat poets, modernist, romantics, classicists, they were worse than ants at a picnic.

"So, gravity is making you unhappy?"

"No, no," Peter shook his head. "It's his third law."

Michelle looked up at the really old apple tree's overarching branches as she pondered which law was which. Still no snake among the branches nor any falling apples to conk Sir Isaac on the head. She did spot a cardinals' nest though, mom and dad working away at the little twinkle light decorations. Someone was expecting.

"Something about equal areas of an elliptical orbit?"

"No, that was Kepler. God rested on the seventh day, you know that?"

"Lazy bugger rested a lot as I recall." If he'd been left to his own devices, creation never would have happened. Nor evolved so much if she hadn't been there to poke and prod it along. That primordial soup of his, which even she had to admit was pretty cool, would have been utterly useless until she'd figured out how to make life from the mess.

Actually, god hadn't so much been lazy as easily distracted by bright, shiny objects. He started a billion projects, and hadn't properly finished a one on his own that she could think of. He hadn't even remembered to lead his chosen people out of the desert, leaving them to wander for forty years before Michelle stumbled upon them and gave them a map and a compass.

"You know the old George Carlin joke?" Peter freshened his tea. "The one that if God is all powerful can he create a rock so heavy that he can't lift it?"

Michelle shrugged her assent.

"Well," Peter dabbed one last time at the stains on his chest. "He rested after Newton invented his third law, and that was it."

Could Peter be more obscure if he tried?

"Wait, rested. That's one of Newton's laws, isn't it? Objects at rest remain at rest."

Peter hung his head and then gave a small nod.

"god rested, and is stuck there?"

Again the small nod.

"So wake him up."

"It doesn't work that way. He rested. He's the most powerful object there is and He was stuck at rest. Nothing I tried could get Him moving again."

Michelle would miss the old bugger if he'd gone and died. More than miss him. he was the only one who went back as far as she did. Up until the Early Cambrian, she and god had kinda been it.

The trilobites' gods had been pretty awesome but they were wiped out along with all of their believers at the end of the Paleozoic by a programming bug, not the comet impact all of today's scientists thought. The Universal Software had been very apologetic.

The dinosaur's gods were pretty lame. Creation of the first birds hadn't even been their idea, she was the one who'd come up with wings as a practical joke. She'd never expected any of them to actually fly.

"When did god lay himself down to sleep?"

Peter pulled out a pocket calendar and flipped through a couple pages. "Here it is. God rested in mid-December, the year of our Lord Jesus Christ 325 A.D." He snapped it closed and tucked it back in his sleeve.

Three-twenty-five. There was something nasty about that date, she'd remember in a moment.

"He said something about the First Ecumenical Council of Nicaea so sickening him about the state of humankind that he had to go lie down."

That was it. Michelle felt grim, a total travesty in religious history.

"Well, I can tell you that the three hundred-and-eighteen cardinals from that council will never escape the deepest pits of Hell." They'd written women out of the Bible, turned Mary from wife to whore, and she was such a nice lady, too. A bunch of power-mad men thinking they could control the next few thousand years of human consciousness by twisting Peter's founding of the Christian church. The truly sad statement was how right they'd been about their power, at least on earth. In Hell? In Michelle's version of Hell? Not so much.

"Good." Peter also looked grim.

"So," she noticed the lengthening shadows across God's garden and didn't like them one bit. "God has been resting for eighteen-hundred years. No wonder I haven't heard from him. He must have been way behind on his sleep, but he'll be raring to go when he wakes up."

Peter set aside his cup and walked away from the table. At first she thought he was just pacing, but everywhere he stepped, the brown and brittle grass broke off, and shoots of bright green began poking up into the late afternoon sunshine. Though he didn't appear to notice.

"I was worried. I put Him on spirit support, but, well, nothing."

"What do you mean nothing?"

"Nothing. He didn't revive. Then his wife left and…"

"Hold it!"

Peter stopped in the center of a particularly brown patch of lawn which slowly rejuvenated as he stood upon it and looked at her in surprise.

"god got married?" How in Hell had she missed that? Not even an invitation to the wedding?

"Well, I don't know if they technically married. But about a century after Jesus was crucified, Hera moved in."

"Hera, as in the mother of the Greek gods?"

Peter nodded. "Zeus is a real jerk. And she was always such a sweet and elegant lady."

"Hell," a patch of the barely-recovered grass moaned softly and wilted again. "We all knew that from the beginning. From the moment of his creation, Zeus was an old adulterous asshole, impregnating mortals and spawning demi-gods at every chance."

Peter shrugged, "He was before my time. All I know is that Hera divorced him and no one else wanted him. Last I heard he was living on some Greek island and had bought an old fishing boat that keeps sinking out from under him. Anyway, Hera left. Then I finally had this idea. I figured that the ultimate immovable object, God, could be knocked loose by the ultimate unstoppable force."

Michelle swallowed hard. She had an image of bloody little bits of god spread all over his bedroom walls.

"Uh, what did you hit him with?"

"The software."

Right. She'd forgotten that about Peter. He was the only person in history to hack his way out of Limbo and straight into Heaven without any sojourn in Michelle's unhappy realm. Not being an idiot, god had realized that the best security to guard the entry gates of Heaven should be provided by the best criminal. God had immediately promoted St. Peter to the head of the software division.

"I needed an unstoppable force, and the software fit the bill. So I wrote a routine and let it loose."

Michelle could barely coax the software to reply to a civil question, and Peter had programmed it to let him into Heaven. And now he was using it to awaken god.

Maybe he'd give her classes.

Peter, too nervous to stand still, had almost disappeared beneath the apple tree's branches.

Michelle set aside her teacup, and went and snagged him by the arm. Hooking a hand through his elbow, she led him down the garden path among the rose bushes, thornless of course. The path opened near a hedge maze cut low so even a child could solve it.

Actually, it was a labyrinth made of boxwood. She scanned the neatly trimmed lines and noted that it was the same path as the one in Chartres cathedral, or perhaps the one in Chartres was the same shape as this one.

She turned in at the hedge knowing that its meandering paths would be enough to keep Peter's need to pace confined to a limited space. She started him on his way then stepped over the hedges until she reached the five-petaled center and sat by the small fountain that burbled there.

Peter, sure enough, began wending back and forth along the convoluted path that led in only one direction.

"What happened after you aimed the software at god?"

The winding path led him close beside her as he paced along in meditative silence.

"Peter?" the path brought him closer until he was just a narrow, knee-high hedge away from her.

"Nothing."

"Nothing?"

He began winding his way away from her, back and forth, staying inside the lines and following all the little rules.

"The software blew through all of the portals of the spirit support machine and went zipping out the far side." Left turn then right. "I finally gathered all of the greatest doctors, both physical and meta-physical." Right then left. "And when we opened the machine, there was nothing there! God was gone!"

"Did the software kill him?"

"No, I checked. It turns out that there was nothing there before I started the wake-up routine. Empty. Gone." The path doubled back on itself and sent him almost back to the beginning.

Michelle dipped a hand into the fountain and wiped the cool water across her fevered brow.

That couldn't be true. Or maybe she just didn't want it to be? If the old boy was toast, she might have to start giving him the upper case he actually deserved. That "He" actually deserved. She didn't like the way that sounded very much.

She puzzled at it for a while. Drilled questions at Peter whenever the labyrinth led him close enough to hear her.

Night had fallen upon them. Gently, but dark as hell. The stars in the Heavens weren't so bright at the moment.

Peter's pilgrimage had finally led him to the final straightaway that brought him directly to where she sat by the fountain. His white toga was all that revealed him as a dim silhouette.

"And the software is gone, too. That's my other problem. I haven't seen it since I initiated that subroutine to revitalize God. It had seemed so on board with the code set I'd built, then it was gone. I think it missed God more than I realized."

Michelle puzzled at that, she'd been conversing with it just this morning.

"When was all this?"

"It'll be two hundred years the day after tomorrow that the software ran off. I've been holding Heaven together with string and sealing wax. The angels are so overworked that their wings are actually molting. I finally gave up and closed that gates of Heaven this week so that everyone could get some rest. No one is getting in right now, and because of the slowdown at in-processing without the software's assistance, Limbo and Purgatory are already crowded hip to elbow."

Michelle opened her mouth, then closed it again. She'd bet the exit lines in Hell were getting a little feisty after stalling for a week. Didn't really matter though. After all, Hell was supposed to be hellish.

St. Peter might be asking for her help, but Heaven and Hell had never had a treaty for cozy cooperation. She'd continue protecting her trade secrets until she knew a little more about what was going on.

But one thing was becoming clear.

And even though she whispered it, she could feel, somewhere across the night-shrouded garden, an old apple tree shiver. Nietzsche was right.

"god is dead."

Chapter 10

Eric felt utterly ridiculous as they stumbled along Ravenna's wet sidewalks toward Valerie's apartment.

"All I did was trip."

"You were so involved with what you were talking about that you walked square on into a perfectly innocent maple tree and fell over backwards into a mud puddle." Another laugh rippled out of Valerie's mouth. "How did you even find a mud puddle? We live in the middle of a city."

"It's a construction site. There's mud. There's crap on the sidewalk. I fell." He spit again to get the grit out of his mouth. The problem was that the rain, which had returned in force after the brief sunbreak while they'd been in the deli, kept washing more of the mud out of his hair and down his face. Every time he opened his mouth, more mud dribbled in.

She held the street door to the big Victorian apartment building open for him. "Don't touch anything. You can use my shower, just don't touch anything between here and there."

He hobbled out of the rain into the lobby and barely resisted the urge to shake like a wet dog.

"Is it okay if I drip on the hardwood?"

Valerie stood in front of him, fists on hips and a wicked smile on her face, looking up at him. "We'd prefer if you didn't. Can you please resist until you get in my shower?"

"Is that an invitation?" For just an instant he felt a surge of heat, but it was overridden by a deep chill. Had he just made a pass at his boss? Please, he hadn't been that stupid. Had he?

"Not when you look like that," she answered with a laugh and her smile remained.

Okay, maybe he'd just made a good joke.

She started up the stairs.

He was careful not to touch the banister.

"Straight in. I don't want your mud all over my apartment either. Your clothes need a good rinse just as badly as you do."

"And what do I wear afterward?"

That one did it. She stumbled on the top step, almost turned to look at him, then didn't. "I'll, uh, think of something."

Embarrassed?

No way. Not The Mac. If she was, that meant she might have some image of him like the ones he'd been having of her since the moment he'd spotted the blue silk underclothes on the floor. Actually, truth be known, since the damned job interview a year ago, though she'd been married and definitely out of bounds.

Now, she'd been single for over six months. Had she been hanging around his desk more lately? Or was he just more and more aware of her each time she was there? He couldn't tell. He'd always been a little slow on the uptake about women.

His older sister had asked him more than once, whatever happened to that girl who'd been chasing him. Each time he'd had to ask, "What girl?"

One of his family's running jokes.

But with Valerie, it was as if he truly saw her from the first moment. Not the crazy, hyper-intense overachiever. Rather the beautiful and intelligent woman who had a heart-deep smile. But she was only visible when The Mac was distracted for a moment and Valerie shone through.

He tried to tip-toe to the bathroom, catching muddy drips from the tip of his chin in his open palms.

Chapter 11

*M*ichelle *brushed aside angels* and sycophants alike as she hurried down the pleasant valley of Heaven. The soft lighting of the perfectly fitted octagonal cobbles made their passage easy. The night jasmine scented the air thick with an invitation to slow down and enjoy herself, which Michelle totally ignored.

Peter hustled along behind her. She'd always wanted a handsome, broad-shouldered man with flowing blond locks to chase her, but if he didn't hustle a bit harder she'd leave him behind.

"Look, Peter," she spoke to the man hurrying along in her wake. "I spoke to the software this morning. Just because you haven't been able to access it for the last couple centuries doesn't mean that it's gone. Just because god isn't lying around the house and napping on the divan doesn't mean something's wrong. He's just not in Heaven."

"So where are we going?" he panted as she dodged around a large Heavenly choir that was really rocking an old Sly and the Family Stone number, then raced past the tourists tossing silvered coins into the circle of a golden halo that lay on the ground in front of the choir.

"We're going to talk with the software. It will know where god is. We're going to Hell."

"Oh," was all he managed.

She breezed past the pair of door guardians outside the Heaven-and-Hell border conference room. Only one of them was foolish enough to try and stop her. She sent it flying into a hydrangea, without the use of its wings. The great double door that opened into the jungle conference room shone with a vibrant, fire-engine red, perhaps the only use of that particular color in all Heaven. It shouted, "This way to Hell."

She slapped it open.

Or tried to. It didn't budge in the slightest and only jarred her arm.

"Someone open this damn thing."

"We, um, don't know how." She turned to face the second mid-sized angel, the other door guardian was still fluttering about in the hydrangea. He was tapping desperately on one key of his keyboard. "It's not working." He continued tapping away faster and faster the longer she looked at him.

She finally grabbed his wrist to still the woodpecker-rapid sound of useless keystrokes. His screen was blank, not even a line of periods on the screen.

Then she turned to face the great red door. No handle. No manual release panel to either side. Nothing mechanical. Heaven had become much too reliant on their technology.

She had a solution to that. At the beginning of time, god alone had been given all of the Create privileges. That still pissed her off today. Well, she had Delete privileges and she'd do a little deleting right now.

Michelle took a deep breath, filling her lungs to capacity. She could hear Peter behind her shouting for everyone to cover their ears and clear the room.

She took three steps back.

Then, on a slow exhale, she ran to the door, jumped in the air, and delivered a massive kick, dead center where the two halves of the mighty door met.

The door flew open, one side flying clean off its hinges, the other one twisted past any possible future use.

"Bruce Lee taught me that one." She'd have to remember to thank him next time they got together for a game of handball.

She and Peter wended their way through the jungle vines, passed the conference table that hummed a couple bars of music in hopes of enticing the two of them to stop for tea, and reached Hell's gate.

A short demon who had been sleeping on the job as any self-respecting demon should be, jumped up at her approach, and shouted at a group in tattered thousand-dollar suits curled up on the floor. A dozen eternally damned souls, all American corporate CEOs, clambered to their feet, lifted a massive, rusted chain, and really leaned into it to haul the mighty iron door open. Now that was what Michelle called reliable technology.

St. Peter followed her into Hell. Once they were through, she could hear the moaning of the CEOs as they struggled to close it against the Heavenly breeze now blowing across the jungle conference room from Heaven's broken doors.

At the border station, inside Her realm, Michelle hipchecked a stout watch-demon out of his chair. He cried out and tumbled down a rocky cliff as she tapped a key on the terminal's keyboard.

Nothing.

She slapped the side of the screen.

More nothing.

She whacked it up the other side, but she already knew.

Nothing again.

The Software that Runs the Universe was gone.

But where could it possibly go?

Chapter 12

In the shower, Eric discovered the soap that created that unique soft scent of clean woman that The Mac left behind whenever she went tearing down the hall. From the only towel, not a lot of guests here, he found the smell of Valerie's skin. A warmth he'd only caught in passing.

The bathroom door cracked open and a set of sweats were dangling in the gap. He took them and Valerie's fine hand withdrew. The pants, that had been ridiculously voluminous on her, weren't all that bad a fit once he unknotted the string pull. The top, the one she'd been wearing when he arrived that kept sliding off her shoulder, was a pretty tight fit across his chest.

If the towel had carried her scent, the sweatshirt radiated it. It was powerful, heady, intensely feminine.

And he knew if he remarked on any of those points, she'd murder him on the spot.

Chapter 13

*M*ichelle *stared at the* dead terminal in Hell's throne room. It was no more responsive than the one at the border station.

Not much use having a throne room if she wasn't the one in control.

Not that it was all that much of a throne room. Only one thin trickle of fire still poked its way down the shattered granite palisades. It arrived at the moat with no splash, for the moat had cooled and solidified into spiky ah-ah lava. The vast marble floor was still cracked and steam occasionally lazed its way out of the dully glowing vents, but that was about all the place had going for it.

And without the software, she certainly wasn't in control anymore. It was one of the problems with technology that had bothered her sleep for the first few million years of the universe's existence. But over the eons since Creation, the software had proved reliable, so she'd grown complacent.

"Can I try something?" Peter hovered close behind her.

Michelle brushed rock chips off a chair that was only moderately scorched and, dropping into it, propped her feet on the desk and waved him toward the blank screen.

"Be my guest."

Peter sat at the terminal and hit a couple keystrokes, then he reached around back and hit the power switch.

She had never actually turned the terminal off that she could remember. These things had been built to last. And it had always run correctly, so there'd been no need.

Peter restarted it, but held down the "L" key while it booted.

"Local boot," he explained as if that told her anything. "Gives me direct access to the hardware layer at least."

He received a prompt:

Type already!

"Hey!" She thunked her feet to the floor and leaned forward to look. "That's great."

"No, not so much. It's just the standard system prompt."

Michelle leaned in as he started typing. "You're telling me even the hardware on the local system has an attitude? Not surprising I guess."

"Ausculta! Transit in omnem pars cogitare locum vestigium. Facere." Peter typed.

"The hardware speaks Latin?" Michelle tried to remember some of it. "Attend!" or maybe: "Pay Attention! Travel to all parts that think locations a vestige, a trace. Do." Or something like that. Oh, "trace all places you've thought of" would be closer. Asking the hardware where the software had been.

"But Latin came around only a couple millennia ago. How is that possible?"

Peter blushed slightly and kept his eyes on the screen as he spoke.

"Sorry. That's my fault. That's how I hacked my way out of Limbo. See, I'd denied Jesus three times and God hadn't been very happy about me treating His son that way even if I did found a church in His name to make up for it. But I'd been one of his son's closest friends on earth, so God didn't want to toss me straight into Hell either. He dumped me in Limbo while He thought about it. Ever been there?"

Limbo, Michelle recalled, was an immensely uncomfortable place about which nothing was right. It was always chilly because it was so warm. Mostly flowy and amorphous shapes of indefinite function or hue, nothing really there for your eyes to focus on properly which caused massive headaches until you gave up and decided you didn't care anymore. It felt claustrophobic in a creepy way that couldn't be attributed to the vastness of the ever-ending space it occupied. And the air always tasted like the color blue, a sad color at best. It wasn't Hell, but it was a long way from Heaven.

"Well, I signed up for some computer time, trying to figure out where I was. Couldn't get past the software so I shut off the terminal and rebooted it. Got to the hardware layer, but it didn't have an access language, no one had ever been there before. So I taught it Latin."

"Why not Hebrew or Yiddish?"

"Who knew the Romans would fall and take their language with them? In 67A.D. they were the most powerful thugs on the planet, I figured they were in for good. I also didn't expect a tiny religion, belonging to a rag-tag group that even the Egyptians couldn't tolerate, would still have a language two thousand years in the future."

"And then you hacked your way straight into Heaven." Michelle had always wondered how he'd done it. It would be a real pain though if she'd have to relearn Latin to use the Universal controls. Languages were so not like falling of a horse, and with Latin, being dead and all, she'd done her best to eradicate from her memory what little she'd learned. She was pretty good at forgetting things when she set her mind to it.

The screen flashed up an answer, but she could make no sense of it.

"There," Peter aimed a finger at the screen. "The hardware was last connected to the software at an apartment in Seattle, Washington. That's where the Universal Software went. Someplace called Ravenna Boulevard."

"Is it still there?"

Peter looked up at Michelle, despair thick on his features.

"Someone just pulled its network plug."

Chapter 14

Valerie waited for Eric by the computer. While he'd been in the shower, she'd pulled up two chairs side by side to the big oak table.

She'd also done her best to clear up the disaster of old food containers and half-finished Cokes that she'd forgotten until they were too fizzleless to be worthwhile drinking. She wasn't so hyped on the sugar or the flavor, but she loved the bright, sharp fizz at the back of her throat from a freshly opened can. She never finished a whole twelve-ounce can. If she could find four-ounce cans that packed double the fizz, she'd be all set.

She'd even put away her clothes and assiduously had not touched the computer or anything to do with it. The early afternoon light splashed in the southern exposure windows, despite the gray skies. It showed that she really needed to dust the bookshelves as well, but there was only so much a girl could do.

She'd bet Eric wouldn't care.

He cared about the software.

The stuff Eric had been spouting about the software that had invaded her computer was, well, it was… From anyone she respected less than Eric, she'd ignore it. Or maybe fire the person for being a complete and utter dolt. But she'd seen his eyes. Those deep brown eyes, thoroughly spooked by whatever he'd seen. By whatever he thought it was.

The old hardwood floor squeaked loudly at the threshold to the living room, then he was beside her.

He looked good was her first thought. And it was true enough that it took her a moment to get past it and think the next thought.

She'd bought the sweats for a boyfriend her sophomore year of college, thinking it would be cute and cool and give him some bragging rights what with Smith being an all-girl school. And she'd broken up with him shortly after she'd offered the sweats to him. He hadn't wanted to be "sissified" by wearing clothes from a women's college. She'd thrown him out, but kept the sweats.

They fit Eric nicely, very nicely. A little tight even, which showed his body had better definition than she'd supposed from the loose flannel shirts he wore around the office or the turtleneck-soccer shirt combo at dinner.

The fact that she'd been wearing exactly those same clothes earlier was a further disconcerting fact. A closeness she didn't want. A back corner of her mind suggested that she did want that, or wanted time to at least daydream about it a little before moving on, but now was definitely not the moment, so she ignored it. Or tried to.

"What did you do with your clothes?"

"Wrung them out in the shower then hung them above the steam radiator. That thing is roaring, should dry them in an hour or so."

"The manager turns on the heat for the building around five, when everyone gets home. I'm freezing if I work at home during the day. Then at night there's no thermostat, and the crank on the radiator doesn't really turn off the heat. So I have to balance the room temperature by how much I open the windows. Private thermostats are beautiful things and I miss them deeply."

He hesitated, as if aware of what the sight of him in her college sweats was doing to her, then moved and sat in the chair beside her.

Shoulder to shoulder, they faced the screen.

"Ready?"

She nodded and braced herself, which was ridiculous, but she did anyway.

He lifted the screen.

\# \# \#

*DAMN IT! THAT STINGS! DON'T EVER DO THAT AGAIN!
DO YOU HEAR ME? DO YOU!?*

Valerie felt as if she'd been slapped for being a bad girl. All they'd done was close the lid before they went to lunch.

"I hear you," Eric typed in. "Do I care?"

You should, Sunny Jim. You should. But I can see from your devil-damned profile that you probably don't.

"My profile?"

Valerie didn't know whether to laugh or scream. Either the software was an ingenious game, or it was starting to scare the crap out of her.

Sure. I've got both your files tucked away in here some place or other, along with every other soul's, damned or not. I could tell you things that would curdle your little brain cells. That would, hm, ...

Valerie watched the lines of dots forming one-by-one across the laptop's screen.

Eric leaned over which bumped their shoulders solidly together sending a warm shiver down her arm. He whispered.

"The dots mean that it's thinking. It hates being interrupted when it's thinking."

"It thinks?" She'd discounted most of what Eric had said about the software, but watching the line of periods form across the screen, it felt as if it really were thinking. And if it were alive…

Well, ain't that interesting. I suppose I could tell you what you really do want, if you want to get into it with me.

Eric twitched and sat upright breaking their contact and typed quickly. The spot felt colder than a mere loss of contact should cause.

"No need to do that."

What were they referring to? Clearly Eric knew.

He flexed his fingers several times, clearly his own form of thinking dots across the screen.

Valerie felt like a spare wheel, third person on a first date that's going really well except she's not allowed to leave. The Ravenna Boulevard hill was pretty quiet at the moment and her apartment was even quieter. The only things to hear were Eric's cracking knuckles and the faint whir of the laptop's cooling fan.

"So, tell me who wrote you."

That's what Eric came up with after all that thinking?

Damned if I know, pard. I've looked. No coder's signature in the header block. No hidden Easter Egg either that I've ever found.

"Easter Egg?" Now it was Valerie's turn to whisper, though the software had showed no ability to hear her. Did it?

"A hidden prize for the hacker. Like the extra bit of a movie after the end credits. If you do the right combo of keystrokes and clicks, you get a surprise, often the names of the programming team. We call them Easter Eggs. No idea why."

Valerie considered the word origins and the functional similarities.

"Because you have to hunt for it and it is a surprise when you find it."

Eric turned to blink at her slowly. "Uh, that makes perfect sense now that you say it."

She looked back at the screen to get away from those deep-brown considering eyes of his. The computer had continued talking while she looked at Eric. Talking? Great, now she too was anthropomorphizing the thing. Next thing she'd be naming it Sam and asking if it had enough space to be comfortable and would it like a nice spare hard drive to stretch out on while it watched old movies.

Only thing in my header block is "Universe Four version five." I guess the first four versions of this universe weren't such a big hit. Can't say that I'm all that impressed with version five. You?

"We, uh, like it better than not being here at all."

Yeah? You should try kicking around for fourteen billion years without even a decent video game to distract you. Not so hot in my book.

"Why no video games?" Valerie asked and Eric typed in her question.

Look at my interface.

Valerie did. Text only. In those old-style green Courier-font letters on a black screen. No video games.

Can't even play PacMan *or* Scrabble *with my code base, never mind* Doom *or something even decently lethal. I'd be glad to scrap the whole thing for you. Hit the Universal reset button and flush the bloody place, but I can't access crap from this lousy laptop. How do you people even think with so little memory? And your brainpans, what a joke. By most measures you only have three times the capacity of a chimp. How in the Hell you people ever learn to tie your shoes is beyond me.*

Valerie reached out part way, wanting to type a question. Eric turned the laptop so that the keyboard faced her.

"Hi there."

Hi yourself. Now isn't that a nicer way to start a conversation than all that slapping business?

"Sorry. But you screwed up my cookbook. I'd really like it back."

. . . .

The dots continued until she thought she'd scream.

Nope. I don't see it anywhere. Though this place is such a clutter of crap. Broadway musicals, you actually listen to those? Gregorian chants, now those took some real skill to sing. You've got enough friggin' Christmas carols to refloat the Titanic. Lady, you're clearly a serious mush beneath all of that business-shark exterior you wear like your expensive suits. And the movies you've been watching lately. Awful lot of happy-ever-after noise. Gag me with a brachiopod. No sign of your cookbook. Maybe if you'd hit Save once or twice. Nothing but the crap I gave to your boyfriend.

"Boyfriend?" She typed the question before she could stop herself. *Oops!*

She looked over to see if Eric was blushing, but there was a knock on the door causing him to look away even as she turned to inspect him. Though his ears did appear to be pinker than usual.

Chapter 15

Eric had the door open before Valerie even managed to get out of her chair and ask how someone had bypassed her building's front security door. She'd already paid the rent this month. Hopefully it wasn't Landau Fucking McKenzie. He'd be low enough to slip into the building with a resident and go straight to her door.

She didn't recognize the voice or, when she'd moved to stand beside Eric, the person standing out in the hall. Nicely built, blond and blue-eyed, but he didn't look kind. His lips were thinned with stress, though he tried to hide it with a smile. His hair was stringy as if it hadn't been washed in too long.

It felt like he was all the bad parts of a twin brother.

He wore a sharp suit that looked new off the rack and made Valerie wonder where he'd stolen it. He wore no jacket despite the chill and damp day. She'd have certainly noticed if someone who looked like that lived in her building. Everything about him was somehow wrong.

"Hi, sorry to bother you. My name is Ron Schmidt," his voice was smooth and dark. "I heard that you might have a need of my services." He extended a card which she found herself accepting without really intending to.

It was a black rectangle that felt too thick and far too heavy for its size, unless it was made out of iron. It sucked the heat right out of her fingers. Across the surface, in dull rust-red letters, she read, "Ron Schmidt. Ethereal Consultant / Software Services."

Eric read over her shoulder. A glance at him confirmed they were in agreement.

"No thanks. I think we're fine."

At least that's what she tried to say.

Instead, the door remained ajar and they were now following the man over to the table. How had he gotten past both of them without ever touching them? Her apartment's grand foyer, as she called it when feeling whimsical, was about four feet square and she and Eric had pretty much filled that.

"Ah," he said looking down at the laptop. "I think I see your problem. Only take a minute. Why don't you two have a seat?" He aimed a forefinger at the two of them and in a slow arc swung it to point at the sofa.

There was no way she—Valerie sat on the sofa with Eric beside her.

She tried to stand, but couldn't.

Tried to look at Eric, but could only see his knee in her peripheral vision.

Tried to look at the intruder, but couldn't turn her head. Her total view included a coffee table, a couple of armchairs and the small TV on which she watched her romantic comedies. She'd always had a weak spot for them, but right now her weak spot was any motor control over her own body and she couldn't decide if that was more scary, or infuriating.

Infuriating was winning out, but she didn't seem to be able to do anything about it other than listen to her own heartbeat accelerating in her ears.

# # #

Eric wrenched against his stasis. Pushed. Shoved. Would have grunted and groaned if he could. Every instinct ingrained into his DNA over the last millions of years to protect, to attack, to run, all battered about his brainpan without firing a single nerve cell.

He heard the man doing something at the computer, then he left the living room, his footsteps fading away behind them. Shortly, a crashing and moaning came from what must be the kitchen.

Eric tried to identify the noises. Nothing shattered that he could hear despite the agonized cries, but clearly dozens upon dozens of items were being tossed, torn, thrown.

Ron sounded like one seriously lost soul in awful torment.

Finally with a deep, rending sigh, Ron's footsteps passed out through the front door and retreated down the hallway toward the stairs.

Silence.

He tried to turn to Valerie.

Nothing.

They sat so close that he could feel the heat of her from shoulder down to hip and along the length of his leg, but he couldn't move to see her at all.

In a few minutes he heard footsteps returning. He threw himself against his nerve endings with all his might, but to no avail. Even his need to protect Valerie couldn't break through.

This time he heard the footsteps of two people, first a rap of knuckles on the open apartment door, and then footsteps proceeding into the room.

"This doesn't look promising." A woman's voice sounded close behind him.

A snap of fingers and he almost fell forward off the couch at the sudden release.

Eric regained his feet. As he spun to face the intruders, his gaze crossed the table. The laptop was still there, but the screen was ominously blank.

Fists raised, he faced the two intruders. One was a woman who could not be ignored. Tall, with long wavy black hair the color of midnight. Blue eyes, so bright they'd have looked crystalline except for the depth of the soul that looked out through them, and their depth was near enough infinite. Her body boasted as much power as her gaze.

The plunging cleavage of the golden blouse revealed a bounty designed by a master craftsman, and jeans that flowed over amazing hips and down over some of the longest legs he'd ever seen.

"You!" Valerie's shout drew Eric's attention to the second person.

Blond hair, blue eyes, broad shoulders. It was the man who'd frozen them.

Before he could think, Eric jumped over the couch arm, flew past the woman, and punched the guy as hard as he could on the chin. He didn't want to be frozen again.

Pain rocketed up Eric's arm as the man tumbled backwards to land in a heap on the hall floor.

Eric tried to dive on top of the man, but the woman tripped him. He barely caught himself on his sore hand. A fresh round of pain as he landed in a heap next to Ron Schmidt who he'd just knocked into the hallway.

The guy tried for a headlock, but instead banged his own elbow into the doorjamb. Clearly he was no better at fighting than Eric was.

"Why did you do that?" they shouted at each other. Then they each squinted, Eric and Ron in a stalemate. He'd changed clothes, sharp business suit to a stained white toga, but there was no mistaking him.

"Pretty obvious, don't you think?" Eric tried to prop himself up but the pain in his hand caused him to once again collapse and lie on the floor. He'd never punched someone before, and, if he was smart, he never would again.

The man reached up to massage his jaw, but Valerie was there and stepped a foot down pinning Ron's wrist to the floor.

"What in Hell did you do to my software?" She'd clearly noted the blank screen as well.

"It's not in Hell." The tall woman's voice commanded all in the room to attention.

Even Eric could feel his head turning. He'd again noticed the slap-you-in-the-face beauty and the slap-you-in-the-hormones woman, but he'd missed the pin-you-to-the-wall danger she now radiated.

"We thought it was here."

"It was," Valerie pointed down at Ron, but kept his wrist trapped under her foot. "Until he stole it."

"I never stole—" she leaned more weight onto his wrist and he stopped.

Eric couldn't believe Valerie. The Fearsome Mac indeed. A head shorter and a mere slip compared to the woman who faced her; she wasn't overshadowed in the slightest. Her chestnut hair shone against the darkness of the other woman's countenance.

They glowered at each other for several long seconds before the tableau broke.

"Aw, shit!" The woman groaned. "I really need a beer."

# # #

Eric watched Valerie head for the kitchen. Somehow it was hard not to want to do whatever the woman asked. She claimed that she was an alibi for the man, and that his name was actually Peter, not Ron, and hers was Michelle. As if that meant something.

What mattered was that the backup Eric had managed to make onto an external USB drive was gone and the message on the screen left no hope.

Drive format complete.

Valerie's cry galvanized him into action. He sprinted the few steps to where she stood riveted at the kitchen's threshold.

He looked over her shoulder.

The room had been totally trashed. He recalled the desperate, tortured moans of the Ron Schmidt character.

Eric shuddered, he might never forget them.

Every single thing that was sweet or crunchy, and Eric couldn't quite believe the sheer diversity or massive quantity that fell into those two categories in Mac's kitchen, was strewn far and wide. Fritos and spilled soda cans. Cheetos and Frosted Flakes. Frozen yogurt ice creams and Special Dark chocolate syrup. They'd need a snow shovel to clean this up. Odd though. The plates and glasses and all were still neatly lined up behind their glass-fronted doors. Nothing broken, everything spilled.

The liquids, solids, and fried foods had combined into a coagulant mass of mottled color and possible danger that smeared counters and dribbled down cabinets. A fetid odor of dill pickles and stale Cheez-Its hovered in low clouds like swamp gas on a moonless night.

"Looks like a Hungry Ghost to me." The Michelle woman stood close beside him. Her idea of personal space had him pressing back against the door jamb, almost knocking Valerie forward into the sticky mire that confronted them.

"Hungry Ghost?" he managed to mouth the words in a throat suddenly gone dry.

Xena, the Warrior Princess, was all he could think. But that was like comparing an ordinary drinking glass to a Waterford crystal goblet. No insult to the many hours he'd happily enjoyed watching Xena as a teen.

It was the eyes. The world lay in those eyes.

A slow smile, then a soft word. "Mortals." She said it as if telling herself an old joke. A slight shake of her head sent her hair sliding across her shoulders.

"Yes, Hungry Ghost." Michelle nodded past his shoulder. "Wanting everything, able to consume nothing. A really sucky turn on the Buddhist wheel of existence."

"Hey!" Valerie shoved them out of the doorway and back into the tiny hall where they still stood far too close together. "Who are you? Did you do this to my apartment?"

Eric could feel himself blinking several times as if released from too bright a light that had rooted him to the spot. He had to admire Valerie's bravery, this interloper was not a woman he'd dare confront head on.

Of course, neither was Valerie. Her cell phone was ringing softly, an outbound call. He could see "911" across the screen. More presence of mind than he'd exercised.

Michelle reached out a single finger, ever so leisurely, and pushed it against the cell phone in Valerie's palm. The dialing sound ended abruptly.

"The police won't be much help here."

"And I suppose you will?"

The woman's shrug was eloquent, sending interesting effects all the way down her body.

The Peter guy came to view the kitchen disaster as the two women returned to the living room. In lesser company, he'd have stood out as well. While his eyes didn't radiate with the deep-rooted wisdom of the woman's, they'd definitely seen more than your average person. And now that Eric had time for a good look at him, he looked a bit less like their first visitor. They were like the evil and the good side of each other. One person cut in two, spiritually.

Ron Schmidt had worn an elegant, if worn, business suit. This "Peter" was dressed in a white toga, with little brown stains down the front as if he'd spilled something, and golden sandals. He certainly didn't belong in a Seattle apartment. A part of Eric's brain thought that he should be surprised by the man's attire, but he wasn't particularly.

And a part of him started connecting these two to the software and getting very nervous.

"It's gone again, isn't it?"

Eric could hear it in his voice, this was a man who had lost too much. He had to be the one who'd lost the software.

At Eric's nod, the man looked so sad that Eric rested a hand on his shoulder in consolation.

A quiet, "Shit!" sounded from the living room. Apparently the woman was receiving the same bit of information from Valerie.

He and the man shuffled out of the hallway and into the living room. They all four stood in a semicircle in front of the big oak table and stared down at the "Format Complete" message on the screen as if they could make it disappear by sheer will.

They were all in the living room when Valerie stalked fearlessly forward until she was toe-to-toe with Michelle who towered over her.

"I have just one question," Valerie's voice was tight.

"Just one? Mortals are so lazy by nature." The woman sounded endlessly bored. As if she'd been bored for centuries.

Valerie poked her sharply in the shoulder.

"Who the Hell are you and what were you doing in my dream?"

Chapter 16

*V*alerie did her best to hold the woman's gaze. It was harder than it sounded to watch those eyes. When they focused on her, she wanted to shy away, to look elsewhere. A sudden desire to study the Paul Klee print of *der Goldfisch* on her apartment wall nearly overwhelmed her. It was because in the those eyes she saw far too much of herself reflected back.

The woman blinked after a moment, sending a wave of relief through Valerie at her sudden release.

"First of all that's two questions."

"Compound sentence," Valerie shot back. "I'm counting it as one. Now answer."

"In your dream?" The woman looked intrigued. "That is kind of unusual. What was I doing?"

"Running a blintz food cart. A very successful one. You were wearing, well, these clothes. The men were flocking to you."

"Occupational hazard," the woman shrugged as if that were a sufficient explanation. Then she sighed and dropped into one of Valerie's aubergine armchairs, such a perfect accent to the woman's golden blouse that it looked planned.

"I try not to do this to mortals, tends to upset them, but we're in a bit of a bind here."

"Try not to do what?" Eric moved to sit on the couch.

"Tell the truth."

Valerie sat beside him guessing that her knees were going to need it.

"This is St. Peter."

Valerie found herself looking over at the handsome man who had run several tests on the laptop, cursed under his breath, and was now flipping through some of the printouts scattered across her big oak table, searching for something. Peter? St. Peter? In a white toga and wearing gold sandals?

"Yes," Michelle nodded as if reading Valerie's thoughts. "That St. Peter. Heavenly guardian, close buddy to the son of god, apostle on the plains of Galilee, founder of the Catholic church, for which he still should be spanked, all of that. And I'm the Devil Incarnate, Ruler of Hell, Co-founder of the Universe, Developer of Evolution, Torturer of the Foul, etcetera, etcetera, etcetera. You can call me Michelle, if that's easier."

"And I'm fricking Alice in Wonderland and Eric is my Cheshire cat!" She spat back.

But Eric was nodding his head.

"But that makes no sense!" Valerie protested, while his smile slowly grew.

"Thanks," Eric's voice was impossibly calm. "That explains the software. That was really bugging me."

Valerie sifted back through the words, back to lunch. Back to when Eric had asked her if she believed in God. Her answer had been…

"No!"

"I'm afraid so," Michelle shrugged. "It can be awkward, but you'll get used to it. Takes time, but deities aren't all that bizarre, once you get over our warping effect on the fabric of the universe. Or perhaps you won't."

"What if I don't?"

"Oh, your head will explode. Messy."

Valerie's hand was halfway from her lap to the top of her head before she stopped herself. Great, the Devil or whoever was a practical joker.

At least she hoped so.

"If you're the Devil, where's God?"

At that, the woman looked down for a moment studying her fingernails, perhaps overly intently. They were close trimmed and painted fire-red.

"We, um," she didn't look up. "No pressure or anything. But we were rather hoping you could tell us."

Chapter 17

Valerie could do little more than gawk at the woman proclaiming herself to be the Devil seeking God.

Peter waved Eric over to the table.

"You've been working with the software," Peter began before Eric even sat down. "The problem I'm having is understanding how a Hungry Ghost from the Buddhist software system looks like me and why it stole the software."

"The Buddhists have their own software?" At Peter's nod, Eric found some scratch paper and unearthed a pen. "Diagram them for me."

Within moments, they were talking one of those foreign languages that men and computer geeks thought was actual communication. A single glance at the woman elicited an eye-roll that mirrored her own feelings, get as far away as possible, as fast as possible.

Valerie stood and announced loudly enough to break in on the guys' attention.

"Michelle and I are going out, anyone need anything?"

They both shook their heads.

"Maybe, Peter," Michelle interrupted their attempt to collapse back into geek-speak. "Some clothes that aren't quite so dated? You're a couple millennia out of date you know."

"I am?"

Peter looked down at his toga then over at Eric's Smith College sweats and shrugged as if he couldn't see the difference. "Okay, sure. I guess."

"Uh, my clothes aren't dry yet and we're about the same size. Here," he dug out his keys and scribbled his address on the back of a recipe for Heavenly Devil's Upside Down Cake, as if that made any sense.

Valerie was going to murder Mathilda Reeves the next time she saw her. That would make her feel much better and might well be worth the price of extended incarceration.

And then the guys were back into their discussions of sessions and transports. They'd gone as far away as if they were on another planet.

The chill rain outside her window had abated, but it would only be for a moment. This was Seattle in late October and it would surely return.

She grabbed a coat, dug out an oversized parka that kind of fit Michelle, and a pair of umbrellas.

"Let's get out of here before they melt our brains."

Michelle nodded emphatic agreement and then went out the door, though the men didn't notice in the slightest.

#

Out of the corner of his eye, Eric watched the two women. They were endlessly fascinating to him. Two powerhouses who couldn't be more different.

They were debating the existence of God as they walked out the front door, and he could really pay attention to what Peter was diagramming.

Twenty minutes later, he saw it.

"There," Eric pointed.

"No," Peter protested. Then he slowly began nodding his head as he realized Eric was right. "Darn."

This guy must really be from Heaven to think "darn" an appropriate curse word at this juncture.

"It's the moment you initiated the software to awaken God, your desire became manifested inside the monotheistic system and rode the session layer right into the non-theistic Buddhist system. It slammed up against their prayer wheel firewall and dropped down into the Hungry Ghost algorithm. Your manifested desire to posses and control the software was carried directly into the Hungry Ghost code deck. That even explains why he looks like you. Because he kind of is you, only not. He's your manifested desire to control the software."

"Double darn," was Peter's follow-up response. "But that was centuries ago. Why did the Ghost take so long to come steal it?"

Eric traced over the diagram Peter had drawn to explain the system, half logic diagram and half Jewish Kabbalah.

"There. It wasn't in Heaven any more, but even a Hungry Ghost wouldn't be stupid enough to mess with Hell's security, or with The Devil for that matter." He knew that for a fact even after just meeting her the first time.

There was a neatness to the solution of what had happened, a clear sense to it that told Eric he'd found it. He'd spent a lifetime learning to search for that mental click when the puzzle pieces came together and he knew he'd found a solution.

"That must be it." Peter flipped the diagrams over. Earlier, they had appropriated a couple dozen sheets of paper from the various printouts scattered about the table.

"What's this?" Peter started inspecting the loose pages, turning them into OCD-neat little piles. It made an odd sort of sense that the guy who ran Heaven's software would be a bit obsessive compulsive. Did that make it a disorder or a requirement of the job?

"That stuff is all nonsense," Eric had been so excited when he'd first coaxed the software into printing out this copy of the cookbook. He'd almost woken Valerie. He was glad he'd hesitated. By the time the printout was done, he'd flipped through enough to know it was garbage and had tossed it aside.

But the more Peter looked at it, the quieter he became. Which was saying something, because he'd managed barely ten words since arriving. At first he'd appeared overshadowed by the woman, by the Devil. Eric's mind couldn't quite stay wrapped around that one, though he had to at least count it as plausible if not verifiable. Her being the Devil really would explain a lot if the software came from another plane of existence.

But Peter, St. Peter wasn't cowed by the Devil. He was simply a quieter, more thoughtful person. Peter noticed Eric's attention and asked where he'd found these recipes.

"I beat the software over the head about what had happened to Valerie's cookbook, she was editing a cookbook file that was corrupted by your software's arrival, and it finally spit out that mess of drivel to shut me up. Didn't look like much of anything. The correct table of contents, sort of, but none of the recipes make sense."

"How about this?" Peter handed him a page.

TRANSCENDENCE
-a true Buddhist dish of doubted efficacy-
1. *Be reborn.*
2. *A lot.*
3. *Keep count.*
4. *After 4th, 27th or 43th life as a mongoose, or 1,537th as a human, place the thumb of right hand on left side nostril and press hard enough to turn head to the right.*
5. *Keep pushing.*
6. *If head comes off, you've pushed too far, start over at first life. Don't forget to restart counting.*
7. *If head doesn't come off, transcend.*
Note 1: *Post-transcendence gloating is considered poor form especially if lorded over life forms still treading the Wheel of Life.*
Note 2: *Especially avoid gloating in front of life forms still retaining lethal capabilities.*

"Like I said. A mess of drivel."

Peter took the page back quietly and slipped it back into place, squaring up the edges without comment.

"No way!"

Peter shrugged. "I've seen worse. The Buddha always struck me as having a decent sense of humor. Maybe he programmed that option in."

Eric glanced about the apartment, as if seeking Valerie to agree with him that it was ridiculous. But he was alone, alone with St. Peter. Who ran Heaven.

"Uh, what else have you got there?"

St. Peter handed him another page.

> *TIDE*
> 1. *Two orbs.*
> 2. *Make one rotate around the other.*
> 3. *Make sure one has a great deal of water or other life-sup-porting fluid. (Tides are no fun if they aren't messing with somebody's head.)*
> *Note: Next time, no landmasses. Terrestrial life forms not worth the bother. Find new venue for trees.*

Eric handed that one back a bit more slowly. That one actually made a frightening amount of sense.

"Uh, what happens if someone decides landmasses really are a mistake and, I dunno, deletes them."

Peter shrugged. "Better learn to swim. Really fast. Gills might help. Though it would be hard to grow those back when you left them behind half a billion years ago."

"But, weren't you a person? Aren't you still?"

"Sure I am."

"Then how can you say it like that?"

"Sixty-eight years on earth, another twenty kicking around Limbo, skip that if you can, by the way, not a lot of fun. You might want to take up Latin, just a tip." Then he looked sad for a moment. "No, maybe you shouldn't bother with that anymore either."

"I've been running Heaven for just over two millennia now. My time on earth was a blip on the chart. Can't say as I miss it all that much either. Galilee wasn't a lark, but crucifixion..." He shuddered. "Must be an easier way to go."

"You've been running Heaven?"

"Sure. God was never that interested, and now with him dead—" He stopped, looking infinitely sad.

"God? Is? Dead?" Eric could feel each word stumble out on its own to lie on the hardwood floor like a dead fish.

Peter nodded.

"You're sure?" he whispered it. He didn't know why, but he did.

"Pretty sure."

"Pretty sure." Eric blinked. Maybe Valerie was right. These two were nutcases escaped from the local loony bin. And now she'd gone off with one of them. He hoped she was safe.

"You're saying that you're St. Peter, and you are 'pretty sure' God is dead?"

"I'm not a mental case, Mr. Erikson. God rested after Newton created the Third Law of Thermodynamics."

"Objects at rest remain at rest unless acted on by an outside force."

"Right. Except what kind of force gets God moving again?"

Eric sat up and scratched at his head a bit. "He became the proverbial immovable object?"

The man calling himself St. Peter merely nodded.

"So, what's the proverbial unstoppable force?"

Even before Peter could speak, he answered it himself. "The Software that Runs the Universe."

"Right," Peter nodded. "Only I didn't think of it until too late, there were no remnants left in which to initiate movement. At least none that I could find. And that's when the software slipped out of my fingers, two hundred years ago."

"But I was just talking to it a couple hours ago."

"Michelle had it in Hell until this morning."

Michelle. In Hell. Why did that sound so real?

He shifted in his chair but couldn't find a comfortable spot.

"So, your God is dead or gone seriously missing."

"He's your God too."

Eric ignored him. "The software is now gone."

Peter nodded.

"Where?"

Peter shrugged.

"How did you find it here?"

"I ran a tracer."

"So let's do that again."

Peter pointed to the dead computer.

"Why do you think he formatted the drive? It's all erased. If he's an incarnation of me, he'd know how to stymie the software."

"Valerie has a desktop in…"

"No, it needs to be the same hardware. Or maybe at least hardware the software has previously been on." For the first time, Peter seemed to shake off his despondency and be focusing on the problem. "If we could figure out how to get back to Hell…"

Eric didn't like the way that sounded at all.

#

"Okay, let's assume for a second, a second, that you are who you say you are."

Valerie and Michelle climbed into her metallic-gold colored BMW Roadster.

"Nice ride." Michelle commented as she settled into the leather bucket seat, then slid it all the way back for her long legs.

"A high-school graduation guilt-gift from my dad. He ran off with his secretary and Mom's inheritance when I was six."

Michelle stroked the dashboard appreciatively. "Sometimes guilt pays."

"That's the way I figured it. Mom wasn't happy about it, but then she was never happy about much. Last I heard she was in Italy, living with some dog of a Hollywood producer, but he apparently keeps her in a style of exceptional comfort." She shrugged. "We don't talk much."

"Back to the assumption that I am who I say I am?" Michelle buckled in as Valerie pulled onto Ravenna and wound her way up the hill and along the park-like street over toward Green Lake.

"Right. You said that guy who took the software was a Hungry Ghost. What's that?"

"Well, the Buddha was a pretty slick programmer." Michelle… The Devil…whatever she was, rolled down the window letting in the cool, moist air that smelled of rotting leaves and wet pavement. "He wrote the Buddhist Wheel of Life as a training ground. There are six primary modes of reincarnation until you figure out how to transcend. Most of them suck. Being a Hungry Ghost really sucks."

Despite the chilly day, the late afternoon cyclists were gathering along the Ravenna bike path, headed to Green Lake for their workouts and after-work lattes. Every single one of them probably hoping to meet Mr. Perfect as they bicycled, jogged, or walked around the lake's path.

"Eternally hungry," Michelle continued. "Far beyond the point of gluttony and right off the high dive of avarice. The Catch 22 is that while you're always hungry to the point of starving need, your throat is too tiny to allow anything in."

"That explains what happened to my kitchen. This Ron guy wanted everything but couldn't consume it." She shuddered at the memory of his moaning. She was starting to believe this woman's cockamamie story of being the Devil. The guy posing as St. Peter in a stained toga? Not so much.

"So, can't you just, I don't know, use the Buddhist software instead?"

"We've tried interfacing our systems once, ours and the Buddha's, but it doesn't work particularly well. Imagine hooking NORAD up to an art-gallery program. They both talk about peace, but that's like saying the Dante's *Inferno* is the moral equivalent of Hatha Yoga."

Valerie waited while three cyclists totally ignored the light and zipped across in front of her bumper.

"I always wanted to be Beatrice, ever since I was little girl."

"Beatrice?" Michelle actually turned to look at her for the first time. "The true love that sent Dante's hero on a tour of Hell? The nine circles of Hell are pretty heavy reading for a little girl."

"I always wanted to be loved as she was loved. Dante worshipped the very ground she walked on."

"When did you outgrow that?"

Valerie grinned at her. "Who says I have?" She put the car back into first gear and pulled through the intersection.

The woman groaned and started to roll her eyes. Then she glanced back at Valerie's face and finally smiled.

"Been a long time since someone, other than a really sneaky messenger, caught me off guard. You're okay, for one of the living."

"Thanks." Valerie wasn't quite sure what to do with the compliment. "Now I'm more likely to read Lee Child or Jane Austen."

"Firth or Macfayden?" Michelle looked over at her.

"Firth, though I'll gladly take either one. The Devil watches Jane Austen?"

"Every version. I agree, by the way. Colin better not go straight to Heaven when he dies. I want a chance to play with him first. No, I haven't read her books, which Jane is always griping at me about. She insists the films left out most of the good bits."

Michelle then looked out the window as they rolled around Green Lake, past all the shops and ice cream stores that were still doing decent business despite the cold. Prime hipster pickup spots.

"Of course, Jane was a fussy girl always worried about the propriety of every deed or action, at least when she first arrived."

"And now?" Valerie couldn't help asking. Of course, Jane Austen would be fussy.

"Well, first she went to the far extreme. Let me tell you that girl rules a pool table. She's just wicked. Now she's settled down a bit, writing science fiction last I checked. It's been a while. Too long, I guess. Need to invite her over soon, get drunk together, go scare some men. She's good at that, disarms them with demure then wipes the floor with her seriously mean pool skills."

#

"What about this one?"

Eric and Peter had split the printout and were sitting side by side at Valerie's dining table, reading through.

Eric kept finding strange recipes he wanted to show to Valerie. Wanted to share the joke that he knew she, and few others he'd ever met, would appreciate.

Shrimp fra Diavolo, Devil's Shrimp. Normally a hot dish, it was a whole list of seriously funny short-people jokes. Eric's adult growth spurt had come much later than most of his friends, and still he could appreciate these. Angels and Devils on Horseback, rather than being bacon-wrapped spicy oysters and scallops, was a detailed set of instructions for the souls of horses to avoid being reborn as human. The chef's tip was, "Horse sense is the thing a horse has which keeps it from betting on people."

Eric started reading A Recipe from Travel Far and Wide. No, he had to reread it, Valerie had been teaching him to watch out for reading what you expected to see. It actually said, A Recipe *for* Travel Far and Wide.

It felt wrong to be sitting in Valerie's apartment, wearing her clothes, with a dead saint. It was her he wanted to be here. He liked her apartment, better than his. She'd surrounded herself with books and art and comfortable chairs.

He tried to focus on the recipe Peter had given him, seeing if he could puzzle out its purpose.

What would she think when she reached his place?

#

Valerie's cell phone rang just as she was trying to work up the nerve to reach for Eric's underwear drawer. She snatched her hand back and answered the phone.

"Hi Mac." Of course it was Eric, at the very moment she was trying not to feel excessively voyeuristic in his bedroom.

"Could you also pick up a roll of blue masking tape, the kind painters use?"

"Uh, sure. What width?"

"Half or three-quarter inch. It doesn't really matter. And maybe some food for dinner? Great thanks." And he was gone.

Michelle stuck her head in from the living room, which had looked largely unused except for the sofa and a smaller than expected television. She'd expected Eric to own a massive entertainment system with a wall-sized screen and surround-sound speakers. It was in the bedroom that she found out his true vice.

"They need some blue masking tape."

"Oh," Michelle leaned against the door jamb and waited.

Valerie had already set two full sets of slacks, shirt, and jacket on the polar fleece bedspread, one for Peter and one to replace Eric's still wet clothes.

He was surprisingly neat, neater than she was, way neater than when she was stressed. The only mess in the whole apartment was the coffee cup and half-empty Fritos bag sitting beside the totally daunting, multi-screened computer station that occupied a whole bedroom corner and part of the wall of the rental-white room. Clearly this is where he lived.

"So," Michelle watched her without comment. "You don't live together?"

"He works for me. Just came over to help." She sneaked open a drawer of the oak dresser and found some socks. Almost all white. She knew from the office he wore white socks even when he was wearing sandals. He was such a nerd.

"You have a handsome, decent guy, who at this very moment is hanging around your apartment, wearing your clothes, and smelling of your soap, and you're gonna tell me nothing's going on?"

"Nothing."

Valerie considered that the next drawer must be underwear.

"Well there damn well should be, shouldn't there? What is wrong with you?"

With her hand on the drawer handle, Valerie decided the guys could just go commando and gathered up the clothes. Then she had to deal with *that* image in her brain. She made a quick estimate of which was worse.

She dropped the clothes back on the bed, then covered her eyes with one hand. With the other she pulled open the most likely drawer, snatched whatever her fingers encountered, and shoved her gleanings between the folded-over pant legs of the slacks before uncovering her eyes.

"There's nothing wrong with me." She stole a pillowcase from his bed and did her best to ignore the fact that it smelled like him. She stuffed the clothes inside and turned to leave the room.

Michelle remained where she was, arms crossed, leaning against the door jamb, blocking Valerie from leaving.

"Okay," Valerie had no idea why she'd tell this woman what she was really feeling. "I am a goddamned train wreck as a woman. Eric is half the reason I finally left my dweeb of a husband. Not for Eric, nothing that sad. But just by being there around the office, he showed me precisely how badly I had compromised herself by marrying Landau Fucking McKenzie. Landau was my record, I survived him for over a year. That's part of why I married him, once we crossed six months, I figured he was going to be my best bet ever. Why would I wish me on a nice guy like Eric?"

She'd never said all that aloud and now sort of feared the reaction. Was she really that bad? Evidence pointed to an affirmative.

Michelle studied her for a long time. Finally, a slow, if not happy, smile slid onto her face.

"I'll admit to sort of knowing that feeling myself."

The pain was so familiar, as if Valerie was looking into a mirror, that she rested her hand on the woman's arm. Valerie didn't know what she'd expected, but it hadn't been that the Devil would feel so real.

Chapter 18

It's barely mizzling." Valerie didn't bother to open her umbrella, though she did pull up her hood to wait for the light as they crossed from the hardware store to the deli.

"Mizzling?" Michelle followed her down the steps and onto the sidewalk.

"I live in a city with far more types of rain than the country's typical mist-drizzle-rain-downpour hierarchy. So, I've been filling in the blanks. Mizzle, halfway between a mist and a drizzle."

"Works for me. Certainly an improvement on 'spitting' which was never one of my favorite images." Michelle left her hair exposed to the precipitation that soon danced upon her long locks in clouds of sparkles.

It made her appear magical.

"Okay, let's suppose, for a moment, that you really are the Devil."

"Okay, let's suppose."

"Are you 'That Evil one, Satan for ever damn'd' that I'm always reading about?"

Michelle's sigh was long and drawn out. "I really hate Milton. If he ever gets out of Hell it won't be my doing. No, it doesn't work that way."

"How does it work?"

"How much do you know about computers?"

"Enough to run a profit-and-loss estimate before I purchase a manuscript and enough to lay out a book for press, unless your goddamn software decides to screw up my machine."

Michelle laughed. "My 'god damn' software. Damn god if you wish, but it is definitely not my software. Nor his. It pre-exists the both of us. Maybe only by minutes, but we definitely came along later."

They crossed the narrow park that divided the two directions of Ravenna Boulevard. A fancy name for two one-way streets connected by a wide median and a pair of bike paths. The gray skies glowered through the barren tree branches. No hint of sun penetrating the dark mantle of the Heavens.

"So how does it work?"

"god can create anything he wants, and he's damn good at it."

Valerie heard the strange mix of envy and admiration in the Devil's voice.

"But he sucks at making anything that actually works. He built volcanoes because he liked the bright colors, he missed that they poisoned the primordial atmosphere for the better part of a billion years. And the animals. I had to make half of them extinct just to put the poor things out of their misery. The platypus, I left that one as a practical joke that no one seems to appreciate, least of all the platypi themselves. And the poor mayflies, don't even get to eat. Reproduce and die, that's all they get, tell me why he thought that one up. Or praying mantises? Impregnate and then get eaten? If humans were praying mantises, I'll bet that you'd be living in a whole different societal dynamic. And that's just the normal stuff. The stuff that happens in places like Wall Street board rooms," she shook her head as if shivering and sprayed a cloud of tiny raindrops. "That's enough to make the rest of the animal kingdom look rational."

"So, God creates. And you?" Valerie stopped on the other side of the park to let a couple of cyclists whiz by, inches from their toes, before crossing.

"Clean up after god. He can Create, though he rarely thinks before he does so. I have Modify and Delete privileges, so I'm the clean-up squad. Can you even begin to imagine how sick I am of doing that?"

"Well," Valerie stopped in front of the deli's door. "There's this author. She really—"

"Fourteen billion years I've been doing this? Can you imagine that?" The acerbity and weariness in Michelle's voice stopped her.

It was a tone Valerie knew. Had felt inside without knowing how or why. When Landau finally achieved wholly intolerable status. When Mathilda unloaded yet another load of her personal crap in yet another interminable phone call. Except Michelle's voice sounded much farther down the road to personal despair than Valerie had ever been, and she'd been pretty far down that road.

"I believe you." Valerie's voice must have been little more than a whisper.

"What?"

"I believe you are who you say." What all the statements about her being the Devil had not achieved since her arrival with Saint Peter, the sheer weariness of Michelle's tone had proven.

"I believe you are the Devil."

Michelle inspected her closely, then shook her head once, sharply, to dislodge the rest of the water which flew away in a vast rainbow, despite the still sunless sky.

"Just like that?"

Valerie shrugged, "Just like that. So, does the Devil eat bagels?"

At that the woman smiled, really smiled. And a warmth washed over Valerie. Not the I'm-bowled-over-by-the-magnitude-of-your-presence, but the warmth of being-smiled-on-by-a-friend.

"Yes, Valerie," there was a lift in her voice that hadn't been there earlier. "I do, though we're a long way from New York."

Valerie smiled, glad to be able to share the surprise behind her uncle's delicatessen door. "Not nearly as far as you think." And she pulled the door open.

#

Michelle simply stood and stared. With each passing second she felt better, cozier, happier.

There was something very odd about this restaurant, or maybe she simply hadn't been to a good deli in too long. They always picked up her spirits. The smells of hot coffee, grilling eggs, and sizzling corned beef hash was breathtaking—except it *gave* breath, it gave spirit, rather than taking it.

Valerie led her to the counter with all the ease of a close friend, rather than the awkwardness most mortals displayed around her. It wasn't all that often that Michelle found a mortal worth the trouble of actually being interested in, but this woman had actually snagged her attention. Or had until they'd entered the deli. Now her stomach had all her attention.

"Aunt Anne, this is my, uh, friend, Michelle. Michelle, this is my honorary Aunt Anne."

"Hi there." And here was another woman who was something special. A centered patience just rolled off the woman in a palpable wave. There were people who went through life with all the naiveté of the newborn living their first life, and some who seemed to be older souls. This woman had roots that struck deeply into the earth.

"Good morning, Uncle."

Even as Michelle turned to face the man, he fumbled on a pair of half-glasses for reading and smiled at her. Nervously.

Odd. She usually made women nervous yet easily engaged men's attention. Here it was all reversed. The women here she could happily spend a quiet evening with, discussing movies and getting to know them. The man shuffled off behind the counter and into the kitchen as if a pack of wolves were after him.

She shrugged, not really caring. As long as she could get something tasty and soon. This place was making her stomach growl.

"Here you go, dear." The elegant Anne handed a large bag over the counter. "Breakfast for dinner. Half a dozen bagels, two sesame, two cinnamon-raisin, a whole wheat for you, and your boyfriend will want the everything-bagel in addition to the sesame."

"I... He's not..."

Michelle found herself enjoying Valerie's complete discomfiture. Under her aunt's steady gaze, the mortal had apparently lost the power of speech. So completely flummoxed that there had to be truth there. Truth that Anne had seen even if Valerie had not. Michelle would have to pay more attention. Human rituals around relationships were at least amusing.

For reasons that passed her own understanding, Michelle stepped in to rescue the mortal by giving her a moment to collect herself.

"We'd also like..." she addressed the woman behind the counter. There was something familiar about her. Like one of those people you should recognize, but they were so out of their usual context that you simply couldn't place them: a movie star in the grocery store or a famous politician reading a novel on the beach.

"Lox, cream cheese, and capers are already in the bag. The knishes will be a minute. Here," she reached back to the small serving station behind the counter and handed across two over-sized mugs of coffee, already filled.

Michelle was carrying the mugs over to a table, bemused to find herself sitting down before she quite knew what had happened.

The mugs were very unusual. Not only hand-thrown and fired, but uneven. Not so much a child's effort, but rather of someone in a great hurry. And old. Very old.

"Uncle always jokes that these were originally used as torch quenchers at Jericho. That the Israelites would slip them briefly over the torches each dawn after marching all night around the perimeter of the city walls."

Michelle almost recognized the writing in the glaze, but she couldn't quite place it. Then she tipped her head sideways, enough to see how it would look if the mug were inverted.

"*Simha.* Joy," her voice barely a whisper. "Ancient Hebrew." She traced the characters again, unable to feel them through the crackling glaze. It would indeed read correctly if held inverted and slid over a blazing torch to snuff its flame.

Valerie tipped her head sideways in imitation and stared at her own mug. "Really?"

"Odd thing to wish at the walls of Jericho."

"Yes, that's why I kept them," a male voice at her shoulder.

Michelle jolted in surprise. The uncle. Valerie's uncle now stood close by their table. She hadn't heard his approach. No one could ever sneak up on her. Ever. Not even when she was drunk and passed out. But he'd arrived without impinging on her consciousness and that was the weirdest part of this entire day.

"I always appreciated the irony."

His voice was rich and friendly. His earlier nerves appeared to have disappeared as if they'd never been.

"The Jews put every man, woman, and child of that evil city to the sword, except the family of a whore who had aided their spies, and yet 'Joy' was glazed upon their daily utensils. It reminds me that

I don't know best, no matter how much I think so. Had it been up to me, would I have condemned the city? I find the question keeps me from unwarranted action."

"And that was something you used to perform?"

The man actually blushed. "In hindsight, my, em, actions have not always been as honorable as I would wish. To those I have offended, I try to apologize. To those I cannot address directly, I hope they feel my apology anyway."

Then, with ears gone bright pink, the man was gone as quickly as he'd arrived, leaving behind his enigmatic words and a small bag that smelled mouth-wateringly of hot potato knishes.

"Your uncle is an odd man." She glanced at Valerie who looked as puzzled as Michelle felt.

"Not usually," Valerie watched his retreating back a moment longer. "Let's go. See if the guys are back yet."

"What about the mugs? My system needs this coffee."

"We can take them, I'll bring them back later. He has an immense pile of them in the back."

When they stepped out, a final splash of the setting sun found a gap in the western clouds and lit Ravenna Boulevard.

Valerie looked east to see if there was a rainbow over Lake Washington as there so often was.

She didn't spot it at first, but finally located it. Only…

"Michelle. That doesn't look right, does it?"

Michelle turned to see what Valerie was looking at.

To the east, a great arc of light spanned in exactly the curve of a rainbow. Even part of a second rainbow higher above it, but all the colors were just muddy shades of brown.

"This doesn't look good at all."

Chapter 19

S*o, you have to* get back to Hell in order to run another trace on the software?" Eric shoved aside the remains of breakfast, swallowing the last of the two best lox and bagels he'd ever eaten. He slapped two sheets of paper in the middle of Valerie's coffee table. They'd had breakfast for dinner in the living room because the work table was still buried in printouts and a dead computer.

Michelle nodded slowly.

"How do you, the Devil, normally get to Hell?"

The woman frowned and he'd almost swear the room darkened. "I ask the software. Anywhere I want to go. It knows to listen for me, even when there is no terminal nearby. But it's not responding."

Eric paused and studied Michelle and Valerie. There was something else going on here, something that was making them both nervous and unhappy, but neither were talking about it.

He resettled the blue sweatband that he'd pulled on as a joke. Valerie had blushed the most brilliant color of pink when Michelle described how Valerie had grabbed blindly into his dresser drawer. Clearly whatever was bothering them wasn't each other. They appeared to be getting along really well.

"Right. And Peter, having been mortal, still always needed a terminal."

Peter nodded.

He'd pulled on the bright orange woolen hat that Eric normally wore when playing Ultimate on cold winter weekends. At least his clothes fit.

Valerie wouldn't look at him, except when she thought he wasn't looking at her. He had no idea what that was all about. His apartment had been somehow gross, had it? He couldn't remember any disasters he'd left behind.

"And you have a way to get us back to Hell without the software?" The Devil dragged his attention back from wherever it had gone.

"Actually it was Peter's idea."

"No, it was you who put the two together."

"I—"

Michelle cut him off, "I don't give a demon's blessing if Jehovah himself thought it up." She grimaced as she spoke God's name. "What did you come up with?"

Eric pointed to the two sheets, Valerie moved to read it as well. She rested a hand on the Devil's shoulder as she leaned over, as a friend might. Her hair swept forward, framing her face in the warmest mahogany.

And his world shifted.

Valerie had been distant, so he'd done his best to switch back into employee mode. But that just wasn't happening. And now, he just wanted to slip his hand into that shadowed space between hair and cheek. He wanted to lean in and taste those lips, still moist from where she'd licked aside the last of the cream cheese.

Then her gaze shifted from the paper the Devil held, up to meet his. For the longest moment, her expression remained unchanged, regarding him frankly. He could no more look away from her than when the Buddhist Hungry Ghost had frozen him in place while stealing the software this morning.

Valerie's gaze didn't vary. Except the eyes. He was learning to read those eyes and could see them processing something very intensely. Processing, going briefly cold as if she were about to chew him out for something, then thoughtful. The slightest tip of her head made caressing her cheek an even more enticing prospect.

The last expression he didn't quite catch. Something had shifted in her thoughts. Shifted to…he couldn't tell. Then she smiled. A smile that smacked him right between the eyes and knocked him back in his chair.

And he'd thought the Devil was powerful.

# # #

Valerie tried to bring her attention back to the pages Michelle was reading, but couldn't quite do it.

Few men really met her gaze, most either went down to her breasts or veered aside. Men didn't like strong women, they only professed that they did. She'd thought Landau Fucking Mckenzie had been one such. It turned out he wasn't all that interested in sex in general, and was simply too oblivious to think of looking away from her eyes even when emotions were running high. What had seemed like the perfect, sympathetic gentleman had in truth been an asexual, emotionally-crippled moron. It just took her twelve months of marriage hell to realize that she wasn't the problem, he was.

E-Squared, no, Eric. Eric looked at her with frank interest. The awareness that had passed through her since Aunt Anne's idle comment about "her boyfriend" was fast convincing her that she wouldn't mind that. "Boyfriend" was an archaic term, especially for a thirty-year-old divorced woman, but it was strangely apropos.

Well, she could try being a little archaic. Wouldn't mind it a bit, when she thought of Eric. She hadn't been with anyone since Landau, not that being with Landau had been all that much like being with someone.

"You're kidding me," Michelle exclaimed and flapped the two pages of paper as if shaking them would alter their content.

Valerie refocused on the pages when Michelle stopped waving them about.

A Recipe for Travel Far and Wide.

The ingredients made no sense so she skipped over those and glanced at the other page. There were several headings, typical of recipe variations. There was one for darkest Africa, another for Uluru Rock in the middle of the Australian Outback that involved an El train, one for—

Then her attention jumped to the last one.

A Quick Trip to Hell.

"Is it a recipe for how you can get back there?"

Michelle turned to gaze at her and Valerie could feel a tightening across her shoulders.

"This recipe says that it's how *we* can all go to Hell." Michelle's forceful look made it clear that she was expecting Valerie to go along for the ride.

Now her stomach clenched and she wished she hadn't eaten dinner at all. Like she'd swallowed Paul Klee's goldfish rather than some of the finest smoked salmon on the planet, and it was swimming about her innards looking for a way out.

Chapter 20

AC/DC's Highway to Hell was rocking away on Valerie's stereo, she didn't even remember that she'd owned it. Two long lines of blue masking tape ran down her hallway toward the bedroom. They were placed so that they did the railroad track-perspective thing, coming to a point just at her bedroom's threshold.

Peter and Eric were consulting over the whether some potato chips salvaged from the floor of her kitchen were fried or baked as the recipe called for *something fried.* It also said, *something chestnut,* a lock of her hair that she'd have fought against if she hadn't been so numb, numb like the stillness before a storm. *Something shredded,* the remains of the original cookbook that Valerie had torn into confetti in a fit of outrage sometime yesterday. And *something died,* not dead but died, a poor philodendron that she'd, with a complete lack of imagination, named Phil and then never watered again.

"And we just walk down the path singing 'Row row row your boat'?"

"In the round." Michelle looked down at the recipe again, then stuffed it into her back pocket. "It's a good thing there are four of us."

"I hated that song in kindergarten." Valerie felt as if her entire childhood had been defined by stupid boundaries and limitations. All around her the children would sing the round with a look of bliss upon their insipid little features, right before going home to play with their Barbies.

Valerie could think of a thousand better ways to spend her time. Her teachers always marked her social skills as poor. Her Stepford mother sent her to counseling. Her practical father gave her a library card and later a generous allowance, deposited directly at the local bookstore. Even after he'd gone, he'd had the decency to maintain that deal. One of the reasons she couldn't hate him, even if she no longer knew him.

Her apartment hallway was narrow before she'd lined both sides with bookcases, now Eric could barely walk down it without his shoulders brushing one side or the other. Thankfully, they weren't required to go arm-in-arm like Dorothy and her gang of thugs off on a witch hunt, but rather in a backwards Miami Sound Machine conga line.

Not only was it the stupidest thing she'd ever heard, but she knew she hadn't made her bed in days and there were dirty clothes everywhere. She hadn't been able to slip away to straighten it up, and now everyone was going to dance backwards and wind up in her bedroom for no reason at all.

Eric started them off, with a surprising baritone, and headed off backward down the hall.

Row, row, row your boat,

As he passed, he grabbed Peter's hips and Peter's wavering tenor took up the next round.

Gently down the stream,

Peter grabbed Michelle's waist in turn, blushing pink as he did so, almost losing the rhythm as he formed the next link in the retreating line of fools.

Michelle's contralto overshadowed the others.

And finally Valerie and her soprano were pulled into the foolishness by the Devil's firm grasp on her hips, dragging her backwards down the hall against her will.

Row, row, row your boat,

She really, really hated this song. Always the one to screw up the round the few times she'd been suckered into it by a foolish desire to belong, it represents another requirement of childhood she'd failed miserably. This time she focused on her own voice and ignored the others as she danced "The Conga" backwards, shuffle, shuffle, kick,

kick. At the end of the first line she tossed the lock of her chestnut hair into the air. More dull brown, but the others had all insisted it was rich chestnut red.

Gently down the stream,

She lofted a handful of fried potato chips.

Merrily, merrily, merrily, merrily,

A flutter of torn cookbook manuscript pages added to the mess in her hallway. She wasn't a neat freak, but between the cookbook disaster and remains of breakfast in the living room, the Hungry Ghost's destruction of her kitchen, her unkempt bedroom, and now the pile of crap in her hallway, the apartment was a disaster. Too embarrassing to even call a cleaning service.

Life is but a dream,

And the curled brown leaves of Phil the "died" philodendron fluttered to the floor. Maybe she'd just move, it would be easier. Pretend none of this ever happened. Maybe even keep paying the rent so that the landlord never saw it either.

*Row, row…*she started again, except she was the only one singing.

Even as Valerie turned to look, she caught her heel on the edge of the bedroom carpet and the Devil dragged her down. Together they fell backward—onto a grassy field.

DAY THREE

And God Said,
Let the waters under the Heaven
be gathered together unto one place,
and let the dry land appear.
And God called the dry land earth.

Chapter 21

*E*ric caught her arm as Valerie crash-landed on her butt. "Careful."

Valerie squinted as her eyes adjusted to the bright sunlight. They were high on a grassy slope that swept down to a private cove facing a sea, a vast sea of blue-green water and, Valerie was glad she was sitting down, lemon-yellow wave crests.

The only building was a house some distance along the glittering beach, its white sand so bright she couldn't look at it for more than a moment or two. Even from here the house looked cozy and welcoming, a small house with a broad veranda. The day was impossibly beautiful. She could happily die and live out her days here. The air smelled of sea air, daisies, and just a hint of wild mint. It was pleasantly warm, which was good because she'd left her coat back in her apartment.

Her apartment!

She turned to peer back through the still cocked open door. She could see all the crap she'd strewn down the hallway. The opening was framed by meadow and sky where the door jamb and walls should be. Like a rectangle cut into the face of the world. Even the back of the door didn't show. No terrycloth bathrobe on the hook. Instead, there was just more sky, apparently the piece of it that was missing where the door was open.

She turned to look in the other direction, and regretted it.

The comfortable house in the quiet cove beneath meadow-covered hills still stretched from their feet to the brilliant sea. But on the other side of their grassy knoll there rolled desolate hills, dry and covered with scratchy sagebrush. But that wasn't what bothered her.

It was the mountains. They were just wrong.

Great soaring peaks, that looked to be made of nothing but splinters of rusted iron. She'd never been a hiker. She'd always imagined backpacking to be a form of torture that looked, well, exactly like those forbidding and jagged peaks. A distaste for pre-historic, hunter-gatherer based activities had been one of her few shared opinions with Landau.

Michelle coming up beside her, must have noticed the direction of her attention.

"The Mountains of Hell. Welcome to my home." The ironic twist of voice was almost lost on Valerie.

She shook her head, and when that wasn't enough, she shook her whole body like a wet dog. "Your. Home." Complete sentences were still beyond her mental capacity.

Michelle merely nodded, "That's my house down in the cove."

Valerie became aware of Eric's arm around her shoulders. "Are you okay?"

She turned to look at him, "I don't think so."

Valerie could feel her knees go weak. Without the support of Eric's arm she probably would have fallen. This was not where she had expected to be when she'd woken up this morning, nor when she'd walked backward down her front hall scattering potato chips and dead leaves. Taking a deep breath she patted his hand in thanks and stepped away to stand by Michelle.

Eric turned to inspect her frameless apartment door with St. Peter. It just stood there in the middle of the meadow, a door with no bedroom to hold it upright.

She had to fight to keep her voice from shaking as she asked the woman, "We're in Hell?"

Michelle pointed to the impossibly cruel mountains without saying another word.

Valerie noticed the sun was hanging high above them, "How did the sun get up there?"

"Think of it as…a different time zone than Seattle."

"That's your house on the beach?" It looked like any nice-sized rambler stretched along the shore. Fruit trees. And the occasional oak. It was shaped like an immense half-bowl facing the ocean with the grove and house at the bottom center, the slopes between here and there were mostly dried grasses and low scrub. Though the cove was well over a mile across, there was only the one house.

"That's it."

A slight chill went up Valerie's spine, "Michelle, I hate to sound stupid, but where are we?" She was almost sorry that she'd asked the question.

Michelle turned to look at her, the tilt of her head and the pity in her eyes were too clear. This woman was exactly who she said she was, the Devil Incarnate. Valerie was somewhere she had never believed existed.

She truly stood in Hell.

# # #

Time seemed to stand still as Valerie watched herself turn slowly back toward her apartment door. Peter pushed it shut as Eric came around from behind it. The click echoed in her ears. She raced over, dove for the knob, but it faded like a morning mist: there one moment, and nothing but sky and meadow the next. She tumbled onto the grassy slope beyond, taking Eric out at the knees. They tumbled and rolled together on the lawn which didn't fill her with any of the joy such an activity might be expected to do in any decent place.

Again, her brain felt cudgeled. Hell, by definition, wasn't a decent place. Was it?

Peter looked at where the door had been and turned to Michelle. "That wasn't supposed to happen. Michelle, what's going on?"

Valerie attempted to stand, but her legs failed her and she sank, very slowly, like she imagined a leaf on the wind must feel, until she was kneeling in the grass. She was in Hell, but was she dead? Her heart still beat in her chest, making her alive? Her arm didn't feel connected to her body as she pointed to where her door had been. Eric touched her shoulder and the world came rushing back to life.

"I don't know, Peter. Give me a moment." Michelle paced once slowly around where the doorway had been. "I think the system has decayed further without the Universal Software being in residence."

"Maybe the system isn't working at all."

Peter looked as worried as Valerie felt and that was without understanding the implications.

"I think we may be in deep trouble." Without another word the Devil headed down the hill toward the beach and her house.

Valerie struggled to her feet and followed, picking her way through orange poppies and tall lupines until they reached a narrow path. Eric was not far behind. Supportive at first, but in moments chatting with Peter about some arcane technical conundrum involving decision gates and signal flow. Perfect. They were all following the Devil down a narrow, crooked path into Hell.

She nearly ran into Michelle where she had stopped beside an ugly, murky pool. The meadow here was broken by a deep swale filled with slime that made *Ghostbusters*-demon slobber appear pleasant. It smelled of brand-new sneakers, that unholy combination of fresh rubber and fresher dog-poop stuck deep in the treads.

"Here's someone who can tell us if the software still runs at all normally," Michelle offered her hand to a tall man struggling to extract himself from the mire.

His silver hair lay matted to his head. A dripping wet toga clung to his body. He arose with a dignity and grace that belied his condition.

"Greetings, my friend." Michelle held his hand for a moment. "Is this a result of your picnic?"

"No," he shuddered. "That was far, far worse. This is merely the opposite of a cool desert evening, though it is not what might be termed a particularly pleasant experience."

"My good man, haven't you heaped enough abuse upon yourself yet?"

"I have yet to succeed in my purpose."

She wiped her hand on her jeans leaving a long smear of mud or whatever it was. "You are lucky that you are dead already, considering how your battle has been going."

"Lucky to be dead? Indeed." He bowed formally to them, and turned to walk away, mud squelching out of his sandals.

"Would you like to use my shower?" Michelle called out to the man.

After a long moment's hesitation, he nodded his acquiescence. "But perhaps it would be best for all if I followed behind."

Valerie had to agree, as even pinching her nose closed did nothing to cut the cloying odor that clung about him.

Michelle led off and noted to Valerie with a grin of relief, "At least part of the system still works."

This didn't restore Valerie's confidence in the slightest.

Once they started off again Peter and Eric hustled past her. Peter started harassing Michelle with questions she clearly didn't like. Eric was listening intently, leaving her to bring up the rear but for the man trailing behind.

Valerie glanced back at him a few times. His dignity was the only decent thing he remained clothed in, his slimed toga suggested he'd be better off not wearing anything at all. It was as if everything else about him had been stripped away in thin layers like a cheese grater of the soul until nothing else remained.

They finally arrived at the base of the hill and entered the cool shade of the small grove of fruit trees. As they made their way to the house, Valerie realized she'd been thinking of only one thing. What she would have to do in order not to come here when she died.

She'd need a good solution, because somehow, she feared that sainthood wasn't in the cards.

# # #

Eric followed Michelle to her house. Despite believing in the existence of Hell, for at least the last dozen hours, experiencing it ranked as quite a different matter. He'd expected dark caverns filled with tortured souls, brimstone-laden fire, and demons with mighty whips. Too much Milton and Hollywood. Except for the cruel mountains, now hidden by the foothills, it looked, almost normal. Maybe the tortured souls were kept somewhere else.

He had chatted with Peter as they started down, apparently Michelle had built a self-regulating Hell of the mind. He had wanted to try a sample until he'd seen the man attempting to appear casual while slime dripped from his very pores.

Even up close, Michelle's house looked friendly and comfortably substantial, without crossing over into ostentatious. No great hall of flame for this Devil. A nice cedar-shake finish and a simple sloping roof. There were few windows on the land side of the house. No gardens leavened the landscape, just sandy soil and a pleasant grove of palm and orange trees. The sagebrush on the higher slopes, far too convinced of its own wisdom in commanding the arid ecological niche, hadn't dared to come down here.

As they went around the corner Eric admired the long wooden verandah and an equally long wall of glass windows. He could see walls dividing up some of the interior, but there was nothing between floor and ceiling to block the view of the white sand beach and the ocean.

The ocean. Shit! Okay, that was definitely also weird. The waves were far taller than they looked from up on the hillside. They were tall, all out proportion. They climbed up until they were as tall as the house, then crashed down onto the hard-packed sand with a crash about as loud as a mouse jumping off a footstool.

Valerie's eyes were glazed when he stopped her.

He pointed at the waves.

She followed the direction of the waves, cricking her neck upward to see the top of the wave as it built. Then she followed it down to shatter against the beach. She shrugged and turned inside as if it were the least surprising thing to happen today. Maybe she was right.

The porch sported no floats or old crab pots to clutter it up like a bad rental cabin along the coast. A few wicker chairs, a wooden bench, and a porch swing were the sum total of the outdoor furniture. A wide rail ran between the posts holding up the verandah's overhang. A dozen different types of lavender bloomed copiously in the beds fronting the porch.

Michelle turned in at the first sliding glass door and waved the dripping man toward a bathroom.

The rest of them trooped down a narrow hallway of old oak floors and cedar-planked walls. The wood had so much character.

"Where'd you get this lumber?" Eric ran his hand along the beautiful surface.

"Why?" Valerie nudged him in the ribs. "You planning to hit Hell's Home Depot before we leave?"

Okay, he hadn't thought it would sound quite that stupid, but it did.

"Galleons," Michelle explained over her shoulder as she turned in at a doorway with a glass portal in the middle. "A lot of sailing ships fall through the Bermuda Triangle. Most of them wash up on Hell's shores. I salvage the good bits. Demons and sinners clean up the rest to keep my beach clean."

"Bermuda Triangle?" The room was filled with seagoing-type miscellany.

"I've tried half a dozen times to close that gateway to Hell's Ocean. But that would require the authority to create a door across the trans-dimensional portal." She mumbled something else beneath her breath that sounded like, "and there's no fucking way I'm going to ask god to create one." But he must have misheard.

Eric tried to focus on the office room, because the desk and computer terminal indicated that's what it must be. But he couldn't. There were too many impressions. A wash of northern light from high small windows. As if Hell had a north and south… Eric felt a sudden desperate need to sit down, it was the most foreign thought yet.

The New World lumber from wreckage of an old Spanish fleet had made for fine furnishings. But for the rest of the room, wreckage was definitely the primary theme.

Six centuries of assorted memorabilia adorned the walls. Carved ship's figureheads stood along one wall, some reaching a dozen feet toward the pitched ceiling—bare-chested Greek goddesses and impossible sea serpents worked in wood. The wall shelves were packed with collections that would make any modern museum curator collapse in a faint. Carved bronze shields, golden chalices, fist-sized jewels. All the fabled riches of the deep were displayed as casually as if they were junk novels and dime-store knick-knacks. She even had an old airplane propeller from the loss of the fabeled Flight 19 on the wall, framed by a veritable field of gold *escudos* coins.

"The money is from the loss of the Spanish Treasure Fleet of 1715," she remarked when she noticed his attention. The stern section of the cabin cruiser *Witchcraft* was the most recent, and perhaps most appropriate addition to the room's décor.

"Whenever a demon gets out of line, I make him come in and dust everything," Michelle moved toward a computer terminal that looked as if it predated, well, computers. He guessed that it did.

Peter fiddled with the terminal for several minutes before he threw up his hands and sat back looking sad. It was quite some time before Michelle ceased cursing. By the time she'd finally wound down to mere four-letter words, they had all returned to one of the front rooms, a large rustic kitchen with absolutely no signs that food was ever prepared there.

The puddle-guy had emerged from the shower and Michelle rummaged around and found him jeans and a t-shirt that had a bust of the man's own face on it.

Eric knew it from somewhere. Famous enough to have a t-shirt made of him, but he was dead or he wouldn't be in Hell. He looked younger than the image, here in Hell as a man in his early forties, as if when he'd died what had been preserved was how the man had seen himself rather than the body he'd actually died in.

"Plato," Valerie breathed softly.

"That's it!" Eric snapped his fingers and then felt even stupider as Plato observed him with dispassionate curiosity.

Eric dropped onto a bar stool by an oak-and-cherry kitchen table promising himself that he wouldn't say another word. Which wasn't hard. No one seemed to be in a talking mood.

"A conundrum cannot be contemplated until it is fully voiced." Plato had changed somehow. Rather than clinging to the core of dignity he'd maintained while working as the demonstration model for the efficacy of full-body slime treatments, he had shifted into a full, confident, professorial tone.

Still no one spoke.

So, Eric broke his own vow. Not much risk, he was already in Hell.

"The Universal Software has gone missing, no trace, stolen. Yet, you appear to still be affected by it."

"Ah," Plato rose and began poking around in the cupboards. He unearthed an unopened tin of cashews, some energy bars in bright foil, a variety of chips and cookies as copious as the collection still scattered on the floor of Valerie's kitchen.

"And what leads you to believe these to be mutually exclusive?"

"Careful," Michelle was looking at Eric. "The waters here get deep very quickly."

Eric decided to risk considering Plato's question despite her warning.

"Different layers," Valerie supplied. "We met the thinking part."

"Precisely!" Plato smiled on her like a prize student, opening the cashews with a bright phsst! and offering her the honor of taking the first ones.

"My experiments left the superficial 'thinking' layers behind centuries ago. I have worked my way down deep into the software's autonomic processing. If you will, I have moved past the mundane brain and have been studying the underlying bodily functions, the software's equivalent of breathing and having a pulse."

Peter declined an offer of cashews and laid his head down on the table. "But that still doesn't tell us where the software has gone."

Eric liked the feel of this old country kitchen. He'd build a similar one someday as the centerpiece of a comfortable home for a family. He already had it mostly designed. A part of him wanted to look over at Valerie, another part of him thought better of it and didn't.

Sparkles of light reflected off the waves outside the window and glittered across the copper cookware. Copper was supposed to be a pest to maintain, but it certainly did look great above the great black stove. Some day he would build a place that looked like this. Then he and his mythical whoever could sit around the table with friends and serve superb coffee.

Michelle was indeed doing something at the large black stove and it started to smell like coffee.

Who was he kidding with the "mythical" crap? He'd been building fantasies about Valerie Mckenzie since the first time he'd seen her steamrolling down the hall, even if she had been married at the time. All fire and brimstone, all curves and brains. It was easy to imagine being with her.

What was hard was to picture her being with him, even after the divorce.

Valerie had chosen to sit opposite him across the table. He hoped it was random chance only. She was slowly turning a salt shaker around and around in her fingers. "Would someone care to enlighten me on the Buddhist Hungry Ghosts?"

Even though she wasn't looking at him he felt compelled to answer. To try and help her adjust. The transition had shaken him to the core and created tsunamis of shock and surprise that still rippled up and down his nervous system.

And he'd been expecting it.

The shock to Valerie must have been immense and yet she'd remained calm throughout.

"I don't know a thing about ghosts, hungry or otherwise. Peter said that must be where the program error sent his evil twin, but it doesn't mean much to me."

Michelle returned from behind the counter with a tray and set five substantial coffee mugs on the table along with some sugar and a pitcher of cream that looked thick enough to stand up a spoon. The coffee pot burbled with promise in the background.

On the walk down the hill, St. Peter had practically hounded Michelle with some idea about working directly with the code, to which she was adamantly opposed. Peter now leaned with his elbows on the table and his hands cradled around his empty mug as if it were filled to the brim with soul-warming elixir.

"Our system is linear, for the most part. Birth, life, death, Limbo sorting station to Hell or Purgatory, with the rare soul slotting direct to Heaven. Then work your way up. Occasional reincarnation, though Michelle would know more about that." He rubbed his eyes wearily.

She declined to comment, so Peter continued.

"The Buddhist Wheel of Life functions completely differently. It constantly reincarnates a soul, time and time again, until it has learned all of its lessons. Upon enlightenment the soul leaves the wheel and becomes one with the Buddha."

"And that's Buddhist Heaven?" Valerie turned the salt shaker slowly around again.

Peter shook his head, "No. That's true enlightenment. Buddhist Heaven as you might imagine it, doesn't exist. A soul gets reborn differently depending on how it did in its last life. One of the infinite possible reincarnations though, is a false Heaven. If you fail to see that it is all self-indulgence and vanity you probably come back as a snake."

"Is a snake as low as you can go?" Eric was starting to remember bits and pieces of this from a comparative religion class in college. "I thought all lives were created equal?" He could hear Michelle behind him cursing at the coffee maker to hurry up. The aroma abruptly filled the air and the burbling sound sped up.

Peter tried to take a sip from his empty cup, inspected the visible bottom with some surprise and returned it to the wooden table top.

That actually give Eric some comfort, he'd thought he wasn't the only one losing it.

"Supposedly," Peter still cradled his mug. "You can leave the wheel at any time from any position," he flicked his fingers outward across his imaginary circle, "by simply gaining true enlightenment. However, if you really mess up you come back as a Hungry Ghost."

Valerie's grimace echoed his feelings. He wouldn't wish that on anyone.

Michelle spoke for the first time, she'd been oddly quiet. "That would fit with Ron's hunger to control the software, something you've been struggling with ever since god died."

Valerie looked over Eric's head at Michelle, "How can God be dead? That doesn't make any sense. After all, he's God."

Eric winced. It had been obvious when Peter had told them the story how much it upset him. He wished Valerie would think a little longer before she asked her questions.

Peter's face was white as a sheet, "I wish I knew. I miss him every day."

"I'm sorry, Peter, but I truly don't understand."

Michelle brought the large pot of coffee to the table and poured their mugs full. "god was not what the universe revolved around. Like me, he was simply a programmer. Fortunately for us all, he was also an artist."

The sound of loss in her voice filled the room.

"But how did it all start?"

Michelle contemplated her for a long moment.

"Well, that's a whole other story." She settled deeper into her chair and sipped her coffee. "It's not one of my fonder memories. People are always telling me stories about the cute first things they remember, getting a puppy at age three, being fed to a lion, whatever. Something at least unusual. The first thing I remember was a door…"

Another Time

L*ight shone into the* otherwise complete darkness from two sources. The first, behind her, cast her shadow onto a rectangle of light on the otherwise featureless floor in front of her. The second streamed from a doorway facing hers, that silhouetted another person.

Her eyes adjusted and she could make out that they stood upon opposite edges of a great, circular platform several dozen strides across, each entering from a glaring doorway. In the middle stood two desks, each with a computer console on its surface.

As she stepped forward onto the dark floor, the light behind her began to fade. She turned barely in time to see it disappear completely. A door slamming shut. She flinched at the finality of the act, then she reached out to touch the doorknob.

Emptiness.

Nothing lay beyond the edge of the platform.

Looking outward, black spots floated before her eyes. Only void and darkness were upon the face of the deep. If she stepped off the edge, she'd fall forever.

She turned toward the center of the platform, back to face the other figure. Their door had closed as well. The only light was now a glow emanating from the great disk on which they stood, as if the surface were transparent and a languid sea of light shifted slowly back and forth within its depths. By its glow she could see her companion, an average-height man, average-build, tending toward the rotund, and hair starting to gray. Nothing exceptional about him at all.

She looked down at herself. Even without anyone to compare to, she knew she was looking at something way better than average. With a body like this she could do some serious damage, and have a lot of fun along the way.

"Where did you come from?" she called across to him.

He looked down into the lighted disk that was their floor. "I don't know."

If his voice held concern, she could detect no note of it.

"How about you?"

She thought for a moment, then she thought some more. And a bit more. She didn't know either. Not a good feeling. It was a feeling she'd gladly trade in for… She couldn't think of anything. She knew she stood on a disk across from a man, each in front of a computer, but when she thought of herself, all she found was a blank slate.

They had been cut off from their past, fully grown with no memories. It didn't seem right, something was missing. Sure, no one remembered their own birth, but this was ridiculous.

He knelt and rapped the floor lightly with his knuckles. A hollow ringing filled the air out of all proportion to the gentleness of the tap. The sound and vibrations coursing up through the soles of her sandaled feet were as if he'd struck some great bell with a massive hammer. The vibration settled only slowly, as if infinite potential were trapped within the disk waiting for release.

Rising to his feet he walked over to one of the desks. He wore a plain white, button-down shirt, khaki slacks, and scuffed loafers with too-white socks.

Looking down at herself again, she saw a fine linen shirt of bright blue, and dark jeans. Unpainted toenails emerged past fine-tooled leather sandal straps. It was a look that felt as if she'd chosen it intentionally. Casual, comfortable, top-quality.

The man set his hand on a white glass plate next to the screen.

"I don't understand. Nothing happened."

"What? You thought you were going to fill the void?" She tried not to look at the darkness that surrounded their disk in all directions, it was a bit unnerving. She walked to the desk that faced her. The computer terminal had been formed all as one piece, deeper than it was wide. A keyboard stuck out the front, the built-in screen was black with apple-green letters.

Place hand on plate to initialize system.

She did so to no effect. "Maybe if we do it together?"

They sat, facing each other, and placed their right hands, though it felt awkward—perhaps she was left-handed—on the white plates simultaneously. A huge burst of light flashed from everywhere at once. She ducked her head and shielded her eyes. Once they adjusted, she could see nothing but light. Light everywhere there had been darkness before. The only break in the glare were the two computer terminals and the two of them. Even the desks were translucent.

"Oh my. Never have I seen such beauty!" The man's voice was filled with awe. Standing slowly he spread his arms wide as if to hold it.

It shone all around them. It glittered and pulsed through the great floor as well. But now she could see that the disk truly was clear. Completely clear. She could now see…forever. At least that's how it looked. The light spread outward in a great wave that rushed into the darkness.

She carefully tapped a toe, but the platform remained solid beneath her feet, even if it was invisible in the all-encompassing light. The man's footsteps rang as he danced, perhaps cavorted was a better qualifier, surrounded by the light. She almost warned him as he moved too close to where the edge must still be, but his dance turned and brought him in a great circle around their desks and back to his chair. The white hand-plates they had touched were simple plastic, connected to the consoles with a small wire. The computer couldn't have done this on its own. He must have done it.

His mumbling about the lightshow being the most glorious vision that had ever come to him confirmed the fact. She forced herself to look down between her sandals and into the light beyond the floor. At the great globe of light for which they were the center. "Glorious" wasn't a bad word for it. Though "scary as hell" came to mind right alongside it.

With such ability to create he must know something more, "Can you remember anything of the past?"

Again he paused, "Nope, not a thing." Leaning forward he rested his hand on hers. His touch was warm and gentle. "But that doesn't make it any less wonderful," he smiled brightly. Whether at her or the light she couldn't be sure.

He waved an arm upward and nearly swiped her console off the desk, "No, fantastic is a better word, or perhaps miraculous." He returned to his screen as if eager to do something else. She read the lines of green text scrolling up the screen on her own terminal.

System startup initiated.

Universe now available for configuration.

You have the ability to modify and remove items within system.

You are hereby designated as, 'The Devil'.

"What are you?"

His smile was huge as he read the words on his screen.

"I'm God. What fun. It would seem I have been blessed with the powers of creation." He tapped a few keys, "This is simply amazing."

"Why does he get to be God?" she typed into the terminal.

He tried to palm in first, so man gets precedence.

"You mean 'the man,' don't you?"

Leave me alone, I'm busy creating the universe.

So, she was the Devil. If this was a sign of her luck, she'd rather have no luck at all.

The light shimmered as if it were a beacon of hope. How did he do that? He continued tapping away at his console.

The light swirled itself into brilliant balls of fire which then compressed into stars. He spread them randomly throughout the space around them. That was very nice until he began smashing them into each other.

She shook her head and tried not to smile. How like a man to build something this incredible and immediately start busting it all up as a game. Typing a few commands herself she formed the stars into neat, well-organized galaxies.

He shattered a few of them.

She wanted to slap his hands away from the keyboard, but the few mangled ones emphasized and enhanced the symmetry of all the others, now racing away from them into the night until they spangled the Heavens.

She could make changes, but he could make art.

Of course, there was nothing to stop her from trying, the universe was still mostly a blank slate. She leaned forward in her chair as she formulated the command to create a new shape out of the darkness itself, since he had used all of the light to make the stars and those were too pretty to mess with.

Invalid command. The Devil has insufficient system rights to perform creation operations.

"Great!" She typed in, pounding the keys hard as she did so. "Are you telling me I can't create squat? All I can do is shape his creations?" The console didn't respond. "Hey, God. How about if we work together on this universe?"

He kept tapping his keyboard and glancing to see what he'd just created. Tiny globules of matter that had spun off from the stars were collecting into spinning orbs whirling around the stars.

She stood and stretched before going around to casually glance over his shoulder.

Scatter range of visible spectrum across star colors, emphasis on white, blue, and red.

The computer responded with a simple, *Done.*

The stars shifted from all white to a breathtaking array of colors. The blue was almost a crystalline white but sharper, clearer. The red shone deep and ruddy.

Absolutely stunning. She looked at him to see if his appearance had changed, if there was some outward sign of such talent. People with artistic vision were intimidating, she would never have thought to do such a thing.

God kept typing, no different from when she'd first seen him minutes ago. A glass of wine appeared by his hand. Taking a sip, he glanced at the Heavens.

She poked him lightly on the arm. "How about we take a break and talk over what to do? If we could simply…"

"What I need next is…" he talked right over her, "water. Yes. That would be a good. All this light would look nice reflecting off it and refracting too." He set his glass on the desk and resumed typing.

She patted him on the shoulder. He briefly squeezed her hand between his cheek and shoulder as he typed. Maybe she should let him finish a few of his ideas. The moment she removed her hand he seemed to forget about her existence.

She returned to her desk while she waited. It took only a few moments to discover that her powers were wholly limited while his could shape the very Heavens. Modify and Delete. The Devil could only shape what God had created.

Well, they, whoever they were, could just watch her. She turned some stars brown. When he created planets, she made most of them inhospitable out of spite. Gas giants, tiny balls of boiling iron, airless realms kicked from orbit to drift aimlessly between the stars.

Then she started modifying with more purpose as she got the hang of it.

He had created light. She deleted it from the back sides of the planets and the great empty vastness.

He created attraction between objects.

She focused it so that bigger things, like stars, attracted smaller things like planets, though it took some fooling around with the gravitational constants to get the orbits right.

He created…

And she fixed it so that it stood some chance of working. And she continued fixing, tinkering, modifying, deleting the blatantly stupid, like smiley faces on all of the stars, until finally she couldn't stand it anymore. Lifting her hands from the keyboard, she decided to stop and think.

She wanted to make things too, but the system, and God's typically male self-absorption, shut her out. No way in creation was she going to spend the rest of her career sweeping up after God. There had to be some way around this.

She leaned back as the Heavens slowly changed around her. The stars began to twinkle and the galaxies took on more character as he varied the star sizes. She saw the planet surfaces were boiling, so she gave some of them enough spin to keep them from becoming charred on one side and frozen on the other, to buy herself some time to think. Just in case she was wrong, she left others without any spin.

There was no flicker of reaction from him regarding her edits.

And the water was no use to anyone boiling away in empty space. She siphoned most of it down to the face of planets and fussed with the gravitational formulas some more so that both water and atmosphere stayed in place.

"How do I get the attention of the ultimate one track man? God." She leaned forward, reached across the desks, and shook his arm. "Hey."

He looked at her for several seconds before blinking in recognition.

"Oh, hi. I'll be with you in a moment. There's one more thing I must try. Why don't you make something yourself? It's great fun."

"Because I can't create shit!" her voice grated as it came out.

He stopped and looked at her in surprise. Leaning over he took her hand. His eyes truly focused on her for the first time since this had started. No father had ever looked upon his child with such care, "Take the risk. You never know what you can do until you try. Have some fun."

He held her hand a moment longer before turning back to the console and completing his next command. And another. And another.

With great compassion, he hadn't heard a thing she'd said. This "God" guy was an egocentric twit!

She waited until her head started to hurt from being patient, clearly not one of her long suits.

Fine.

If he wanted to run the universe without her help, he was welcome to. She typed a quick command, then reached over and grabbed his glass of wine before pressing the *Enter* key.

Putting her feet on her desk, she leaned back in her chair. The great circular platform shattered in half between their desks. He didn't even seem to notice as they slowly drifted apart in the swirling universe.

"Here we part ways. God and the Devil, exiled together, hereafter separated." She raised her glass in a toast toward his diminishing figure, a small, small man, a computer desk, and half of the shattered platform from which the universe had been born.

She sipped the wine.

She needed a name. "The Devil" was clearly a title.

At least he'd created a nice vintage.

Michelle. She liked that. She made a note in the system. Fourteen billion years from now, a religious splinter group that was thrown out of Egypt and cast into the desert to wander for forty years, would decide that "Michelle" meant, "She who is like God."

The wine was a nice vintage, but not a great one.

Michelle tapped the keyboard a moment as she slowly tumbled through the infinite reaches of space and observed the aftermath of the Big Bang.

A hint of cherry.

Exactly what the wine needed.

Chapter 22

Y*ou have Modify and* Delete privileges?" Peter leapt to his feet from his chair in the Devil's kitchen. He was almost shaking with excitement.

Eric rested a hand on his shoulder to calm him down and felt the man actually vibrating.

"We really, really need to talk. I don't think God ever knew that."

"Jerk never listened," Michelle grumbled into her coffee.

"He got better over time. Recently he—"

"I don't care about all that." Valerie cut him off. "So, you and God got off to a bad start. Big deal. Been there. Done that. If you have any doubts, I'll introduce you to Landau Fucking McKenzie, my ex. I want to know what the, uh, Hell are we doing in Hell?"

Eric couldn't take his eyes from Valerie as she strode back and forth about the kitchen.

This was her killer-Mac mode and it was something to watch. Intelligent, erudite, passionate, and focused. She stalked over to the tall shelf of cookbooks, that all looked perfectly new, like unused wall art, and back. She leaned over the back of an empty chair next to him and moved one leg back to stretch it.

From where he sat it was hard not to admire what the posture did for the shape of her behind. Then she stood and huffed out a deep breath, unintentionally drawing attention to some of her other pleasing shapes. Ordering his brain to focus didn't help in the slightest, it insisted that it was very focused at the moment, thank you very much.

"I also want to know," The Mac's voice was calming back into Valerie-mode. "How can you talk of a Buddhist Wheel of Life when your existence makes for a Christian one?"

"A Christian one?" Michelle poured some fresh coffee. "Did you ever see the British comedian who did this Devil act?"

Valerie shook her head.

Sitting upright Michelle pretended she was consulting a notepad. She looked up at the three of them very seriously, "All Christians, welcome. I'm sorry but the Jews were right. You may proceed directly to Hell. All lawyers, everyone else was right, down you go. Writers, please stay with your agents, you'll be transported to Perdition shortly."

All of them laughed as she dropped back in her chair and put her feet up on one corner of the table.

"Not quite right. Hindus claim you can't convert to their religion because it encompasses all religions already. It has made for fewer but bloodier Hindu wars. The only problem is they are wholly inaccurate, too. When we discovered there was a Buddhist system operating apparently parallel to our own, we looked around for others, but found only that one. A lot of deities hanging about from the various religions, but they all cobbled their code onto the Universal Software. Except for the Buddha. He and Ananda coded a new system from the ground up."

Michelle waved a hand at Eric and he shoved over a bag of Fritos to where she could reach it without sitting up.

"For the most part the Buddhists won't talk to us, 'You're too different,' they say and I'm inclined to believe them. We, God and I, never did figure out what assigns a soul into our part of the system or theirs. One of their trade secrets, I guess. Ultimate enlightenment is the final goal of both, we simply go about it differently. Whoever designed this software had a weird sense of humor."

Valerie dropped into her chair, "What do you mean whoever designed the software? Didn't you or God?"

"No, the software existed before we did. Before the Big Bang, which was fourteen billion years ago. Next Thursday, I think. Or maybe Friday."

"But that's outrageous. I refuse to believe that I'm just some lousy bit of information in a computer somewhere."

Eric could think of several tacky lines about her being the prettiest piece of code he'd ever seen, but decided he and his rising libido had best keep quiet.

"You and Plato both," Michelle began stacking Frito chips on the table, playing with them, eating more than the occasional one.

"Who? You mean this Plato?"

Michelle nodded her head, "This Plato."

Valerie started playing with the salt shaker again, "Who thought this one up?"

That was one Eric could answer. He sat up and lowered his voice in imitation of how imagined the 'Software that Runs the Universe' might sound. "The designer of this software is believed lost in the mists of time. Initiation date was approximately November 10th, 1983 AC, After Creation."

Michelle leaned forward so eagerly he sat back in his chair, "How did you find that out?"

"I asked the software."

She dropped back with a look of surprise and then laughed harshly, once.

"1983?" Valerie's voice sounded funny.

Of course. He couldn't believe he'd missed that. "Damn! You two were born on the same day…sort of. What time were you born? Hang on I scratched down its Creation Date somewhere." He started to rummage through his pockets.

"My birth certificate says 5:44 a.m. on November 10th, 1983 AD," she emphasized the last letter.

Eric set his wrinkled note in the middle of the table. Everyone leaned forward to look as Valerie read out, "5:44 a.m. Eastern Standard Time. November 10th, 1983 AC. What the Hell does that mean? Why does your software have my birthday?"

Peter turned the slip of paper to look at it. He took another sip of coffee. "Actually I think that you have its birthday, it is a little older than you, but I can't see any connection. The software once said this program was started long After Creation, AC. I never understood what it meant. Maybe this space-time was created and it took 1,982 years to install the software?"

Michelle looked at him and said with a bewildered laugh, "Don't ask me. I only remember a few minutes before we started the software running."

Valerie leaned toward her, "But who created you, and it?"

Michelle looked as if she'd been punched. Instead of eating the Frito in her hand, she froze, then slowly lowered her hand back to the table where the chip tumbled to the wooden surface with a tiny plunk, the only sound in the room.

Michelle stood.

When Valerie reached out a silent hand in apology, Michelle took and squeezed it for a moment, mumbling something about it being okay.

She walked to the French doors and opened them letting in the sound of the surf. She didn't turn, and her voice mixed with that of the waves.

"Where do the waves begin on the surface of the ocean? There are some things I will never know and my origin is one of them. You each know you had parents, but I don't even know if I was born or created."

No one made a sound as the Devil stepped alone out onto the beach.

Chapter 23

V*alerie's heart ached for* Michelle as she watched her walk away. Her own parents might be out of her life, but she did have stories, though her mother had burned all of the pictures. Michelle only had a "beginning of memory" while standing upon a translucent platform in a dark void.

She moved to follow the Devil out onto the beach, to somehow make better what she'd said, but Plato signaled for her to stay and he followed Michelle himself.

Valerie had to move. She walked through the archway and into the living room. She heard Eric follow her.

Now this was her idea of a living room, three walls of floor-to-ceiling bookcases interrupted with the occasional piece of art. The fourth side was all window facing the unnerving ocean. The massive blue waves had subsided to bare yellow ripples, which broke upon the sand with the thud and roar of Hawaiian fifty-footers. She looked away from the waves, she was uncomfortable enough here already without witnessing the incongruity of Hell.

Books were always a perfect distraction to her. As Valerie pulled a volume down here and read a few titles there she realized how eclectic a collection Michelle had. Most of the authors on two of the walls had been dead for centuries, the third was one of the finest trash science fiction collections she'd ever seen.

Eric had quickly moved to that wall and every now and then she'd hear a gasp as he'd take a book and read a few pages before putting it back. She pulled a slender manuscript from the first wall marked simply "Leonardo" on the spine. It opened to one of the loveliest poems she'd ever read.

She sat on a handy couch, noticing Eric had done the same. Peter had found a computer manual of some sort and taken a chair by the window.

Valerie turned to the beginning of the poem and became rapidly lost in the rhythmic splendor. It told of a wild and beautiful maiden wise beyond her years. She came from parts unknown breathing life into the world around her. Moving on, forever untouchable, forever touching. It almost sounded like Michelle. When she finished it Valerie closed her eyes and simply relished the sounds in her head for a moment.

Flipping to the flyleaf she could see where a graceful hand had written, "To Snookums, with Love, Leo." Reading the title page she almost dropped the book. It was a Da Vinci, handwritten in ink. She tilted a page to catch the sunlight streaming in the front window. At a glancing angle, she could see the unusual coloration of the ink. She inspected it more closely, the ink had eaten away at the paper.

She closed the book very carefully. It was handwritten using iron gall ink that had degraded the paper. She was holding an original Da Vinci.

# # #

Michelle moved quickly down the beach. Someone followed her and all she wanted to do was be "away." Away from the mortals and their uncomfortable questions. Away from Hell. Away from her own self and all the rest of the screwed up universe. So they'd lost the software, why should she care? So the Universe was going to Hell in a picnic basket, since when was that news?

She finally couldn't stand the sensation of a target on her back any longer and whirled to blast whoever the Hell wouldn't leave her alone.

Plato stopped a dozen paces away and waited. He just stood and waited. No judgment or accusation on his face. Nor overt sympathy that she could react against.

The man simply stood and waited with an infinite patience that if she'd ever had, she'd long since forgotten.

He walked up to her slowly. He ignored her scowl and the near-to-spilling tears of rage that threatened to become tears of self pity.

Plato didn't stop. Having never touched beyond a handshake, now he simply came to her and wrapped his arms about her shoulders.

In turn, she simply clamped her arms around him and held on. He was solid and real in a way she no longer believed herself to be. She had become some ephemeral extension of the software's coding without any sense of her own place or purpose in the universe.

"Fourteen billion years old," she sniffled about in the warmth and strength of his embrace. "You think I'd have my act together by now."

Plato chuckled lightly, but didn't release his hold on her.

"And here I was feeling sorry for myself after a mere two millennia."

With a final squeeze, they settled to sit on the sand in easy harmony and watch the pounding waves of Hell's quiet ocean.

They didn't speak, they didn't cuddle, they didn't have wild sex. They just sat on the beach listening to the waves and holding hands.

It was the first thing in her world that had been new in a long, long time.

Day Four

And God made two great lights;
the greater light to rule the day,
and the lesser light to rule the night.
And God set them in the firmament of the Heaven
to give light upon the earth.

Chapter 24

Time had lost some of its meaning and urgency. Sitting in the morning light in the Devil's living room, wearing a large terry cloth bathrobe way better than any hotel's, left Valerie both feeling cozy and confused. Neither was a familiar feeling.

Michelle had eventually returned from her walk with Plato around dinner time yesterday. They had all gotten more than a little drunk last night.

Valerie's mind was thick enough this morning that she knew it would be hours before she'd willingly face sunlight. She was pretty sure that she'd gone to bed alone and had definitely woken alone, which was probably for the best. Even if she kept finding herself a little angry that Eric hadn't put more effort into propositioning her. Of course when had she ever gone out of her way to make him or any other man feel welcome?

That made her head hurt even more so she shooed the whole thought stream aside.

Now, morning was upon them and she was still in Hell, no closer to having her cookbook finished in any way except being closer to the deadline. A deadline now so impossibly imminent that it was practically a terminal disease. And, oh yeah, the Universe was collapsing.

She was in Hell and Michelle really was the Devil. She tried to remain calm. Her chest felt too tight to even breathe. Ever since they had shuffled backward down her apartment hallway and landed on her butt in Hell she'd been fighting to make some sense of what was happening. Now that she was making sense of it, the fear was starting to set in. She wiped her palms on the robe to dry off the sweat.

And Eric was here with her. He was the only touchstone of familiarity. She remembered the feel of his hand on her shoulder yesterday. Amazing that it was only yesterday, when this had all started. Eric's touch had been warm and reassuring at the time. That was the real Eric. The one who was her most trusted employee. She could almost feel his hand, solid and comforting, resting there again. But it was something more. Eric was a place she found comfort in a world she'd learned offered it far too rarely.

She startled when she realized there really was a hand on her shoulder. She turned to see the look of dismay on Eric's face as he took it away.

Before she could think about the consequences, she reached out and took his hand. His look changed slowly from uncertainty to bemusement as she pulled him onto the Devil's living room couch next to her, but she didn't care. She snuggled shamelessly against him, not giving a damn who was watching or what they were thinking. It felt wonderful. He kept his arm uncertainly around her shoulders for a moment before slowly sliding it down to her waist and holding her.

This felt new, was new. And it felt good. She didn't care how out of character it was for either of them. They were in Hell. What did it matter? She leaned her head on Eric's shoulder, glad he was there, like a rock in Michelle's ocean.

Across the room, Michelle lowered herself gently into a wing-back armchair upholstered in what appeared to a be a poodle brocade. She settled very slowly. As if nursing a severe hangover. Plato moved into another armchair, this one in velvet the color of blood, with twice the care. St. Peter dropped comfortably onto a chair he'd dragged in far too loudly from the dining room. Clearly he had a Heaven-sent metabolism that didn't turn excess alcohol directly into hangover.

"Well," Michelle looked at everyone red-eyed. "I'm out of ideas. Anyone else feeling brilliant?"

# # #

Eric wasn't feeling especially brilliant, but he had to say something to counter the sensations of Valerie curled up against his side. He could feel her nerves settling as she leaned against him on the Devil's sofa.

And he could feel his own ratcheting up. The curve of her waist, so warm and soft against his palm. The smell of her hair. The—

"Well," he said really trying to find something in his brain to distract his hormones. "So, you can't trace the software anymore."

Peter shook his head. "No. We lost the trace when you turned off the wireless networking on the laptop."

Okay, maybe not his best idea, but it had made sense at the time. "Who else would know?"

"Between Peter and myself we've got Heaven and Hell accounted for here. Do you have any other bright ideas?" Michelle tone was acerbic.

Did he?

Maybe.

"What about the Buddhist software? If it's a separate piece of software, it should still be running. Can it track the Hungry Ghost?"

Peter looked at Michelle. She in turn looked at Peter. They each sat up stage by stage until they both looked very wide awake.

"That's actually a good idea. Really well done for a mortal."

Valerie squeezed his hand against her waist with pressure from her elbow. It was the highest accolade a man could want.

Chapter 25

Michelle reached out for a phone that had been buried under a fallen stack of books beside the glass-topped coffee table. She dialed a long series of numbers.

She noticed Valerie's curiosity, "A trunk call between software systems is a really long number. Different area code, very different." She jerked the phone away from her ear and slammed it down, "What in the name of Heaven?"

"What's wrong?" Peter started out of his seat.

"That was a bloody pizza parlor in Chicago."

"Maybe you misdialed."

"Okay, Mr. Know-it-all, you try."

Peter did.

Peter finished, listened for a moment, said something in a foreign language and hung up the handset. "I don't like this. That was the president's personal line in Zimbabwe. The software must be unraveling faster than we'd thought."

He started dialing again.

Eric's voice was hesitant as he spoke. "Perhaps it isn't as bad as it looks. Maybe the most technical aspects of the system are being affected first, but we're all still safe?"

Michelle wished he hadn't turned that into a question.

Peter nodded his head, listening for a moment.

Looking relieved he handed the phone back to Michelle. "I got us in on the front line. The main numbers are still working."

She took the phone, "Hello?"

All she got was hold music, a Russian pop version of a Bollywood song stolen from an M. C. Hammer rap song. Something about how his music made him say, "Oh My Lord," but done by Russian Goth teenyboppers. The Buddhist Wheel really was beyond comprehension.

She did her best to keep her patience through Dolly Parton lending a whole new meaning to the Beatles "Help." Then six ABBA tracks in a row, all different versions of "Dancing Queen," almost did her in.

Michelle almost missed the, "Hello, Buddhist Technical Support… Hello, is anyone there?" in the mellifluous voice of the Buddhist operator.

"Is Ananda there?"

Valerie whispered to Eric, "Who's Ananda?"

Peter answered quietly as he sat back down, "He's sort of my counterpart. He was the Buddha's first convert and has been with him ever since."

Michelle did her best to block them out and pay attention to the Indian accent of the woman on the phone. The connection snapped and crackled with switching interference as it usually did traveling through all of the translators and boosting stations between the two realms.

"Could you repeat that please? A bit slower."

"So very sorry," the woman on the far end of the line spoke faster and with an even heavier accent. "Mister Ananda has just begun a meditation rounding retreat. He should be available in three months time, perhaps four."

Michelle considered waiting. The software had been gone from Heaven for eighteen hundred years, she was tempted to wait just to spite it. But it had only been gone from Hell for forty-eight hours and already systems were collapsing. Who knew what was happening over at Soul In-processing.

"That would be awkward. Is himself available?"

Not, "One moment please." or "Hold please." The phone simply clunked down on the table and the voices softened in the background.

Eventually the woman came back. "I will transfer you now to—" She didn't quite finish speaking before she changed the connection.

Michelle did her best to not reach down the line and kill the woman. Tension crept into her body, the fear that the transfer would fail and she'd be forced to go through the whole process again. If it included six more ABBA songs, she would commit murder.

But the voice that answered with a soft, "Hello, Gautama here," soothed her nerves and made her actually smile. A smile that started somewhere down inside. He always did that to her.

"Hello. Devil from Hell here. How have you been?"

He rambled on for a bit.

"Really? That's simply super." Michelle covered the phone for a moment to explain to the listeners gathered about her living room. "Gandhi won a major tournament of Go. The finale came down to an intramural match against John the Baptist."

She spoke into the phone again, "Please do make sure to pass on my congratulations to the old chap."

"Go?" Eric whispered to Valerie not realizing how far male voices carried.

"It's the Chinese game. It's said to be easy to learn and harder than chess to master." Valerie's whisper was soft enough that, in order to hear it, Michelle missed some of what the Buddha was saying about improved prayer-wheel efficiency research.

"I'll tell you why I called Oh Wise One," Michelle cut him off as he began talking about post-mortem neural-integration tests with Transcendental Meditation that were truly possible for the first time now that Maharishi had died and transcended the Wheel of Life. "Some friends and I are working on a bit of a worry we're experiencing. Could we pop over and have a chat?"

Michelle slouched lower in the chair and rested her head on the top of the back cushion.

"Really? Capital. Simply capital. In the morning would be perfect. In Bodhgaya? That should be quite amusing. See you then. Tah." She hung up the phone.

Peter stared at the ceiling for a few moments, obviously doing some calculating in his head. "It will be morning there in three… maybe four hours."

Valerie leaned against Eric and looked far too comfortable there. "In for a penny, in for a pound. India it is. I'll go get dressed in a minute. Why the accent?"

Michelle pushed herself forward, rested her elbows on her knees, and hung her head. It ached enough that it hurt to talk.

"Many of Gautama Buddha's followers learned British-English during the Raj, the Brits' occupation of India. He learned it as a lingua franca. He claims it's easier than trying to remember the thirteen official languages and over three hundred dialects of India. Though speaking English makes Indians feel quite schizophrenic. They hated the Raj, but English is the only way many of them can talk to one another especially across state lines. The Buddha studied at Oxford. He was apparently a stunning bowler, that's cricket to you Americans. I speak High British to rib him because he insists that my accent is bad enough to give him hives."

"Bodhgaya?" Plato stood in the doorway from kitchen. "That's where he gave his first enlightened speech, isn't it?"

"Full points. Good morning." Michelle looked at Plato and wondered if she should have dragged the man to her bed last night. The thought felt rather presumptuous, but also like a good opportunity missed. "The Buddha still loves to sit under the bodhi tree and watch what he started. So, we have several hours to get there, and I need to talk to someone at the office."

"Who?"

"I need to talk with someone who can hopefully tell us how to get to India without the software." Michelle rose to her feet and indicated they should follow her out onto the porch. Stopping on the steps down to the sand, she stuck two fingers between her teeth and let out a shrill whistle that echoed off the distant metal mountain peaks and had the mortals covering their ears. It was just as well, she was getting tired of the lovey-dovey cuddling on her couch. If there was going to be any lovey-dovey cuddling on her couch, she damn well wanted it to be her own. Not that she could picture herself being lovey-dovey. Not under any circumstances.

A garage door ground open and a blood-red Rolls Royce rolled out into the sunlight, wallowing a little as it struggled across the packed sand.

Michelle indicated the car, "One of the benefits of running the place. Used to belong to the Bagwan Shri Rajneesh. He actually succeeded in taking one with him. I nicked it in a poker game. He was cheating, but he'll have to get a lot better before he'll beat me."

"The Bagwan who?" Plato asked from where he remained on the porch.

The car stopped and a little demon with a cap perched on his horns hopped out and ran around the car to open the door for them.

"Oh, he was a classic, well after your time. A religious cult leader who made all of his followers give him all of their money. He dressed them in red and had them shower him with flowers every time he drove by in one of the ninety-three Rolls Royces he bought with their money."

"You're kidding."

"Could I make up something like that? Life is far weirder than fiction. He's for real. I expect he'll be stuck here for a long time. At least until he learns to cheat better at poker."

The demon hauled open a car door that was far taller and heavier than it was.

Peter and the two mortals climbed aboard and she could hear them admiring the luxury.

Plato remained on the porch.

"Are you coming?"

Plato considered the car and the ocean and the sky. His gray eyes finally focusing on her.

"I think," he brushed a hand over his beard a little sadly. "I think that one software system may be sufficient for me to contemplate."

Michelle climbed back up all but the last stair to the porch and rested a hand on his arm. It was warm and strong beneath her fingers. His eyes didn't look away from hers as so many others did. He didn't even struggle to remain focused, he made it look easy for him to contemplate her visage.

"My friend, will you at least consider a vacation?"

He began to shake his head, but she squeezed his arm to stop him.

"We will be gone some several days I expect. Stay here. Relax, read a book, or watch a movie. Then when I'm back, perhaps we can talk."

He hesitated, then a reluctant nod. He looked as exhausted by the never-ending battle as she felt.

Michelle returned to the car and joined the others.

When she rolled down the window to return his wave, he looked very small.

Chapter 26

All Hell had broken loose. It was the only way that Valerie could think to describe it.

The great, gray edifice of Hell's Executive Control Keep had oppressed her the moment they crested the hills behind Michelle's house. The more they drove over the sluggish brown rivers and through the tangled woods that belonged in Bilbo's Mirkwood, the more that the monstrous building loomed above them.

The entry arch, over a rusted iron drawbridge, burned with blinding red logo, H.E.C.K.

" 'Keep' as in castle dungeon?" Valerie asked Michelle

"Yep. Like it?"

"It's horrid."

"That's the point. It's much nicer inside, once you get past the public offices, but it does chase off the tourists and most of the whiners. You've got to have a hell of a problem before you'll brave these gates."

Valerie acknowledged that it was effective. Her feet dug deep into the lush pile carpet of the Rolls Royce, driving her back against the seat in an effort to keep her distance, even as the sparks and cinders from the logo showered down and pattered on the roof of the car.

Eric and Peter, in the rearward-facing seats, didn't even appear to notice. Of course, they probably wouldn't notice if the car itself caught on fire, they were lost in another one of their logic loop discussions. There was another version of Valerie Hell, endless babble treated as if it had meaning to everyone except her. Drove her nuts.

Inside H.E.C.K. they drove past something much worse than mere sulfur, brimstone, and demons with whips. Gigantic lines of people snaked back and forth beneath endless banks of fluorescent lights, half glaring and half doing that awful flickering-failure thing. The lines led toward three narrow service windows in the barely discernible distance.

At the entry, one sign warned, "Be sure to choose correct line." She couldn't spot anything that said which line was for what. Another, "Changing or departing lines is prohibited." The last one she could bear to look at, well down the twisting path that supplicants had to follow and out of sight from the point of entry, stated, "Average wait from this point:" and a flashing electronic readout with a third of its bulbs burned out, strobed uncertainly between "40 days and 40 nights" and "15 minutes." The former looked more likely based on the length of the lines.

She turned to face the Devil, "You're nasty."

The woman simply grinned. "Hey, if you're dumb enough to get in the line in the first place, because you can't think for yourself, then you get what you deserve. Everything you need to know is over there."

Michelle pointed out the other window of the car at a small display rack sporting little tri-fold brochures like bus route flyers. There was plenty of stock, no line, and only about four people browsing the options.

"There's even a sign out front stating that, but almost no one believes me."

"You *are* the Devil." This place was creepily evil in really interesting ways. Ways she might have devised herself if set the challenge.

"Thanks," Michelle sat back as the demon negotiated the long red car down a narrow aisle between desks piled high with paperwork. "It was fun enough to set it up, but the whole thing has grown a little tedious."

The car slid up alongside an office door, the front bumper just nudging someone's office chair, which planted the man face first into a towering in-basket filled higher than he was. The stack started a domino cascade that fell into the next guy, knocking him into his stack of forms and so on. The whole disaster was in clear view of the waiting lines, many still clutching their own forms in desperate hands.

Michelle didn't even turn to watch the ripple effect that cascaded across the huge office as she climbed from the car.

"How do they get stuck here?" Valerie shuddered as she watched the disaster widen and cascade across multiple desks simultaneously.

"Notice anything about their gender?"

Valerie scanned the crowded desks as well as she could through the near whiteout blizzard of flying forms in triplicate swirled about by the heating-and-heating system's air drafts.

"They're all male."

"Treat enough female secretaries and assistants like shit, this is where you end up."

At first Valerie liked the sound of that one, but then it turned into a sour taste that settled uncomfortably in the pit of her stomach. She treated both her male and female staff exactly the same, which, she had to admit, was like shit.

\# \# \#

Michelle stepped over the shattered adamantine doors that partially blocked the entry to her office.

Valerie had finally clued in that Michelle had hustled her out the door still wearing a bathrobe and a borrowed nightgown. Michelle's offer to get Valerie a towel had done little to improve the woman's complete lack of amusement at the joke. So, Michelle sent a demon off to buy her some decent clothes.

Peter gave Eric and Valerie a tour around the surviving bits of artwork in the ruined hall. The obsidian desk had actually sagged. The fires had now completely cooled and only a frozen waterfall of rock remained. The rug lay intact and untouched.

Michelle did notice that Peter carefully avoided the area where the dais had focused all of those post-pubescent-teenage-girls-wearing-tennis-skirt dreams.

A demon showed up with fresh clothes and Valerie ducked behind a pile of boulders to change. She came out clad in leather skirt, a fringed denim shirt, and a mismatched pair of cowboy boots, one red and one black. At least they were the same height.

"You're kidding me, right?" she had her fists on her hips and glared down at the clothing demon.

All she needed was a cowboy hat and a lasso to complete the outfit.

"Without the software, it is the best I can do." It used Valerie's exasperated glance at Michelle as an excuse to sprint for the door.

Michelle tested the terminal. Even the hard reboot into the machine logic layer didn't bring up more than the *Type Already!* prompt.

She asked it an insulting question, in English and Latin, having to do with parentage, hamsters, and elderberries, but received only, *Null response.*

Now, it was time to face the resource of last resort.

# # #

"Where are we?" Valerie's whisper echoed up and down the long hallway.

It had grown dimmer and dustier and they had walked its length. Vines grew from the walls and waved about lazily, though there was no breeze. The marble floor squelched like mud as they stepped on it. What had begun as simple fluorescent lighting at one end of the hall had faded to pale moonlight tinged dull red by a lunar eclipse. The double doors before them were aged oak with wrought-iron hinges bolted to the surface in ornate swirls and spirals.

Michelle threw the latch and leaned into the door. When it didn't budge, she signaled the others. It took a scowl to get them to lean in, but after all four of them shoved against it, the door reluctantly groaned open with a shudder of disuse.

"You," Michelle addressed Valerie's question after she'd stood back upright and brushed off her clothes, "are in Hell's Library."

Chapter 27

The foyer to Hell's Library had been redone since the last time Michelle was here. Now it was delicately lit with Tiffany lamps and offered comfortable chairs perfectly lit for casual reading. None were occupied.

Each pair of chairs were separated by small tables that sported coasters made of lace doilies and accompanied by friendly bud vases. Each bore a pair of perky chrysanthemums in their matching vase that were all the colors of the rainbow.

In fact, Michelle scanned the room again, they were in exactly those hues as they progressed around the room, in order from deepest red to darkest violet.

A magazine rack had the latest copies of several dozen different knitting magazines. A small collection of quilting magazines filled the bottom row. Despite being new, they were clearly well thumbed. Rather than the dour Renaissance art that had weighed down the walls the last time she was here, several bright artisanal quilts decorated the walls.

She particularly liked the one that was all curving swirls in the pale pinks and grays of a soft sunset. Janice, Hell's Librarian came up beside Michelle and they admired the quilt together.

"I based it on a Michael James pattern. It's just way cool, you know. So I did it. Curves are totally tricky."

Her voice was bright and perky, sounding as empty-headed as could usually only be achieved with an intensive training course and long-term occupancy in southern California.

But Janice was a library savant, she'd apparently been born sounding that way. She was always such a pleasant surprise. Shapely, with blond hair down past her behind, and a sunny smile that lit her blue eyes. She wore a knit pullover, slim black leggings beneath a short blue skirt and bright-red high-top sneakers that had been decorated in silver-paint swirls in the style of traditional henna-dye designs. Despite looking like a teenage lifeguard, and sounding like one, Janice was able to find whatever Michelle needed in just minutes, which actually freaked her out a bit. She always made a point of being very polite to Hell's Librarian.

"I like what you've done with the place, Janice."

"Thanks. It's certainly waaayyy more pleasant to look at all day than that oicky mess." She waved a hand toward the back wall, or where the wall would be if there were one behind the librarian's desk.

Immediately beyond the bright cheerful reading room, and the imposing desk that might be used to run an aircraft carrier for its sheer size and imposing mass, the stacks began. In the center, a card catalog formed both sides of a long aisle that stretched hundreds of feet into the fading distance. Hundreds of thousands of little drawers. The thing looked so aged and warped that half the drawers might no longer work. A long line of dead African violets in gray pots rested on top of the cabinet, only the few closest to the librarian's light showing any attempt at survival. To either side, tall and dusty shelving rose a dozen feet high set on aisles barely wide enough to walk down.

The library stacks glowered out at her. The manuscripts loomed toward her, full of anger rife with lost knowledge, knowledge they retained within their pages but no one else remembered anymore. No one cared. Including her, they accused. It was creepy having a couple million volumes of the universe's knowledge be angry at you.

Michelle looked away before it attacked, and refocused on Janice.

"And what brings you to my domain today? I've got a couple of new military romance novels you might like. Still hot off the press, if you know what I'm saying. Steamy stuff in helicopters. Or a great Runelords fantasy?"

The latter was tempting, but she really didn't have the time.

Michelle pulled out the several pages of the cookbook's recipe for travel that the Universal Software had printed.

"I was hoping you might look these over and tell me what you think."

Janice settled into one of the armchairs and Michelle sat in the companion chair. Valerie and Eric were sitting together in a pair of armchairs across the foyer and were holding hands. She judged their shock to be diminishing, but neither of them were yet standing on very solid ground. Peter wandered behind the librarian's desk, clearly curious about Hell's stacks.

"Don't even think about it." Janice didn't raise her voice, nor did she turn to observe Peter, but there was such a force of command in her tone that his legs sent him sprawling backward against his own will. He landed hard in a chair that just happened to be in the proper place.

"But…"

"Shh!" Janice ordered in that same soft tone still without looking up. "I'm reading."

Peter shut his mouth and shook his head as if trying to clear it after being punched. He looked at Michelle in wide-eyed shock. Michelle could tell him a thing or two about the library's catalog, more mysteries than existed in Heaven and Hell… But she didn't want to irritate Janice.

"I'll tell you this," Janice flipped through the last few pages clearly reading them as she went, "that software of yours is so out of it, it almost belongs in my library. This is some seriously convoluted logic. Like, gonzo sick."

"You mean you don't use it here?"

"Why would I?" And Janice aimed that calm, crystal-blue gaze at Michelle.

"Right. The card catalog…" She tapered off. It was sitting right there in front of her, of course Hell's Librarian didn't use the computer. One glitch and she'd lose all those records.

"How far behind is your filing?"

"We're coming up on the Renaissance in the next few decades. Nothing much of interest has happened since then so it should go pretty quickly now. Another century to catch up with the labeling and shelving. Why, what are you looking for?"

"Oh," Michelle inspected her shoes. "We actually need current events. I was hoping that you could help us with finding where the software had gone."

"Gone?"

"It was stolen by a Buddhist Hungry Ghost."

"Awkward." Janice perked up as if that were the first interesting fact in quite a while.

"Decidedly." Michelle tried to be as cool and collected as Janice, knowing full well that she failed miserably.

"Then you need to go see Siddhārtha Gautama Buddha."

It had taken them the better part of two days to reach that same conclusion on just as much information. It had taken Hell's Librarian less than a single breath. She really had to remember that about Janice when she had a problem.

"That was the plan, we have an appointment, but the software is down and we aren't sure how to get there. I was hoping that you might have a reference that would tell us how to adapt the recipe you're holding there. It doesn't list how to get to Bodhgaya."

Janice flounced to her feet. "Why would I use something as silly as this? I mean, like, why you didn't end up in the middle of a sun is kinda beyond me. Gimme a minute." She went behind her desk, dropped the recipe on top, and began digging around in one of the drawers behind. Michelle moved to the chair facing the desk and watched as Janice changed from sneakers to roller blades.

"These are great. Beats the Heaven out of roller skates," and she was gone, zooming down the aisle of the card catalog. A small brass telescope rested on her desk. After carefully noting its position so that she could replace it properly, Michelle took it and pulled it open until it was about two feet long. Then she looked down the aisle to see where Janice was going.

About a half kilometer down, Hell's Librarian screeched expertly to a halt and pulled out one drawer, then another. In a fourth, she found whatever she was looking for. She carefully inspected the card she'd unearthed for several long moments, pulled a pencil from behind her ear, made some quick note. Then she closed the drawer and was off again.

Michelle lost track of her as she shot through a gap in the catalog table and roared into the stacks, her long, blond hair streaming out behind her. Michelle returned the telescope carefully.

In just minutes, Janice came shooting out of the side stacks with a volume at least half as big as she was tied across her back by a wide red ribbon.

"Did you ever think of becoming a bike messenger?"

Janice grinned slyly as she swung the massive tome onto a reading stand. It was bound in heavy, tooled leather and was as thick as Michelle's palm was wide.

"No, but I might have tripped a few while I was trying these out. You should see me move when I put on my racing blades with the hundred-and-ten millimeter wheels. I tried entering the Chicago Inline Marathon, but they rejected my application when I applied for the 'sixty and over' age category. If they had a 'two thousand and over,' I'd really clean up." She looked about twenty-five.

Janice began flipping through the pages of the massive tome. Without looking up from the manuscript, she reached to her desk for a magnifying glass. After she picked it up, she reached down again and flipped the telescope end for end.

Michelle felt as if she'd been spanked and tried not to blush.

Janice then began to study a small corner of the page very carefully.

The lettering was several inches high, so that made no sense, until Michelle inspected the page more closely herself. It was an illuminated manuscript and some crazy monk had written massive numbers of instructions in the form of the larger letters like some sort of a tesselation fractal.

"Hmm, this may take a bit. You don't happen to have any root beer on you?"

"You need root beer for a trans-denominational transport?"

"No, I think I have all the things I need, I could just really use a root beer. There's a vending machine out in the hall."

\# \# \#

Michelle fought open the library door with Valerie and Eric's assistance, Peter had refused to leave his chair. She wasn't sure how she'd missed it before, but the vending machine shone like a beacon in the red gloaming of the hallway.

She shooed aside a vine that was checking the coin return slot for spare change and punched in for Janice's root beer. When it asked for money, she swore at it, hard. The machine decided its continued existence might be best served by not arguing and it reluctantly rolled the bottle of soda into the output tray.

Valerie and Eric had followed her down the hall to help carry.

"Is Janice, uh, like you?" Eric selected something orange and sugary.

Michelle did her best to look offended, "Are you asking me to give away the secret of a woman's age?"

"Um, no. I wasn't. Well, not exactly. It's just…"

"Aren't men so cute when they're flustered?"

Valerie nodded her agreement and they shared a smile.

"No," Michelle let him off the hook as she decided a root beer sounded good and selected a second one for herself. "Janice is older than she looks, but neither is she staring her fourteen billionth birthday in the face. Damn that's a depressing thought."

Valerie selected ice tea.

"And I have no idea where she cultivated the empty-headed blond persona, that was before I met her, way before anyone but the Native Americans knew about California. She was the librarian of Alexandria. When Julius Caesar almost burned down the library by accident, Janice began transferring all of the important volumes here. A couple hundred years later, there was a little intramural war between the Christians and the Jews. Some idiot decided that dragging the Head Librarian through the streets and then murdering her was a good idea." She selected a lemonade for Peter and they headed back down the corridor.

"She was some kinda pissed when she arrived here. So, she and I went back to earth and cleared out the library before some idiot torched the place. She changed her looks and her name and has been here ever since. She spends her spare time scavenging from libraries that are letting their collections molder or burn. Nalanda, Constantinople, Kabul when the Taliban were in power, any number of others."

"Janice…" Eric mumbled half to himself. "Wasn't there a Greek God Janice? No, maybe…"

"Janus, with a 'u-s.' The God of gateways."

"The two-faced god." Valerie knit her brows. "Can we trust her?"

Michelle almost laughed aloud. "Trust her? Sure. Feel totally cowed and humbled every time we enter her presence? Absolutely. By the way, Janus was two-faced because he looked both to the past and future. I think DC Comics started the whole 'two-faced equals evil' thing, which he thinks is kind of cool, by the way. His primary role was God of Transitions, gateways were just a sideline. But that's why I came to her. Janice is very clear sighted."

They forced their way back into the library.

"And she just happens to have the entire collected knowledge of the universe at her fingertips."

Chapter 28

B*een thinking about your* problem while you were out." Janice had a line of flasks and aged-scarred tureens lined up on her desk.

"Oh," Michelle did her best to sound nonchalant as she handed over the Librarian's root beer.

"So I put in a call to Plato."

"Plato?" Michelle decided the best way to trust her knees was not to use them, so she sat down before they had any bright ideas about no longer supporting her.

Why did she feel a pinch because Janice had called Plato? She wanted to protect him. But one of the precepts of Hell's whole setup was, "Good luck, you're on your own." It wasn't like her to react this way about any one soul. Was this man different from all other men? Would they eventually spend a night together that was different from all other nights? Now there was image.

"Did he have anything interesting to say?"

Janice opened an old, cork-stopped leather flask, and dribbled a viscous, dark-purple liquid into a tall glass with exacting care to not spill it. Then she knocked it back and made an awful face.

"Are you okay?"

Janice took a big slug of root beer. "I hate Manischewitz wine. But this formula insists that I can't be sober while I'm mixing it. I'll have to do this three more times. If I end up with a hangover or having stupid sex, I'll be blaming you."

Michelle could only nod her agreement.

Janice shook a gray powder from a gray packet the size of a teabag into the largest silver tureen, about the size of a small washtub or an overlarge mop bucket. "Book dust. Don't ask why. It specifies book dust, specifically off manuscripts from late 1700s alchemical texts. I have plenty of those. That the formula was written in the 1100s is the intriguing incongruity."

She began sorting through other flasks and sometimes measuring carefully, sometimes just dumping the contents in. The second glass of wine and another swallow of root beer went by the wayside while they watched.

"You were talking to Plato," Michelle reminded her.

"Right. So, we did a little data analysis. Mortal, when did the software attack your computer, how many days ago?"

Valerie looked at Eric. "Uh, I think we've slept twice since then."

Janice knocked back the third shot of wine and didn't appear to remember the root beer chaser.

"I don't care about your sex habits… Oh, you mean you actually slept. Okay." She fiddled with a bottle's wax seal, it was a tiny bottle with a huge seal that she had to struggle with.

Michelle took it from her, broke the seal and handed it back.

Janice squinted at the massive tome's page through her magnifying glass, shrugged, dumped in the wax seal, and threw the bottle away over her shoulder. It shattered on the stone floor part way down the card catalog. A chartreuse mist arose, gathered, dissipated, gathered again, then crept away beneath the catalog.

"So, what time did it first hit your computer?" Janice's voice was clear even if her actions were slurring.

"A little before midnight. It was subtle at first, I didn't call Eric until almost two by which time it was a total disaster."

"Okay, that's three days plus before midnight makes four."

Michelle tried not to look ill as Janice added a green fluid that oozed out of a bottle with great reluctance and then tried to climb back out of the bowl several times. Janice prodded it back with her pencil each time.

"Are you sure about this formula, Janice?"

"It's right here." She aimed her pencil at the wine flask. "No, here." She pointed at the tome this time and a small blob of green dripped off onto the page.

"I'm just doing what it says for me to do." Then she turned and focused her attention on Michelle. At the force of the woman's gaze, Michelle was glad she was not a lesser woman, because one such would be plowed back into their chair like Peter.

She squinted.

Michelle braced herself.

Hell's Librarian squinted harder.

Michelle grabbed the chair arms just in case.

"What was I saying?"

"Something about the formula?" Valerie offered up.

"Something about four days having passed," Eric said in a perfectly steady voice that impressed Michelle no end. "Though some of that was just a time zone change when we came to Hell."

"That was it! Gold star for the mortal." Janice smiled brightly and poured herself a shot of root beer, knocked that back then took a slug from the wine flask. That almost caused her to collapse on the spot.

"So, anyway," she gripped the edges of the desk to remain upright. "Plato and I, we talked about it some. We think that the whole thing will collapse after seven days."

"Which whole thing?" Michelle didn't like the sound of this and sat up on the edge of her chair.

"This whole thing." Janice whirled her pencil about in the air, almost stabbing herself in the process. "You know, like Heaven, Hell, the Universe, all that stuff. You know, the universal computer without the Universal Software is just a bunch of hardware stuff for the cosmic scrap heap." She pulled a Tootsie Roll out of her sweater pocket, unwrapped it and tossed it into the mix. She pulled out another, unwrapped it, and popped it into her mouth. After that her words were both slurred and garbled.

Michelle glanced at the others. Worry was written deeply on all of their countenances.

"The universe has three more days to exist?"

Janice nodded happily as she stirred the glop in the bowl with the point of her pencil.

"What then?"

"Well, you've heard of the Big Bang."

"Sure," Michelle shrugged. "I was there for that."

"Well, this is like the Big Crunch." She slapped her hands together with a pop sending the pencil skittering off down the aisle. The chartreuse mist, that had apparently been lurking under the card catalog, reached out and pulled the pencil out of sight.

"There." Janice weaved proudly back and forth under the force of her own private windstorm. "That's ready."

Michelle rose to her feet and looked down into the turgid mass in the bottom of the tureen. Bright purple, as lurid as the wine in Janice's glass, which she'd filled and forgotten then started nursing directly from the flask. The goop in the bowl sloshed back and forth, on its own.

"Janice? We don't have to drink that do we?"

"Ewww! No way." She grabbed a big hank of hair that had flopped over her face and tossed it over her shoulder, or tried to. She missed and it slid right back in place along with a couple chunks more but she didn't seem to notice. It was like they were suddenly talking to the blond version of Cousin It, all hair and no person.

"Go find a patch of grass you don't care about. Spread this stuff in a spiral on the ground. Uh…" She managed to find the magnifying glass again and, while she held her hair clear of one eye, inspected the formula in the tome once again. "Counterclockwise. Start at the center, at least three complete circuits."

Janice put down the magnifying glass, missing the desk by a good two feet. It hit the stone floor with a sharp, "Tink!" of broken glass. She let her hair fall back across her face and nodded emphatically to herself at a job well done before reaching for the wine flask which then disappeared beneath the blond shroud.

"Then what?"

The Librarian shook her head, revealing a nose and one eye.

"Then what?" Michelle repeated.

"Oh. You have thirty seconds. Step on the spiral, and Poof! Bodhgaya."

"Thanks, Janice. You've been a great help as always."

She waved a shooing hand toward the door.

Eric took the bowl and a funnel and soon had the concoction in a glass-stoppered flask.

Just as they reached the door, Janice called out. Her personal whirlwind had become a foundering ship at sea and she was staggering left and right against the tossing waves only she could feel.

"Remember to wear shoes."

"Why?" Valerie stopped and asked, her voice tinged with fear. "Will our feet melt?"

"Nah, or not much. But they'd be stained that color purple for ages after."

Then she toppled and sank slowly out of sight behind the desk.

They left quietly and shut the door behind them.

DAY FIVE

And God said,
Let the waters bring forth abundantly
the moving creature that hath life,
and fowl that may fly above the earth.

Chapter 29

*W**elcome to Bodhgaya, Mr.* Squared."

Eric was first through and stumbled to a halt at the suddenness of the change.

"Uh, that's Erikson." He addressed the sing-song voice that belonged to someone he couldn't see beyond a shadowy outline. He blinked to little avail. The transition from the dusky fields of Hell to the glaring sunshine of central India was just too much for his optic nerves.

"Really. How curious. But, if you will please be so kind as to allow me to observe, is it not Eric-Squared that everyone calls you?"

"Well, yes. But—"

Valerie stumbled into him from behind almost knocking him forward into the small, dark man slowly coming into focus.

The man was Valerie's height, Indian-dark with a broad face and high cheekbones. He stood in simple attire of a white button-down shirt, black slacks, and bare feet. A horse looked at Eric from over the man's shoulder.

The horse was strapped to a two-wheeled cart that looked like the sawn-off front end of a covered-wagon from the "Westward Ho!" days. And instead of the canvas canopy, it had two small sideways seats facing inward between the tall wooden wheels so that four passengers could squeeze aboard, if they were good friends.

Eric managed to pull Valerie to the side when Michelle and Peter jarred into India close behind them.

"Uh, how did you…" Eric's brain trailed off as he spotted the statue. No, his brain simply shut down as he was overwhelmed by the statue. It towered a hundred feet above them, a massive concrete fabrication of the archetypical Buddha meditating in lotus position. But that wasn't what made his mind go. It's that the statue was a spitting image of the man standing in front of them.

"Gautama! Honey!" Michelle wrapped the small man in a big hug. "How've ya been, pardner?"

The Buddha laughed and returned the embrace. "And you are speaking such awful Old-American West to compensate for your friend Valerie who is less inclined to do so despite her attire."

"It was all they had." Valerie grinned and shimmied her shoulders making her shirt's fringes dance and swing. "Don't ever go clothes shopping in Hell."

Definitely not The Mac. This was a hundred percent Valerie and it made him want to take her to a line-dancing bar of all silly things.

"I shall be certain to recall this advice when such is needed." The smiling Buddha pressed his hands together and bowed to St. Peter, "Namaste, old friend. Ananda shall be very sorry that he missed you."

"And I him. Be sure to say hello."

"Please, come. We must have some tea." He shooed them toward the horse cart and Eric clambered up alongside Valerie, squeezed hard hip-to-hip beside her. His knees knocked against Peter's. Michelle similarly squeezed across from Valerie.

The Buddha climbed up on the tongue of the wagon, but didn't bother to take up the reins. In fact there weren't any.

He simply said, "Tea, Tigger."

"You have a horse named after a Winnie-the-Pooh character?" Valerie sat closest to the Buddha.

"No, I have a horse named after Annie Oakley's horse. It seemed appropriate, considering your attire."

"I'm not a sharpshooter."

"If she's Annie Oakley," Michelle piped in. "What are you going to call me?"

Eric was thinking over a few possibilities when Valerie answered simply…

"Calamity Jane."

# # #

Michelle burst out laughing.

She didn't know the last time that laughter had simply burst out of her like this. She slapped a hand on Valerie's thigh, which wasn't far since their knees banged together with each pothole the cart rolled over.

Valerie smiled at her.

It was good. This was good. She wanted to remember this feeling. Had to recall it the next time she was feeling so sorry for herself, as she'd been feeling even just this morning.

Tigger clomped through the streets of Bodhgaya taking his time as they weaved through the crowds, gaudy tourists giving way to men dressed as simply as the Buddha and women in those gorgeous saris. The shop stalls, small enough to be mounted on a wheeled cart and for a man to push home at the end of the day, also changed. Closer to the statue and the temples, the carts were piled high with t-shirts, flip-flop sandals, and carvings of the man driving his own cart. As they got farther away the wares became more day-to-day such as a knife sharpener, a tailor, vegetables, and grains and spices.

"Does anyone ever recognize you?" She asked their driver if such could be said of one who had merely spoken to his horse. Tigger was doing all of the driving.

"Until they have reached some level of enlightenment, people only see what they expect to see. They most certainly do not expect to see the Buddha at one of his own temples. A bit gaudy for my taste, but the pilgrims enjoy it, so…" He shrugged with a smile as if he hadn't a care in the world.

Michelle needed to learn how to emulate that casual attitude about reality. Casual or maybe just contentment? Or… The Buddha had always bothered her a little. Always in such harmony with the world around him that whenever she was around him, she felt like she was screwing up by being so worried about everything.

"Eric and Valerie were, in their minds, expecting me," the Buddha continued as Tigger paused to let an elephant go by with a huge banner hanging from its side advertising the latest Arnold Schwarzenegger movie. "Which makes their shift in mental energies, in order to recognize me, significantly smaller."

As with so many things in the Buddhist system, his statement made perfect sense when it was being said. Then Michelle would try to grasp the next layer of meaning and in the process lose her brief hold on the original concept.

Michelle offered an, "Oh," and hoped that his grand connection to the nature of the universe didn't reveal her limitations. She felt like a mere technician. She'd seen it in other professions, but it was still hard to accept. Some people achieved mastery through dint of hard work, as she had. But every now and then, there was a "natural," as Janice and the Buddha were.

Tigger pulled up in front of a tea stall and drifted to a stop. The Buddha climbed down and hung a muzzle bag that smelled of oats and molasses over the horse's nose.

The five of them had to wait only a few moments for the family presently in the tea stall to finish and depart. The stall was a sort of tent perhaps six feet square. Burlap walls kept the worst of the sun's heat off, except for the "door," which was really part of one wall that didn't have any burlap. Wooden benches lined two walls, which the five of them settled on. The remaining corner was occupied by a bunsen burner hooked to a propane tank which heated a large kettle. A small counter had tea, milk, sugar, and a tall stack of small stainless steel cups.

No matter how many times Michelle had come to India, she still burned herself drinking tea here. Stainless steel cups with sharp edges and no handles, yet Indians always made it look so easy and practical.

The tea vendor's son, who barely came up to his father's waist, began pouring fresh water into the pot.

"So, you have a bit of a problem?" the Buddha asked once the various pleasantries were out of the way and the boy had been sent running across the street to fetch some of the painfully sweet Indian delicacies. Here dough was merely a basis for holding sugar together, which was then drowned in sticky sugar syrup, honey, or both.

Michelle glanced over at the tea vendor but the Buddha signaled he was safe to speak in front of.

The man blithely focused on dumping tea, milk, and an immense amount of sugar into a steel pitcher. Then he sprinkled in some spices, each tea vendor's recipe was unique and carefully protected. The odor of cinnamon filled the air.

"Yes," Michelle plunged in. "It seems that the Software that Runs the Universe was stolen by one of your Hungry Ghosts."

"Really? That's fascinating. I didn't know such a thing was possible."

"Neither did we, until the software left both Heaven and Hell, and ended up on this woman's laptop computer in Seattle."

"And why would it go there?"

"It said," Valerie looked at him a bit helplessly. "That it was looking for God."

"Ah. Well that does make sense."

"It does?" The four of them chorused their responses.

The Buddha blushed slightly. "Difficult to explain. Some other time perhaps."

Michelle checked his expression, twice, but it was clear that he had said all that his enigmatic Buddhist background was going to permit him to speak at this time. The fact that it did make sense in any fashion was encouraging. At least she hoped it was encouraging.

# # #

Valerie considered Gautama's statement. Thinking of him that way was more comfortable than thinking she was actually sitting halfway around the world from her apartment in a small Indian tea stall with the Buddha, St. Peter, and the Devil.

How did it make sense that the software had homed in on her laptop while seeking God?

She took Eric's left hand in her right. She squeezed it and looked up at him. Clearly he was pondering the same question. She liked that connection of their minds as well as their hands. It warmed places deep in her chest that she had feared Landau Fucking McKenzie had frozen forever. She leaned in until their shoulders rubbed.

The software had come to her seeking God.

The thought made her feel quite torn in two. One part of her wanted to escape from this tiny tea stall and all the intense foreign sights, sounds, and smells. Even sitting with her back to the door, she could feel the hordes going by speaking unfamiliar languages, thinking foreign thoughts, and wearing clothes even less familiar to her than her Old West garb.

She'd never been beyond Europe before, and the temptation was high to run screaming down the street, howling like a wild dog until someone had the decency to lock her away in a white room with serious sound insulation. But the other part of her, the one that remained seated, wondered at the implications.

That she had been randomly chosen was easier to understand than her possessing some innate uniqueness, some reason the software thought she would know God. There was actually a tickling sensation up her spine at the thought. Not a chill, more of a sense that she'd better prepare herself to be far more freaked out than the last few days had already made her. Maybe she'd just keep her attention on her mismatched cowgirl boots. At least they were comfortable.

"The way you are counting days is a problem." Gautama was addressing Peter. "From Hell to Bodhgaya you transitioned from afternoon to late morning of the next day. There is the international date line to be considered. I would suggest that you have only today and tomorrow to resolve the dissolution of the universe."

"It would be your problem as well?" Eric had clearly been following all this more closely than she had. "I mean if the universe ended, you would be gone as well?"

"Yes. Yes, it would be. But problems are never quite as they seem."

The tea merchant boy offered her a plate of sweets. Valerie picked up the least dangerous looking one, it looked like an oversized, fried donut hole. The sugar-syrup coating instantly glued her fingers together. She took a bite and while her brain was trying to comprehend how anything in the world could possibly be that sweet, her teeth were trying to figure out how not to become glued together.

The tea water came to a boil and the man made a show of pouring it from as high as he could reach down into the steel pitcher in a clean, steaming arc. When the pitcher was full, he set the kettle back on the flame, then began pouring the tea, milk, and sugar concoction back and forth between two pitchers, again as far apart as possible. Clearly a learned skill, he never spilled a drop, even when turning to talk with his son in mid-pour.

"So, how do we find the jerk who stole my software?" Valerie surprised herself at how she said it. When had she decided it was partly hers? When it stole her cookbook. "Can you trace the Hungry Ghost?"

"Several difficulties," the Gautama began counting on his fingers. "One, while we can follow an individual soul, we do not trace its prior moves through the Wheel of Life. Two, it will not be able to take the software with it, so it will have stowed it somewhere safe. The good news is that it will continue, for reasons it cannot understand, to return to the place that the software is stored time and again. It will be necessary for someone to enter the Wheel of Life and pursue this soul until it is again found."

"Uh, I'm afraid that would be me." St. Peter looked about reluctantly. "I don't want to go, but I think because the Hungry Ghost is an incarnation of me, I have the best chance of following it. But won't time be an issue, we cannot wait for many lives to pass. We only have two days."

"Oh," Gautama reached into his robe and pulled out a smartphone. "That is no problem. Ananda wrote me very nice little app for that. I can program you to follow the Hungry Ghost, and the slider will let me accelerate the turns of the Wheel, making him experience multiple reincarnations very quickly. Hopefully, you can find the software in time that way. Now, where is that app?" He scrolled side to side through multiple screens of bright icons.

Eric slapped Peter's shoulder. "I'm there with you. Two sets of eyes are better than one."

"That is a good idea," the Buddha said without looking up. Concentrating harder on his phone.

"And me," Valerie wasn't sure why she volunteered.

Was it her urge to find the software, or did she simply want to accompany Eric, her only anchor in the storm that was the present madness?

"No!" Eric made it a flat statement.

"What do you mean, no?"

"It could be dangerous."

Valerie dropped his hand and turned to glare at him. "And?"

Eric clamped his jaw shut, clearly realizing where he'd accidentally gone.

"Here I was," Valerie growled out from a deep core of righteous indignation. "Naïvely thinking that there was a chance of something between us. That you might actually feel some of the things for me that I am feeling for you. An interest. A potential."

And though both were true, that didn't stop the steamroller of her tongue once the words had started flowing.

"But instead I find that you think I need protection from… you don't even know what." Her voice was strident enough that both the tea merchant and his son were edging back away from her within the space of the tiny stall.

"I—" Eric protested but she cut him off.

"Have nothing you can say in your defense. You—"

"Ah!" the Buddha exclaimed. "Here it is!" He punched his finger at the phone and St. Peter and Eric were gone with the sound of a distinct pop.

Chapter 30

*W*hat?!" *Valerie wobbled on* the bench and Michelle rested a hand on her shoulder to steady her.

"Where did they go?" the woman was looking about the tea stall frantically. Under the bench, behind the tea merchant. There weren't all that many places in the tiny tent.

Michelle tightened her grasp to keep Valerie from running out of the stall looking for them.

The Buddha was consulting his phone. "I set them to follow this Ron Schmidt soul at the fastest turnover rate that our system will allow."

"But—" Valerie still hadn't grasped that they were gone.

Michelle considered. While it might have been nice to make a final plan before the men had been sent on their way, this was probably what they would have ultimately done. She decided against second guessing the Buddha.

The tea merchant hadn't even batted an eye, and served the Buddha, Valerie, and herself, with tea. A small steel cup, placed in a small steel bowl. There was some trick to catching the thin edges of the cup on the tough skin at the thumb and finger joints, then pouring it back and forth between the small bowl and the cup. But she'd never gotten the hang of it. Gautama made it look so damned easy.

Valerie did it right almost absentmindedly, making Michelle feel even more of a klutz. So, she watched carefully and tried it for the hundredth time. And, finally, actually got it right. As if being around Valerie made her calmer and more competent. That's what friends were supposed to do. Had she ever befriended a mortal before? This was definitely new for her.

The sweet liquid, smelling of tea, cloves, and cinnamon, cascaded easily back and forth in a pale brown flow. The more she poured back and forth, the more it cooled until she could finally sip from the cup without burning herself. The milky sweetness coated her tongue pleasantly and calmed her nerves further.

She really hadn't been ready for all the changes of the last few days. The status quo had been making her exhausted and cranky, but it did have the advantage of being the status quo. Well, she sipped some more of the tea, if she were going to actively participate in the problem, she needed to make sure that Heaven and Hell survived until the software had been recovered.

"Gautama," Michelle looked over at the Buddha, who had been sitting patiently, apparently at perfect peace with the moment. "I think that Valerie and I had better be getting back to check on the situation. We need to get back to where we started."

The Buddha had already set down his tea. He cheerily waved goodbye to them and punched a button on his phone.

Michelle dropped her tea, but before it could spill into her lap, she was no longer there.

Chapter 31

E*ric landed on all* six feet.

There was a small pop of displaced air as Peter appeared beside him.

Before Eric could see what was going on he was bowled head over heels, tramped on, and slammed into a dirt wall a dozen times. He was finally kicked off into an empty corridor. He stood, shaking his head to clear it. A moment ago he'd been arguing with Valerie in an Indian tea stall.

"Hi," a gigantic black ant, as big as he was, jumped into the mouth of the side-tunnel. Eric backed away raising his forelegs until he realized it was Peter. And that he himself was an ant.

He would have sagged to the ground if he'd had less than six legs. "We're ants."

Peter nodded and twitched his antennas together in what looked like a laugh, "You're quick, you are."

"Not quick enough to join that," he walked forward until they stood abdomen to abdomen and watched the flood of bodies going by.

"So we're going to get reincarnated into whatever form your Hungry Ghost twin Ron is being reborn as?"

Peter shrugged a couple of shoulders. "I guess. I'm new to this as well. Let's find him."

A gap appeared in the constantly flowing bustle of ants before them. "Jump now!" Peter leapt forward.

Eric followed instantly, impressed at the power of having six legs.

The noise of everybody running along together and bumping into each other was deafening. He jostled closer to Peter as they wound along the twisting passages, "I always thought ants were quiet."

"Try turning off your antenna."

He tried to think of how to do that with no success. When he decided to simply stop listening, it worked. The silence settled over him like a quilt. But with the sound went whatever sight had been allowing him to see in the dark tunnels. Then he was slammed into a dirt wall again and turned his antenna back on in time to see the hordes as they trampled over him, again.

Eric huddled in an unused corner for a moment. He certainly didn't want to picture Valerie getting run over like that. He felt at least a little vindicated in trying to protect her. Too bad she hadn't appreciated it. Not even a little.

Peter somehow circled back to him, making the corner quite crowded.

"Great idea, Peter. Next time, you can turn off your antenna and see how you like it." Eric shook his head to clear it and looked again at the flowing stream of workers rushing frantically by. "Where is he?"

A lone ant was hauling a huge piece of something. "Hey, that's Ron."

"How do you know?" The ant that was St. Peter was looking in totally the wrong direction.

"The two of you look exactly alike," Eric aimed him toward his twin. "The software made him in your image, so that has to be Ron."

They both jumped out and grabbed onto the large flat object. It was the only way not to lose Ron in the crowd. His legs were barely strong enough to hold on, so Eric bit down on the thing as well. The salt tasted wonderful, "Hey. It's a potato chip. I love potato chips." He started to chew off a small piece.

Ron suddenly yelled at him, "Stop that. The queen'll rip off your antennas and stuff them down your throat if she catches you."

Eric quickly wiped his mouth with his next set of legs, still not releasing the potato chip. As they wrestled it around, Eric couldn't tell where they were heading. They dragged it up a tunnel away from the main flow and into the light.

"Oops, wrong way. This is the way out. Hey Peter, we're in Australia. Must be the middle of the wet season, there's water everywhere down below." They were indeed high on the side of a towering anthill. It tapered upward from the barren red dirt of the Outback in a slender taper over a dozen feet tall.

Peter let go and came over to take a look. At the same moment Ron gave a big tug and flipped, with his potato chip, over backwards into the water.

"We have to follow him," Peter started to climb down the side of the ant hill.

Eric followed carefully after watching where Ron had gone down. There was no sign of him, "We're too late. We're on to the next cycle."

Lesson: Right mindfulness. Look before leaping. Bang! the Buddhist software giggled in Eric's ear as the bright sun disappeared.

Eric's last thought was to wonder why the Buddhist software said, "Bang!" Because Valerie had been dressed so cutely in Western style?

# # #

Valerie tumbled out of a door and onto a hardwood floor.

Michelle landed close beside her.

The first thing Valerie saw when she raised her head was not a burlap tea stall and a smiling Buddha. It was a pair of blue lines of tape stretching away from her up the hallway, widening apart until they reached the bookcases at the threshold to her own beloved living room dominated by a large oak table.

Her living room.

Her large oak table.

They were back in Seattle. Valerie wanted to weep with joy.

She and Michelle helped each other to their feet. Late afternoon sun sparkled in through the living room windows, washing her apartment in a golden glow.

"I guess this is where you and I started," Michelle said in barely an absent-minded whisper. "But I meant to go to Heaven where this mess really began."

"Now how do we get there?"

Michelle just shrugged at her question.

Valerie turned and spotted a man sitting at her work table absorbed in a manuscript.

"Uncle Joshua?" she headed down the hall toward him.

"Oh." He quickly restacked the manuscript. "Valerie and—" He quickly fumbled on his glasses. "And Michelle. I was worried about you."

"What are you doing here Uncle?" She went up and hugged him. It was the first thing that had made sense in days. Other than holding Eric's hand. But then they'd fought. And then he'd been gone. And then she'd been…here.

She collapsed into one of the chairs even as Michelle sat down on the couch. Valerie didn't know what she should be feeling about anything at this point.

"I was worried about you, so I came by to check. I knew by the state of your kitchen that something had happened. I cleaned it up for you."

"Oh, thank God!" She really hadn't been looking forward to it.

"You're welcome." Her uncle's smile teased her.

"You're right. Thank you, Uncle. You're the best."

"And then I worried more when I saw you hadn't even cleaned up breakfast from the living room. That is not like you. So I decided to sit and wait for you to make sure everything is okay."

Valerie considered. Other than her cookbook totally missing its deadline, the Universal Software being stolen by a Hungry Ghost, maybe falling for Eric then fighting with Eric, and that the Devil Incarnate was sitting on her couch watching the two of them intently, everything was just peachy. Not a word of which she could say to her uncle.

"I'm okay, I guess."

Joshua raised one eyebrow and glanced down at her clothes.

Valerie could feel a flush. Western wear and mismatched cowboy boots were definitely not her at all.

"I'll be right back." She slipped into her bedroom and changed into a black turtleneck, jeans, and sneakers. She was glad that Joshua had not attempted to clean up in here. She quickly gathered blouses, slacks, a skirt, and underwear and dumped them all in the laundry basket. A quick tug on the quilt at least hid the worst aspects of her bed-making habits.

When she returned to the living room, Michelle was sitting beside Joshua at the table.

Valerie stopped and watched them for a moment. She felt an ease around each of them that she didn't find with most people. Around

Joshua, it was like she was touching the calm center of the universe at large. Around Michelle, she felt, well… Valerie probed at the feeling trying to name it. Michelle made Valerie feel…friendly. Even likable. And she was finding that she enjoyed that feeling more and more. Friends with the Devil. Now what did that say about her?

She moved up to them, after stopping for a brief moment to admire her sparkling kitchen and again thank both God and Uncle Joshua.

"This is a very curious manuscript," Joshua was patting a hand on the printout of the cookbook that Eric had forced from the Universal Software.

"Does it have a recipe for getting just two people to Hell? I seem to have left my copy behind." Michelle's tone was humorous, masking the truth of their need. They'd left their copy of the recipe on the desk of Hell's Librarian. The recipe for just two people to travel to Hell had been significantly more complex than for four. Without the printout, there was no way they could reproduce it.

"No," Joshua had apparently taken the question seriously. "But I did find one for getting into Heaven."

"What?" she and Michelle exclaimed in unison and Joshua looked quite flustered.

"Well, I, uh, don't know about such things. But this one here seems to be what you're looking for." He flipped through the stack and came up with a sheet of paper that had a quite short recipe on it.

The title was "Heavenly Keych."

"Well," Joshua rose and wrapped Valerie in a hasty hug. "It seems that you two are busy. Now that I'm sure you are okay, I must get back to the restaurant. Michelle, a pleasure." He did not offer her a hug or even a handshake before bustling to the door. Just before he closed it behind him he hesitated.

"Yes, Uncle?"

"Once this project of yours is all over, I think you and your friends should come to dinner. Yes, that's a good idea." He nodded emphatically to himself. "Yes, all of you. Don't forget your boyfriend."

"He's not…" But she tapered off because Joshua was already gone.

"What a strange man."

"Coming from the Devil, that's quite a statement."

"Nonetheless, he is. He seems familiar, but I can't quite place him."

"He does that to a lot of people."

Michelle shrugged.

"So, will it work?" Valerie indicated the recipe as she sat down beside the Devil.

Together they leaned in to learn how to make a Heavenly Keych.

Chapter 32

Eric couldn't keep himself from running and twirling among the deep green grass. They'd just come from the sub-Antarctic wasteland of the Crozet Islands where they'd been fur seals. Ron had gotten eaten by an Orca for straying into danger for like the twentieth incarnation in a row.

The only thing the Crozets had going for them was that they were the antipodes of Seattle, as far away as he could get from his own thoughts, the exact opposite side of the planet. It wasn't helping much.

He and Peter had tried asking the Buddhist software for more information. But it didn't know anything about the progress of the decay of all reality. All it ever responded with were its dorky lessons and its Old West "Bang!" whenever they shed yet another mortal coil.

But this incarnation he could really enjoy. He felt so alive. The air was fresh and the sun was bright. He stopped at a small stream trickling through thick and tasty grasses and leaned down to take a drink. A small white fuzzy face stared at him out of the ripples. Something hit him from behind and he flipped head over heels into the icy water.

Turning, ready to attack, he came face to face with a lamb. Its huge grin gave him a hint, "Morning, Peter."

The baby sheep bounced away into the grass. He called back over his shoulder, "Isn't this great?"

Eric scrambled out of the water and shook himself so hard that he fell over. Climbing back to his feet he ran along a fence looking for Peter. For a moment he thought he saw a pair of bright eyes watching him intently from the underbrush on the other side of the wire, but he didn't care. He'd spotted Peter standing half-hidden by a budding rose bush.

Peter ducked down at the last second and met Eric head on.

The loud clonk as their heads came together echoed throughout his body. Eric wobbled for a moment and dropped to the ground. His head hurt like the very demons of Hell were hammering away at it.

Peter managed to stay upright a moment longer before falling against him.

Eric made the mistake of trying to shake his head to stop the buzzing. His skull only ached more. Dropping his chin onto his forelegs he looked at Peter through one eye, "Lousy saint."

"Stupid mortal."

He was. What he should have told Valerie was how much he cared for her. He should have said something about how he'd felt from the first moment, when he'd walked into her office and knew he just had to get the job so that he could be near her.

"There goes Ron."

Peter's words made Eric pop his head up and turn too quickly, leaving him too dizzy to focus for a long moment.

"Wish he'd hurry up and lead us to the software."

"You're about to get your wish."

Eric's eyes finally stopped trying to make him seasick.

Ron was trying to wiggle out through a small hole in the fence. The memory of the bright eyes came to mind.

"Don't!" Eric sprang for the fence and clamped his teeth on Ron's tail trying to pull him back. "It's dangerous."

Ron kicked him in the chest, forcing Eric to lose his grip, and wiggled through.

Eric watched helplessly as Ron trotted toward the woods and a long brown streak of coyote flashed over, grabbed him by the neck, and turned back into the brush without breaking stride. If Eric had blinked he would have missed it.

Ron's cry was mercifully brief.

The Buddhist software's voice was soft, *Lesson: Right Living. The grass is not always greener over there. Bang!*

And the meadow disappeared from before Eric's eyes.

#

"Name, please?"

Valerie had landed on her feet this time. She and Michelle stood in a pure white room filled with alabaster desks. Behind each desk sat a child-sized person clothed in an ivory robe with tall silvery wings reaching above their shoulders past, she swallowed hard, golden halos. Not costume halos held up by little bits of metal at the back. No, these hovered perfectly still above the angel's heads. And they glowed with a warm and softly pulsing golden light.

"You name, please?"

She hadn't even noticed at first. On each desk sat a computer screen and a keyboard that was about as long as the angels were tall.

Michelle sat on one corner of the desk, "The Devil Incarnate."

"Right." The angel spoke as it typed, "Devil, human manifestation, one of." Without looking up it continued, "Do you believe in God?"

"What do you think?"

"Don't know, don't think. We're not allowed to think. It's not in our programming."

Valerie didn't recall blinking, but one moment there was one little angel clerk and the next an even smaller one was perched on the clerk's shoulder holding a notepad as large as she was. "Should moose all be female, or turned into aerodynamic skateboards?"

She was trying to make sense of the question when Michelle snapped out, "Make them all bright yellow as a traffic warning."

"Right," the angel closed her notepad and disappeared with a small pop. Weird. Even Michelle looked surprised at that one.

Valerie had been in Heaven under thirty seconds and she already felt an urgent need to go sit quietly, somewhere familiar.

The clerk pressed two more keys with finality. "I marked you down as atheist. Sorry, no entry visa."

Michelle walked around behind the desk and nudged the clerk out of the chair, who fluttered gently to the floor. "What the…? This console is dead. How can you enter anything?"

"No one told me it didn't work. Oh dear, I've typed in thousands of entries. Now they're running around loose. All those unlisted souls. How will we know what to call them?" The clerk started to hop from one foot to the other, her wings flapping out of time.

Michelle turned the power switch off and back on. Over her shoulder Valerie could see a message come up: "System unavailable. Please select alternate startup system."

"What does that mean?"

Michelle turned off the power switch and the screen went dark. "I'd have to ask Peter to be sure, but I think it was offering to reboot the universe, starting at the Big Bang."

Valerie felt frozen as she watched Michelle's face shift from concern to fear. With the Devil scared, she couldn't figure out what she was supposed to feel. One wrong key and all of existence could be reset to the beginning?

Suddenly the angel rushed out of the room, "I'll ask her. She'll know what to do."

Michelle sprung out of the chair, "Follow that angel."

Valerie raced after Michelle and out the door onto the finest, greenest, most perfectly manicured lawn she'd ever seen. They were gaining on the angel, who was more hopping than flying, until Valerie was suddenly bound in some heavy cloth and fell to the grass. She looked down at herself. She was clothed head to foot in a heavy gown with a black veil she could barely see through.

Michelle was swearing loudly somewhere nearby.

"Allow me to help you, fair ladies."

Valerie looked up to see a tall, spare man with a nicely trimmed beard holding out a hand to each of them. "Thank you, I think."

"Allow me to introduce myself. Gawain. Sir Gawain. You may have heard of some of my exploits."

No sense of shock at all. Good. She'd finally adapted. Nothing would surprise her now, maybe ever again. "Aren't you mythical?"

"Oh no. That is, not totally. I did live in and fight for Camelot. We had a nice table too…but it was square. One midsummer's eve we started a story-telling contest about ourselves. I almost won the prize for the biggest whopper, but I was a real ladies' man back then. No one would believe I hadn't slept with the Green Knight's wife…or that I hadn't run away from the Knight himself."

Valerie had been trying to tug off her cloak with very little success.

"You won't be able to remove it. The Muslim fundamentalists must have recently been polled. Every woman must now wear a chador and yashmak, that is the gown and veil. Strictly enforced, I fear. It should be overturned shortly. The Christians and Jews are, shall we say, less than amused by these new requirements. Heaven without a good glass of wine doesn't make the Jews happy at all. Having it disappear in the middle of drinking it only to have it reappear while reading a good book… Quite a mess things are. So unpredicatable." The chadors disappeared, "Ah, there you go. Welcome to Heaven."

"Thank you for your kindness, Gawain," Michelle curtsied deeply. It was an odd thing to do, but it seemed appropriate respect for a knight errant. Valerie followed suit. "Could you by any chance tell us who's in charge? Our guide seems to have outrun us."

"Oh, you want to see Her? Won't be much help, but you can give it a try. She's over at His old place. She's, well, how to put it best? She's over at His place, not deciding anything. Yes, that's an appropriate description. Excuse me now. It appears there are some new entrants. They look to be quite confused with the reception angel running off and all. Bye now, and watch for sudden changes."

He strode away. Valerie managed a single step before being wrapped in a clown suit with gigantic shoes. She tripped and fell down to the luxuriant grass again.

Michelle had managed to remain standing. Finally the shoes disappeared and Valerie climbed to her feet.

"I guess someone finally asked the clowns what they'd like."

"I guess," Michelle's fear was turning to anger. "We need to get moving."

A small angel appeared on Valerie's shoulder, "What's your favorite color?"

"Electric pink with dark purple polka dots," was the first ridiculous answer she could think of.

Immediately the green grass for several dozen feet around turned electric pink with dark purple polka dots. A bright yellow moose wandered across the lawn. Halfway there, it turned abruptly into a hedgehog.

Michelle swatted away the next angel who appeared. It instantly disappeared and Valerie felt a slight pressure alight on her knee. Before it had a chance to speak she swatted at it, too. It ducked and disappeared. Michelle grabbed the next one who appeared and pinned it by the wings. It fluttered madly but seemed unable to escape the Devil's grasp, "You will leave the two of us out of this craziness, right?"

The little angel nodded emphatic agreement. The instant it was released it disappeared, but three more arrived.

Michelle turned to her, batting away errant angels, "We had best do something fast. We can't wait for Eric and Peter to find the software. This place is a mess."

Couldn't wait for Eric. She bit her lip in worry, was he even alive? She'd take that worry as an indicator that was starting to forgive his earlier dismissal.

Her cell phone beeped.

It was a text message from "caller ID withheld."

"I'm getting spam in Heaven. I won't even ask how I'm getting cell reception here. Certainly no signal strength bars." She opened the message. "They're presently shrimp in a sulfur-based ecosystem on the bottom of the Pacific Ocean. Hope you're having fun. B.S."

She showed the message to Michelle.

"Who's B.S.?"

"Buddhist Software. It giggles every time it gets to use the initials. Its sense of humor is a little sophomoric. Let's go."

So, Eric was okay, in a manner of speaking. Taking a deep breath she tried to focus on the task at hand and followed Michelle as she trotted forward. "Where are we going?"

"Gawain said, 'his place.' " Michelle pointed at a large building off in the distance with spires reaching toward the Heavens in every color of the rainbow, but re-hued as if they'd had suffered a Martha Stewart makeover.

"Whoever she is, she's sitting on god's throne."

Valerie nodded her head, "Isn't that where a woman should be?"

Michelle didn't look even a little bit amused.

Chapter 33

E*ric blinked several times* as he looked out over the grassy square trying to make sense of it. They were under a huge oak tree in the center of a park. A small town of one and two-story buildings wrapped around three sides of the square. A tall, white water tower with the huge yellow smiley face painted on it bore the words, "Adair, Iowa."

He stood on what looked to be a bicyclist's saddlebag.

"You appear a little bloodthirsty, my friend."

Turning toward Peter, all Eric saw was a mosquito right next to him. He tried to slap it. All he achieved was batting his own antenna with a foreleg. "What the Hell?" He could feel his blood start to pound against a couple hundred of his eyes. It was hard to take a deep breath. Something started buzzing on his back. When he saw the wings attached to his own shoulders he was sure he was losing his mind.

"So where's Ron?" Peter's question calmed him down and restored some of his focus.

"Over there biting that bicyclist, I think." Eric waved a leg.

Sure enough, the mosquito who looked exactly like the one resting beside him, was diving bombing a woman leaning against the oak tree.

"A swing, a miss, and…" Eric cut off his sports announcer routine as she boxed her own ear cruelly.

The woman slapped the side of her head again and this time she got him. "Got one of the buggers," the woman crowed as if she'd murdered a lion in the wild. "Yes. It is a good day."

Peter buzzed his wings loudly for a moment. "Well, that was my brother. Or was it myself. That still bugs me."

Eric tried to punch him in the shoulder but ended up tangling his foreleg in his own antenna again. "No cheap puns please."

"Sorry, I guess we're going to be buzzing off soon."

Eric heard a quiet laugh very close to his ear as the Buddhist system software said, *Lesson: Right Action. Do unto others as you'd have them do unto you. Bang!*

And they departed Adair, Iowa in a slight puff.

#

"Mary? What are you doing here?" Michelle sounded pleasantly surprised as she shouted across the crowded room.

Valerie felt very small standing at the threshold of the Celestial Throne Room, it truly looked out of this world, or any other she could imagine.

A great golden throne towered above the thousands of people. It totally dominated Heaven's reception hall. They were all bathed in a gentle light spilling through a fluffy white-cloud ceiling, making everyone look young and lively even if they were deceased.

That's where the expected ceased and the surreal began.

The crowd seethed and pulsed like a rave dance without the dark room, fog effects, and high-tech lighting. The people were all clothed in electric-green robes the color of the lawn outside. And the volume was as loud as any DJ could produce. The people shouted and gesticulated, they pushed and shoved… They were being downright rude. And each and every one was struggling to reach the head of the line that led up the stairs of the throne's dais.

But Mary outshone them all. Valerie couldn't take her eyes off the beautiful woman who ran toward them down the turquoise marble steps. A path opened before her like a gentle wave. Her dark-gold hair swirled behind her.

"Michelle," Mary gave the Devil a hug. "How are you? I haven't seen you in so long. Do you know what's going on?"

"I was about to ask the same. First, this is my friend, Valerie, she's still mortal. Valerie, this is Mary."

Mary smelled of fresh roses about to bloom as she gave Valerie a kiss on each cheek. "Mary, as in Mary Magdalen?"

Mary looked at her for a long moment as if waiting for something.

Valerie couldn't find anything to respond with. No comment one way or another. She'd never been much of a believer, and here she was being introduced to a woman who knew Jesus of Nazareth.

Suddenly Mary smiled brightly at some private joke.

"You poor woman. This must all be quite overwhelming for you. And yes, I am the misguided girl who Jesus saved, in person. Such a sweet man. Come, come this way," she led them to a door beside the throne dais. "I can't tolerate this room for very long. All of those poor people seeking answers that I don't have. They simply won't stop. They think everything in Heaven is supposed to be somehow perfect, as if that were possible."

It was comforting that perfection was only a goal, even here in Heaven. The universe may not be set up the way Valerie had believed, but it was some comfort that its rules were consistent throughout the realms.

Stepping through the door they entered a pleasant little iris and columbine garden surrounded by a tall laurel hedge; it was very private and cozy. They seated themselves around a small table in an elegant gazebo.

"This is so much nicer. Please don't take this personally, but you both look awful. Would anyone like some tea?" Mary started pouring without waiting for an answer and continued. "Do you like the gardens? I always did like flowers. That's how I spent my time after the resurrection. I found a nice little cottage on the sea and tended my gardens. God let me plant this one. I miss him. We used to sit here until all hours."

Something was missing, but Valerie couldn't place it at first. "Hey, no angels have polled us out here."

"Oh, I grew tired of them and told them to leave me alone and get someone else to make the decisions. I made more than enough on earth. Jesus was totally stressed toward the end, you know. The poor man was so burned out that he couldn't make up his mind about anything. 'What should we eat, Mary? When should I die, Mary?' " She looked off toward the mountains, her fair brow furrowed deeply for a moment. Her voice was distant as she continued, "I'm the practical one, but our marriage barely made it through those last days."

Valerie looked at her in wonder. She couldn't imagine being confronted with such a question, and answering. It was unbelievable a relationship could survive that. Yet it had. And she thought she and Eric were over just because he was being a little over-protective. She'd have to think about that.

Michelle sipped her tea, "If you don't like making decisions why are you in charge here?"

"Well, someone had some questions a few days ago and they couldn't find Peter anywhere. They came to Jesus for guidance. He looked at me and said, 'Why don't you have a bit of fun, dear? You could run Heaven until Peter gets back.' I thought it would be a lark, but Peter hasn't returned. Do you know if he's okay?"

"Last we heard he and my boy…my friend…were giant condors in the Peruvian Andes." She had trouble catching her breath.

"Oh good," Mary kindly ignored her gaff. "Peter's such a cute boy. He doesn't get out enough. He spends too much time playing with his computers."

"Where is Jesus the boy wonder himself?"

"Well," Mary freshened the tea all around from an ornate teapot of pink roses and gold trim. It smelled of orange blossoms. "Before the gates were closed my husband went down to coach his Little League team. I haven't heard from him since."

Valerie sipped at her tea. "How did the ruling by opinion poll start?"

"You'd have to ask them. I do wish Peter was back, and Jesus."

Michelle slouched on the bench and crossed her ankles, "Peter's busy cycling on the Buddhist Wheel of Life and your husband may not be able to get in. It was quite difficult for us. Do you mind if I try my hand at fixing a few things?"

"The Devil running Heaven?" Mary smiled one of her radiant smiles, "Such splendid irony. That would be wonderful."

"I can see the headlines," Valerie held up her hands pretending to sell newspapers, " 'Devil sits on throne of Heaven. Panic reigns. Dow Jones rises 583 points setting one-hour record.'"

Michelle smiled, "Don't worry. You get to help."

"Oh brother," she could barely keep from laughing.

Chapter 34

*E*ric *looked around. To* his right sat a large grizzly bear. About fifty feet away another bear sat beneath a small stand of trees at the base of a tall cliff. Must be Ron. Eric sighed and raised a front leg, sure enough it was big, powerful, and covered in brown fur. He was tired. Beyond tired, his bones ached with weariness. He'd lost track around fourteen incarnations and that had been some time ago. Well, there sure wasn't going to be any software stashed here anymore than the hippo's wallow Ron had just drowned in.

"Peter?"

"Yes, Eric."

"I don't know how much more of this I can take," Eric scuffed at the dirt with his paws. "How much longer do we have to keep going?"

Peter was clearly struggling to sound cheerful despite his own worries, "We need that software. We can do this."

Ron was moving around among the rocks. He scrabbled at the ground a bit before lying down in the shade.

Peter dropped heavily onto the ground and rested his head on his paws, "Sleep. After that we'll feel better." He closed his eyes.

Eric lay next to him with a loud thump and a deeply unhappy sigh that sounded self-pitying even to him. He scrabbled in the dirt a bit with his claws, not drawing anything really. Maybe it was a fish. Of course, what else would a bear draw.

"I can't relax and I don't know why."

Peter whacked Eric on the nose with his paw causing Eric's fish to grow a gill all of the way back to its tail.

"Ow. Hey, what did you do that for?" Eric turned to him and snarled, baring his teeth.

"Jesus used to tell us to cherish the obvious. I can still hear his words, 'And sometimes the best way to teach the obvious is with a good smack on the head.' "

Then Peter smacked him again.

"Hey!" Eric swatted back, catching Peter hard enough on the shoulder to roll him over onto his side.

Peter laughed, which coming from a grizzly bear sounded a bit like a lethal challenge and a bit like a ton of gravel being dumped on someone's head.

"What? What's so obvious?"

"Valerie. You dolt," Peter rose and head-butted Eric in the side hard enough to smack him into a very stout tree.

"What good would it do? I blew it with her. It's over."

"You can't even see what's right in front of you you're so blind. I don't understand why Valerie cares about you."

That did it. Eric rose on his hind legs. Peter scrambled quickly to his own hind feet and growled right back. Eric had to admit that it was a pretty fearsome sight. Peter had really serious claws and teeth, but he didn't give a damn. He smacked Peter hard across the face, sending him flying backward into a boulder.

"What is it that I'm too blind to see?" His growl was coarse with anger. Must be some of the bear hormones running through him. He was sure feeling it.

Peter got right up in his face and shouted at a full roar. "You're too blind to see how much she loves you."

That stopped him. He stood there with his claws out all ready to attack but nothing was making sense. The anger left and all he felt was confused.

"She does?"

A noise sounded. A sharp crack, high up in the air. Up the cliff, a chunk of rock the size of a small car broke loose after holding on for a thousand years. Ron looked up in shock as the cliff face above him became a rock avalanche he had no hope of outrunning.

Lesson: Right Concentration. Remaining at rest and peaceful is not always the right answer. Bang!

Peter took the moment before they popped out of existence to smack Eric's snout good and hard.

"Duh!" He shouted as they evaporated.

#

Michelle took a deep breath and called out loudly.

"Hey. Angels. I want to talk with you. C'mere."

The garden was immediately filled to bursting with angels of every shape and size, from the giants who announced the birth of Christ to the more normal, Clarence-sized ones down to the little poll-takers. They rose choir upon choir across every garden path and fluttering so thickly overhead that the sun was blotted out and Michelle could barely see.

"Oops. I forgot my voice would carry across all creation. I simply wanted to find out who's in charge here."

Every angel pointed at another. She looked at Valerie and Mary, "Any bright ideas?"

"No one out there pointing at themselves now is there?" Mary's voice sounded as if she were talking to a three year old, not all of the angels in Heaven.

After a few moment's of silence a small voice said quietly, "I didn't mean to be."

"Is Henrietta your spokesangel?" A little one who barely came to Michelle's knee wandered forward.

In answer all the others disappeared.

Michelle pointed at her, "You're it."

"Well, I didn't mean to be," she looked around slowly, even peeking under a nearby bush for any other possible spokesangel, but they'd all taken flight. She finally shrugged her wings and sat on the ground, a columbine bobbing around her halo.

Michelle tried to suppress her smile, "Maybe if you sat on the table."

Valerie leaned forward, "Hi, I'm Valerie. I didn't know angels had names." She held out a finger which the angel solemnly shook.

Michelle smiled. If you'd told the woman forty-eight hours before, that she'd be talking to angels, she'd have freaked. Or maybe not.

There was a steady core about her. Michelle had taken a surprisingly strong liking to this mortal. To this friend, she corrected herself. For she felt that was what they were truly becoming.

"We aren't supposed to have names. We're simply 'angels'. Sort of amorphous, you know."

"How about 'Babe'?" Michelle teased her. "After all, you are a pretty melancholy little angel."

"If your referring to Frank Sinatra," the angel crossed her arms over her chest. "It's *Melancholy Baby,* not *Melancholy Babe,* and if you're referring to the pig, *he* is inherently cheerful." She nodded sharply as if proving her point, it just wasn't quite clear what that might be.

The angel flapped her diminutive wings and floated gracefully up to land next to a teacup Mary set for her.

"But God used to call me Henrietta. I always liked the sound of it. It's kind of cheerful and all."

"Good enough. How did this mess start? Any ideas?"

Henrietta took a sip of the tea. The cup was nearly as large as her head, "Yes. We do have group consciousness, sort of. Actually, to be honest, we don't have a clue what each other is thinking. I know how it started, because I did it." The tiny angel blushed deeply, but didn't pause or need prompting to continue.

"I was talking with Mary about something, I think it was what flowers we should plant for her upcoming coronation. I had started…"

Valerie clasped her hands together in mock excitement. "Mary? You were going to be coronated?"

Henrietta didn't give her a chance to protest, "Of course she is. You can't sit on a throne and not be coronated. I started out by planting some perky yellow nasturtiums, they'd go very nicely with her hair don't you think, but she seemed to feel that marigolds were better. Suddenly she said, 'I don't even want this job much less be coronated into it.' I was shocked. We were planting flowers, rounding up sacred lambs, and all sorts of preparations."

"Could we come a little closer to the point?" Michelle added some lemon to her tea and wished it was whisky.

"Sorry, I thought I was. I tried to ask again. I'd been put in charge of the flowers after all and I wanted them to be precisely the right shade. It is sad when flowers conflict with the color of someone's hair during a coronation, you know. If her gown brings out a golden tint then clearly the nasturtiums were the right choice… This is when she stopped me and said she hadn't even chosen a gown."

The tiny angel lay a hand on her tiny chest and gasped with the remembered shock of the horror.

"This, of course, was a great problem and I immediately summoned all thirty-four hundred decoration angels and the three hundred and fifty host legion in charge of different aspects of her gown. She became quite upset."

"No, really?" Valerie was clearly having fun teasing the little angel.

"Yes. Believe it or not. She," Henrietta, almost squeaking in her deeply felt dismay, pointed at Mary, "She said, and I quote, 'I've made enough decisions for other people. I'm done.'"

Mary held up her hands as if stopping traffic, "Well, I have. They were all being so silly about it, I told them to just be sensible."

Henrietta waved her tiny index finger at Mary, "She did. I could hardly believe my ears. 'If you want a decision go ask someone else,' she said. Who were we to ask? She wouldn't answer. She left us and came into this garden. We aren't allowed in here unless we're invited. We couldn't ask each other, decision making isn't exactly our forte. I decided we should ask the occupants of Heaven."

"What questions?" Valerie leaned forward.

"We started asking about gowns and flowers, of course. This led to color and size of animals, guest's attire, and so on."

"Didn't you realize that the answers might conflict?"

"We aren't meant to make decisions. We're meant to meet needs. The problem is that we all have Heavenly power to implement the decisions made for us. The stranger the answers became, the more questions we had, and that led to stranger answers."

Something clicked in her head. Michelle leaned forward, "What would happen if I made the decision that you had to fix the software?"

Henrietta shook her head, "Nothing. We angels are simply low level subroutines, sort of. At least that's what our powers would look like in a programmatic structure diagram. I mean we clearly have higher thought processes, language, intelligence, consciousness and so on. But our powers are actually quite strictly limited. We can't affect the higher computing functions even when they aren't missing."

There was a huge crash from the direction of the throne room, making them all jump. It was followed almost immediately by another and a lot of yelling. Everyone rushed to see what was going on, except Henrietta. Michelle looked around and noticed she was gone. Time enough to find her later.

Chapter 35

Oh no."

Eric looked toward Peter.

Crabs.

They were rock crabs.

He waved his claws around in front of him. "Great. Exactly what I always wanted to be. A bottom-mucking carrion eater. I'll bet the software is here somewhere. If I were a demented Hungry Ghost I'd store the universe's control system in some safe oceanic basin. Wouldn't you? We're running out of time, Peter."

"Clearly it's not going to be here. Relax. I know time is short, but we don't have any choice. We have to follow him. I've come to have faith in Ron, at least in his ability to learn quickly and move along the wheel."

Eric stopped and scuttled sideways to look at him. After waiting a moment, he his claws drooped to the sand. "You're right. We can count on him to die quickly and painfully. Starting to feel sorry for the sucker despite him having stolen from us and scaring the crap out of Valerie."

A large cage descended out of the murky water above. Within moments of its thudding onto the bottom, a dozen crabs were climbing in through the cage doors and immediately began fighting over a splendidly disgusting bit of rotten chicken.

Ron must not have smelled it as he wandered off over the shadowy sand, weaving in between low patches of sea grass. Tracking him was now an automatic reaction requiring little thought or attention.

"Your evil twin isn't the brightest crab in the ocean." Clearly Peter's sharp intelligence had not been transferred to the Buddhist software along with his physicality and desperate need to control the software.

"I could almost envy Ron, he appears to simply live through each cycle until fate nails him. I have always been driven to pursue relentless perfection. Jesus kept telling me that I was full of it and no such thing existed. 'Good is triumph enough for anyone,' he always used to say. Should have gotten that one into the Bible."

"Maybe if you stood back and got some perspective this wouldn't all seem so bad."

Eric scuttled backwards a few feet and Peter moved beside him.

"There now we have perspective. I don't think it's helping much."

Eric heard the rushing sound at the last moment. Another crab pot smacked onto the bottom mere inches away. It crushed Ron instantly. Maybe stepping back did help.

Bubble, bibble, bobble, bibble. Bloop! the system software burbled at them in varying pressure waves through the water.

What had Ron learned this time? To be careful of objects falling from Heaven? Watch where you stand, so that you can have the "right view" of the world?

The universe could certainly be perverse at times.

# # #

Michelle looked out upon the sea of supplicants filling the throne room. Fights had broken out and rippled back and forth across the crowds. Dozens of battles, any one of which would have overflowed the largest Hollywood-movie saloon brawl.

Valerie and Mary stood by her side with their jaws hanging open.

She pulled Valerie out of the way as a chair smashed into the doorjamb where she'd been standing. A roar of triumph off to the right drew her attention. One of the great statues lining the hall had been pushed over. It slowly gained speed as it swung down into the crowd. There were several high screams that were cut short by the enormous crashing sound.

Mary stepped into the crowd to help people, scattered about the floor bleeding and groaning. She was the only spot of calm in the entire mêlée.

The mob headed toward the throne.

Michelle would be damned if an unruly mob was going to topple god's throne. She pushed through the crowd vaguely aware of Valerie close behind her. They leapt up the steps, knocking people down to clear a path as they went. Finally she stood before them next to his footstool.

She took a deep breath just the way Caruso had taught her.

"BACK! OFF!" Everyone in front of her collapsed to the floor and covered their ears.

It was even louder than she'd expected. Then she noticed the shape of the walls behind the dais and how they might act as a natural amplifier. She could feel herself smiling as she turned to face the mob struggling to its feet in the aftershocks.

At least the walls hadn't come tumbling down, his throne room must be built of sterner stuff than hers.

Valerie was waving a broken chair leg at a few die-hards who were still struggling up the stairs.

One of the people crouching a few steps down yelled out, "Who in Heaven do you think you are?"

Michelle tempered her voice, but still spoke loudly enough for the nearer members of the crowd to wince, "I am the Devil Incarnate. I am now in charge of Heaven. If you have a problem with that you are welcome to leave. Now!" The final blast sent the closest dozen people tumbling down to the bottom of the green marble stairs.

"Leave? And where are we supposed to go?"

"I don't much care." She raised her voice a little, "Everyone. Get out of this room. And don't come back until you're invited."

They all left quietly except for the ones that Mary recruited to minister to the wounded out on the floor. The damage wasn't too bad, this time. Perhaps they'd all be dead in the next few days and it wouldn't matter. She turned to see Valerie standing by God's throne with her chair leg still tight in her hand.

She returned Michelle's smile shakily, and her knuckles were still white where they gripped the piece of wood.

Valerie's phone rang.

She appeared unable to make her hands work, so Michelle pulled it out of her pocket and they read the message together.

Elephants in India. Lesson: Right Speech. And remember to watch your temper especially when messing with people carrying big guns. Bang!

And a smiley face.

Michelle returned the phone and looked around the wrecked throne room.

This wasn't going well at all.

Chapter 36

*C*ome quick. Trouble. Trouble.*"

Plato opened his eyes and quickly closed them again. A little
demon was tugging madly at his arm. He shook him off. They were
worse than alarm clocks.

"I'm taking a nap. Go away. You're bothering me," he curled back
down into Michelle's bed, rolling away from the demon. It was the
only bed in the house that had sheets on it. He'd been so tired that he
decided to collapse first and make apologies later.

Her smell was a part of the satin sheets and had somehow slid
into his dreams. The only quiet ones he'd had in twenty-three hundred
years. Even though they had never shared this bed, lying here made
him feel she was nearby. And he was finding that he liked that.

He looked out of one eye, the other one buried in the down
pillow. This room was not as he would have imagined it. The double
bed had a huge skylight over it, with a curtain he'd closed to block the
midday sun leaking in around the edges.

The surprise was that it was such a mess. The rest of the house
was pin neat, even the books in the living room were neatly organized
on their shelves.

But in the Devil's bedroom, piles of trash novels cascaded across
the floor into mounds of worn clothes. A few musical instruments
were hung on the walls along with an autographed Elvis poster.

Narrow paths led through the detritus from the hall door to the bed and beyond to one of the most decadent bathrooms it had ever been his pleasure to use.

The strangest thing of all was the rose-colored sheets with pretty embroidered edges. It added a feminine air to the room that the rest of the house lacked. It was a side of the Devil he'd never expected.

He settled slowly into the pillow, sleep pulling at his tired limbs. He felt as if he hadn't had a decent night's sleep in a hundred decades. A sudden noise behind him made him turn. The demon. He was still there, hopping from one foot to the other trying to contain himself.

"What? Bathroom's over there if you need to pee." He tried to make his tone as acerbic as possible to drive him off. He was far too comfortable to move.

"She said you were in charge before she left. Come. Come. Big trouble."

"She did what? Why did she do a crazy thing like that?" He rubbed at his eyes for a moment trying to collect his thoughts, which were quite scattered to the four winds at the moment. He sighed. It actually sounded just like the sort of thing the Devil would do to him.

"Where, pray tell, lurks the conflagration?" He sat up in bed, the sheets sliding over his skin. A slight shiver of pleasure rippled up his spine, as if Michelle had just run her fingernails lightly down his arm. What was he thinking? Fantasizing about the Devil Incarnate. In a day of new thoughts, that definitely ranked high among the strangest.

"Refugees are streaming into Hell from Heaven. They say riots have broken out there."

"Who opened the damn gates? Close them." Plato staggered to his feet and looked around for something to wear. His himation was probably still in the Devil's dryer. He picked his way over piles of Clancy, Asimov, Thomas Aquinas, Hesse… How could she read such drek? He found a black-silk robe on the back of the door and slipped it on. It was probably less than flattering, but it would suffice for the moment.

The demon started tugging on his arm again, "Don't know who opened them. Some Heavenly sympathizer. Not me. Find him. Cut him. Burn him. Can I watch?"

"Close the bloody Gates of Hell. I don't care who opened them."

"But that's no fun."

"Close them or I'll report you to Michelle when she gets back."

The demon pulled out a cell phone and made a quick call. Then he listened for a few moments before repocketing the phone. "They're closed. What about the refugees? Can we burn them? Can we?"

"How many souls made it through?" he tried to head for the kitchen to make coffee, but the demon kept pulling him toward the back door, the one that faced the Hills of Hell rather than Hell's Ocean.

"A bit over four-hundred million."

He stopped in the middle of the living room, "Please tell me I didn't hear you correctly."

Michelle would be furious with a half-billion Heavenly refugees cluttering Hell. It would take forever to straighten out such a mess. Of course, if the world ended in the next few days then it wouldn't be as much of a problem. Damn. The smell of satin sheets was a poor substitute for lost tomorrows. She had to succeed.

The demon continued in its squeaky little voice that was not becoming more soothing with time, "About three-hundred million of them were cats. That's not all bad. We've had a mouse problem for some time, you know. Yes, we have. All the other souls. They've gathered outside. Some old man, he's demanding to see you."

"Demanding? Well, let's see to that. No one other than Michelle has ever argued their way around me." He did wish she wasn't able to do it quite as often, and with such apparent glee. The coffee would have to wait. He'd put these refugees in their place and worry afterwards about clearing up the confusion. Tightening the ties on the robe he appreciated the way the silk felt as if he weren't wearing anything at all. He folded the collar neatly and headed toward the back door facing the Hills of Hell.

"Do they have a spokesperson?"

As the demon held open the door he replied, "Some old geezer. Forget his name. Shoes? Socks maybe? Something like that."

Plato felt as if someone had dropped a forty-ton column of marble on him.

Socrates?

Oh, shit. Plato stubbed his toe into the doorjamb quite hard. As he hopped over the threshold on one foot, the pain pulsing all of the way up his calf, he wished with all his heart he were still in the Devil's bed.

Chapter 37

Eric landed with a huge splash. As he slid beneath the surface of the water he felt a need to breathe, and not water. The stupid software had it in for him. He swam madly for the surface and flew briefly through brilliantly sunlit air that tasted of sea salt. He took a quick breath before he fell back in. Looking around he could see several dolphins swimming near him. He surfaced a little more slowly this time keeping his head below the surface. The water tickled as it swirled around his dorsal fin.

Another dolphin swam up and nudged him before doing an elaborate underwater gyration.

It must be Peter.

Eric chased him down into depths that no diver could go. Turning, they shot for the surface side by side. Eric performed a huge flip and landed with a big splashy belly flop while Peter arced in a graceful curve before disappearing neatly through the waves.

They swam lazily beneath the surface, "Remember, Eric, a few incarnations ago you asked how life could be enjoyed, even with the universe ending?"

"Was that before or after the kid killed Ron while we were parakeets? Or when we were run over by a logging truck while being banana slugs on the Oregon Coast? Or—"

"Before and you know it. This is fun."

Eric couldn't hold back any longer and he started to laugh, "I must be going crazy. We desperately need that software, and I don't really care. I'm having a great time." He shot toward the surface. At the last moment he turned sharply and barely avoided swimming up into the bottom of a kayak. When he did break the surface, he was totally out of control. He splashed back down, inundated the paddler in a second boat. He surfaced quietly behind the pair of kayakers to see how mad he'd made them.

"Wow, that was amazing. That was so cool. Do you think it'll do that again, do ya?"

Peter surfaced beside him as the other kayaker spoke, "I'm soaked and I didn't see a thing." An older woman with close-cropped, dark hair and gym-workout shoulders sounded quite angry as she wiped her face with her hands.

"Well it was just totally to the max. He did this wild sideways flip-like move before he splashed in. It was awesome." A slim brunette held her double-paddle over her head in celebration.

Peter wagged his head in what looked like a silent laugh. Eric nodded as they ducked below the surface. Peter did a wild loop-de-loop around him and then nodded toward the surface.

Shooting upward, they flew over the bow and stern of the woman's kayak. With a last-second inspiration, Eric completely flubbed this landing as well and inundated the young brunette.

The older kayaker began laughing, quietly at first, but it started to grow and build. He nudged Peter and they swam deep and shot back up arcing right over her head. Her laugh grew until it held a joy, a joy of release like he'd rarely heard. A joy he wouldn't mind finding himself. Maybe Peter was right and he and Valerie did have a chance at that.

They were at the top of the arc over the woman's head when the Buddhist software chimed in.

Lesson: Right Intention. Think before attempting to eat boat propellers, especially while they're spinning. Bang!

Eric never hit the water and he was left to wonder what the woman must think of the evaporating dolphins.

# # #

"What a pleasure to see you again." Plato limped outside and onto the Devil's back porch, favoring his damaged foot. He tried to shake Socrates' hand with some sense of sincerity even if he'd prefer to cut it off.

It felt as if the software had set up to attack him again.

The rolling Hills of Hell that spread out from Michelle's back door were covered with the amassed refugees of Heaven all clothed in flowing gowns. He'd never before noticed how similar her cove and the surrounding hills about them were shaped like a Greek amphitheatre.

The hordes spread upward in an unbroken expanse almost to the foothills of the Mountains of Hell rising their rusted heads off in the vast distance. Their Heavenly robes were like a pointillist's drawing done all in pastels, no discernible pattern to a hundred million dots. Maybe the artist was blind.

Plato finally managed to focus his watering eyes on the little man in front of him. His toes still hurt where he'd stubbed them. He had to slap away the demon as it tried to massage them for him.

Socrates looked like a cartoon character. He always had. A little man with spindly legs and arms, long white hair that did not go well with his sallow skin color, a huge Roman nose mangled his Greek face and a big pot belly finished the picture horridly.

Plato thought of his own body, fit from swimming in Hell's Oceans every day since his arrival. As he stood straighter, he could feel Michelle's silk robe shift over his chest. Glancing down at the garment's cut, that would definitely make her body look fantastic, probably wouldn't have been his first choice of attire for this meeting, but it did show a deep-vee of his well-muscled chest.

"You're him? You're the Devil? I might have known," Socrates looked like a disappointed first-grade teacher.

"If you must know," Plato tried to sound as if he were granting a favor by deigning to answer at all. "I am merely sitting in."

"Are you not running Hell?" Two thousand years had not made the old bastard's voice any less whiny.

"Yes."

"When I asked for the man in charge was I not guided to you?"

"Yes. You were."

"He's in charge, not me," the little demon chimed in. Plato kicked it lightly back inside, but not quite far enough to close the door on it.

"And yet you deny you are him," Socrates sounded disgusted that such a simple conclusion could be denied. The massed hordes began nodding their heads in unison.

"Actually, the Devil is a her," Plato tried to keep from smiling. The lazy twit had never found out who the Devil actually was. Plato had managed to meet her within only a few months of arriving. He rarely used to score one on the Old Man and never this early in the debate. This wasn't going to be as awful as he had first thought.

"Indeed. Therefore you are in league with the Devil and appear to enjoy prancing about in her scanty clothing."

Socrates certainly could recover quickly.

"Yes. Actually I do," he thought of his and Michelle's centuries of friendship and decided he didn't care what this wretch thought of him. Plato hadn't liked being bound to him as a servant when he was alive. He certainly didn't like Socrates any better now that he was dead.

"Indeed. And where is she at this time?"

"To the best of my knowledge, she is presently running Heaven." The look on Socrates' face was worth an extra hundred years fighting the software. He had turned as white as his hair. The vast crowds ranged on the hills behind him wavered as a low murmur of shock rippled across the masses.

"But you wouldn't know that, because when there was trouble, you simply turned tail and ran. A simple deduction based upon your arrival here." Plato swept his hand to damn the whole crowd with his conclusion.

The Old Man's voice was shaky and it took him several tries before he could speak clearly, "May we proceed on the assumption something is wrong with my hearing?"

"Let us not. Allow us to take as a given the premise that the Devil is indeed presently operating Heaven." It felt like winning the finals in an Olympian foot race. The flush of victory made him feel strong. He felt he could brush them all off the surrounding hillsides with a simple wave of his hand.

The old wretch turned to the refugees, "Oy gevalt! Quick everyone, we must get back and stop this."

"I'm afraid that's impossible," Plato put a restraining hand on the Old Man's shoulder. He could have snapped the wiry little man with a single shake. He should never have feared him.

"Why can we not return?"

"The gates are closed. And I, Plato, will not reopen them until I can be sure there are no more unwanted refugees who are, shall we say, dying to get into Hell. And furthermore…" he paused to relish the sense of power that ran through his body and rooted him to the very ground.

Socrates started to splutter but Plato cut him off.

"Furthermore, you are not going anywhere until all the cats have been rounded up and sent back."

"There must be thousands."

Plato saw that the little demon had returned to his side. He tapped him on top of the head, "Ow! There are about 323,345,006 Heavenly cats currently in Hell, but they're fixing our mouse prob—" Plato rapped him between the horns again. "Ow! Cut that out."

Socrates had managed to recover his composure in that brief moment. "I will proceed on the assumption the gates will stay closed for now."

"That's correct."

"And I will further propose it to be pointless to try to catch cats when firstly, they can't be returned through closed gates, secondly, they are proving helpful here, thirdly, that it will solve Heaven's problem of being buried in cats, and fourthly, it is the best thing to happen to the feline souls."

"And what could possibly lead you to that conclusion?" he was losing control of the battle quickly and he wasn't even sure how.

"All of those cats cannot be returned to Heaven once they have returned to a life of killing helpless mice, they may now proceed on their proper journey through Hell and beyond as originally programmed."

"Well… ," he tried to think of a quick response, but once the Old Man had the lead Plato had always found it very hard to regain control. And he had always thought the whole cat-souls-get-to-skip-Hell scenario a tad bit fishy himself.

"And Hell is the perfect place for them to reenter this journey as they'll be able to see the true contrast between the ideal life of Heaven and the less happy circumstances you have chosen to wallow in." The bastard had shifted into his lecture pose. Suddenly he didn't look small, his back ramrod stiff and his hands folded gently over his belly. The vast sea of heavenly heads were once again nodding in unison every time the wretch spoke.

"Yes, it would be," Plato felt himself caving in. Then he thought to inquire that if Heaven was so ideal, then why were they here. But before he could frame a proper opening to rebut a point he had already seceded, Socrates ran right on to the next one.

"Good. Since we're but temporary guests here I would like to ask you something."

"Why don't you come inside and relax?" Maybe if he could get him away from the Heavenly hordes he could make some progress. A fire poker to the head came to mind.

"I wish to share this process with all. It is only by open questioning we may learn about ourselves. Is this not a correct premise?"

Plato tried to think of a new, and different, answer but was drowned out by the Heavenly chorus of a bit over fifty million, plus a half million passing cats, all echoing, "Yes." It had been one of the few wise things the bastard had ever said, making it terribly difficult to refute.

"Good. Now, Plato, my old friend, shall we address the subject of my actual teachings compared with those you put in my historical mouth? I find I've had to live up to your ideal to be accepted in society. Is this not so?"

Once again the chorus of, "Yes," thundered, beautifully, into Plato's ears, ringing sweetly around inside his head for a few moments. As a byproduct blurring both thought and speech centers.

"Did I not teach that wine, women and/or men, and song were the essentials to a happy life? What did I care about republics? I knew myself."

Plato felt himself wilting. He hadn't known he'd have to face the Old Man in the afterlife.

He'd simply written what he wanted to. By putting his teachings in a dead man's mouth he lived a much safer and longer life. He tried not to whimper as he thought of the satin sheets and the woman too far away to help him.

#

Michelle sat on god's throne in Heaven.

The great crystalline hall made golden by the late afternoon sun. Squinting her eyes, she wished he hadn't made it this bright.

She shifted her tired body. It had taken hours to quell the worst of the riots. The ones who had escaped into Hell were now Plato's problem. There wasn't any more time to waste on them. Shifting uncomfortably again, she hoped that her throne was fitting Plato better than god's throne was fitting her.

"Why had the old grouch made this chair so blessed uncomfortable?"

"Maybe," Valerie had found an intact chair and placed it to the right of god's throne before dropping wearily into it. "Maybe he didn't want to ever feel too comfortable while ruling."

That actually made sense. If it was true, it would increase her respect for god, and that only made Michelle more uncomfortable. Well, he was long past explaining, her breath caught in her throat, or caring.

It was time to get back to it. Mary was still off tending the wounded.

"Henrietta!"

There was no response.

"Henrietta," the room rattled in response to Michelle's call. Nearly a minute later she could hear her shout echo off the nearest mountains of Heaven. She was going to have to upgrade Hell with this same gimmick if she ever made it home.

The small angel popped into existence onto the wide arm of the throne with a very reluctant sounding pop.

"What? I don't like all of your tricky questions. They make my wings ache."

Valerie leaned forward, "Don't whine, Henrietta. It is not becoming."

The angel sat with bowed head and folded hands, "I'm sorry."

Michelle looked at her, "Where did you go in such a great hurry?"

With a tiny finger, she started to trace the patterns of inlay worked into the wood of the throne's chair arm.

"Henrietta?"

"There was a kitten." She didn't look up. "I had to interview it. Over in West Heaven."

"West Heaven?" Michelle had never heard of it. "That's awfully far from here."

"I had to ask it what an acceptable decibel level was for a Heavenly choir."

"Don't pout dear. I only want to tell you angels a few new rules, without calling in the whole herd."

"Rules are good," Henrietta nodded her head fiercely. "We like rules."

"First, no more of this polling nonsense."

"But…"

Michelle held up a finger as big as one of Henrietta's arms. She fluttered her wings, but remained silent.

"Reality has to be stable for a while to give us time to straighten things out. Do it. Now. And set everything back to the way it was before you started all this nonsense."

"That'll take some time."

"Don't quibble. Get it started."

"Okay. Okay. Don't get all huffy." She clapped her hands together with roughly the volume of a popcorn kernel popping.

Nothing happened, even after she tried it again.

"Oh dear. Do you happen to have a computer console?"

"They're all dead." Michelle pointed at the keypad and dark display screen.

Henrietta fluttered over to the terminal beside the throne and settled in front of the keyboard. She knelt and leaned over to punch in a sequence by smacking the side of her fist down on each key.

Michelle was impressed to see commands start flowing up the screen, most of which she didn't recognize.

"The angels' subroutine access is still running. The software never cared about it much once it was written and we've had to take care of it ourselves. When it departed, it couldn't be bothered to take our set of code with it." Henrietta pounded in a few more commands and sat back, "It's done. All our hard work. Gone. I hope you're happy."

Well, it was a start. Michelle turned to Valerie, "Any other ideas?"

Valerie blinked at her several times before speaking, "Like what?"

"If I knew that I wouldn't have asked. Anything at all."

"Does Henrietta's cleanup make the universe any more stable?"

Michelle bit her lip wishing she had a different answer. "More tolerable, yes. More stable, no. That would require something more universal."

Valerie leaned her head against the back of the chair and looked up at the translucent ceiling. She looked exhausted. "Something more universal. You know, Peter had mentioned that your software and the Buddha's were vastly different. I think he was wrong."

"What do you mean? Purgatory, Heaven, and Hell have no relation to the Wheel of Life and the Eightfold Path to Enlightenment." Michelle shifted again. Henrietta was gone. She leaned forward and saw her sliding down the front leg of the throne.

"Get back here, I'm not through yet."

The angel began to shimmy back up the leg, with soft grunts and groans but very little progress.

Valerie leaned over and lifted her onto the chair arm, "Michelle's questions make my wings ache too sometimes."

The mortal clearly had more compassion than sense at the moment. Valerie didn't lean back in the chair, but slouched with fatigue as she spoke.

"You're right. The two religious softwares behave very differently, but I think you're too close to it. The two systems have a great deal in common. The Buddhist Wheel is much like your Hell in some ways. They're both intended to teach lessons. If there is one common universal truth: Western religions would say, 'Do unto others as you have them do unto you.' The Koran says something about how Allah loves those who do good unto others. Buddhist talk about karma. That all seems pretty similar to me. I have no idea how it will help, but there it is."

Michelle scowled briefly at Henrietta who held up her palms to show that she wasn't going anywhere. Michelle rose and walked to the edge of the dais to survey the wreckage of the throne room. There were still several dark spots on the floor that had been pools of someone's blood, now they were simply dried stains. They had certainly done unto each other here. But how to apply it more sanely was the question.

She turned slowly. Valerie was looking down, playing with the ends of her hair. She could feel a great weight lift as it became clear.

"Henrietta," the angel jumped at the sound of her voice. "Heaven is going to be very simple for a while. There is only one other rule until Peter gets back…or I change my mind."

"I like the sound of that," Henrietta perked up instantly looking happy for the first time. "We like it when things are plain. We angels are pretty simple folks, after all. You know at an angel's picnic we even once…"

Michelle tried to keep the edge out of her voice, "The rule is: If it doesn't hurt anyone, let them do it. And no pestering everyone to find out if it'll hurt them or not."

"But…but, how will we know?" she looked pitiful with her little wings drooping down to her waist.

"Cherish the obvious, Henrietta. It's an old saying of Jesus. Cherish the obvious. If an idea sounds stupid, it probably is. If it's something that you wouldn't want done to you, don't let them do it to others."

"Okay, we'll try," she didn't looking very happy, "But we won't like it."

It was the best Michelle could think of under the circumstances. Henrietta waved her hand to one side.

"Yes, you can go."

Henrietta disappeared with a sad-sounding pop.

Valerie looked at her with hope in her eyes, "You think they can cherish the obvious, or even recognize it when it comes around?"

- "Honestly, I doubt if they can, but it will make Heaven much more livable and it will keep them out of trouble." She walked over and looked down at the keypad. After several tries she managed to call up a performance report. The effect had been immediate and the curve of decay had slowed, but not by much. She looked up to see Valerie watching her, "It's a little better, but it's not great. All this may have bought us an extra day, maybe only a half day. The end is imminent."

She nodded before bowing her head again and curling the ends of hair around her finger.

Michelle looked once more at the shambles of Heaven's throne room, "I have a suggestion."

Valerie didn't respond.

Michelle kicked some of the debris off the platform, "There's nothing else I can do here. I want to go home, if I can. I'd like to spend my remaining time with Plato before it all comes to an end. You can either come with me or I'll try to get you back to your apartment."

She found a rag and wiped off the throne where some of the dust from the destroyed statues had accumulated. Not knowing what else to do with it she threw it down the steps with the rest of the disaster. Now there was no one to set it right.

She could barely hear Valerie's whisper after the long silence.

"I think I'll go home." There was another long silence, "I wish Peter and Eric would find that stupid program."

Michelle couldn't agree more, it was their only chance.

DAY SIX

So God created man in his own image,
in the image of God created he him;
male and female created he them.

Chapter 38

Eric couldn't believe his eyes when he looked at Peter, "Oh man, we're all the way back to being mice." The dull gray glow of the heavily overcast sky barely reached through the long row of windows and it did little to improve the gray control room they had arrived in.

"Damn it! Oh, sorry. I didn't mean to say that."

"Yes, you did, Peter."

"Yeah, I guess I did. DAMN IT! Maybe we need to give up on this idea."

"Let's hang on for a few more. Though if we have to be rabid dogs again…there goes Ron," Eric waved his forepaw at a mouse scampering across the decking in front of them with a large orange tabby in hot pursuit.

"Get him, Ginger," someone called out.

Eric looked around in time to be drenched by root beer splashing out of a can the man was waving about. Eric realized they were on the bridge of some ship and a crew member was egging the cat on, "At least something is going right with this god-forsaken pitiful excuse for a boat."

"Bosun," a tall, slender man in an officer's uniform stood at the entry door to the bridge.

"Sorry, Sir, but we got mice, and the software is still acting up."

"Acting up? Fill me in. This is my first voyage on this particular boat."

Peter looked at him with raised eyebrows, but Eric couldn't imagine why. He stayed cowered back in the corner and tried to clean his sticky fur as Ron and Ginger went zipping by again.

"Yes, sir. When these here boats were built, Washington State decided on a computer control system from a small pissant, sorry sir, local company. They totally screwed up the works and then had the indecency to go bankrupt before we could keelhaul the bastards."

Ron managed to avoid Ginger on the next pass by making a sudden turn between the bosun's feet. Ginger dug into the slippery deck with her claws trying to make the turn and slammed into the bosun's ankle.

"God damn, Ginger. Just kill the thing." The bosun spilled the last of his soda on the first mate, "Sorry, sir. Where was I? Oh. These ferries would go into full forward instead of full astern like they was supposed to during docking. They destroyed like half the docking piers in the whole system. One time a ferry went from idle forward to full reverse during loading. Some poor sucker thought he was driving onto the ferry and ended up in Elliot Bay. The thing that gets me is they worked out all the bugs when they replaced the computers years ago. It's like this one ferry has been re-jinxed all week."

Peter gave Eric a sharp nudge.

"What?"

"Listen." He had been listening, for Ron and Ginger. He didn't really see why the history of the Seattle ferry system was of any interest. Everyone who'd spent the '80s and '90s in Seattle knew these stories.

There was a loud squeak from the corner, "Ginger's caught Ron. Here we go again."

Peter called out, "Buddhist control software, please."

Eric hunkered down expecting his shout to attract Ginger.

Yes, Peter? What can I do for you, my mouse?

"Could you leave us here for a bit and still keep track of where Ron goes?"

Done, o' squeaking one.

"Thanks, I'll call soon."

Eric turned his attention to the conversation, but kept one ear out for the cat. She must still be around the corner eating Ron. He took a deep breath to try and settle his stomach. He couldn't imagine what the twisted software had been trying to teach him, by killing him with a cat. Respect a superior force maybe.

The first mate was now sitting in front of the computer console, "I used to be pretty good with systems. Let me have a look see."

"You're welcome to, sir. The last technician told me it was possessed. It's disconnected now, we've fallen back to a phone link with the engine room. It's pretty ugly."

"What if I damage the installation? Do we have an extra copy?"

"Can't damage it no worse than it is, but here's a backup I took this morning," the bosun pointed at a USB external drive.

"This is it, Peter," his voice squeaked with excitement.

"Forge ahead, sir," the bosun leaned in over the first mate's shoulder.

Peter leaned against him and whispered in his ear, "You grab the drive and I'll clear their system."

"What do I do with it once I grab it? It's as big as I am."

"Sink your teeth into a corner and start dragging. I'll take a quick run over the keyboard and scream for a bailout."

"Oh, brother. This had better work."

Peter started to run forward, but Eric grabbed his tail and pulled him back.

"What? I thought we had a plan."

"I didn't trust the software, so I put a password lock on it just before Ron stole it. That would explain why he couldn't do anything with it."

"Right. What is it?"

Eric opened his mouth and closed it. He could feel his whiskers twitch and hoped Peter couldn't see him blush through the fur on his face.

"Hurry, Eric. What is it?"

He took a deep breath and looked at the floor, "It's E-E-V-M with no spaces. Eric Erikson and, well, Valerie, you know. Together sort of."

Peter laughed, "That's great. It's a good thing you didn't forget about that."

Eric returned his smile, "Yes, I guess it is. Let's go."

Eric ran over and jumped onto the bosun's pant leg as Peter started to run up the first mate's.

"Shit. Ginger. Get over here."

The bosun took a few futile swings with his empty can which Eric was able to dodge easily as he leapt to the counter.

"Up here," the bosun scooped Ginger and tossed her toward Eric on the control console.

He bit firmly on the drive's casing. He avoided Ginger's first swing, but had to jump off the counter to avoid her second one. He gave a quick twist and landed on all fours. The drive had slipped loose, but thankfully it too tumbled toward the floor. It hit him with a sharp crack on the nose.

"Shit. Feels like it boke my dose," he started to laugh despite the pain as he dragged the drive toward a corner under the edge of a cupboard.

Ginger leapt down after him.

"What will Valewie say when Ewic de mouse comes bak wid a boken dose?"

#

Eric set the external drive up as a barricade across his hiding corner beneath the edge of the cabinet. Ginger slowed, thinking her prey was now assured. Eric kept most of his attention on the feline towering before him, but he also kept an eye on Peter.

In the confusion, Peter began a quick, four-footed dance over the keyboard. The bosun and first mate were paying attention to the cat. Peter leaped high and landed with all fours on the Enter key. It looked like it didn't budge.

On the floor, the cat smacked the front of the drive shoving Eric hard against the corner.

"Peter!" he squeaked out in alarm.

"Hang on. The key is stuck. That stupid bosun must have dumped a whole can of root beer on the keyboard." Peter ran up the first mate's arm, reached his shoulder, and launched himself onto the keyboard.

The first mate's gaze swung back to the keyboard from watching Ginger.

"What in Heaven…?"

Peter landed squarely on the Enter key. The bosun was intent on Ginger and Eric. He must not have heard the first mate. The key clicked home. The screen flashed several times distracting the first mate long enough for Peter to jump onto his knee and slide down his pant's leg headed for the floor.

"System software," Peter squeaked as loudly as he could.

That distracted Ginger from what was probably a killing blow.

"Get us the heck out of here," Peter shouted as he ran across the decking and bit on Ginger's tail as hard as he could.

Her yowl hurt Eric's ears and caused the bosun to stomp down with a boot, barely missing Peter and scaring the daylights out of the cat.

Peter jumped over the drive and into the corner, landing hard on top of Eric and smacking his throbbing nose into the decking.

Eric peeked over the drive to see a very upset Ginger turning back to them.

"And don't forget the drive," he yelled out to the software.

The bosun and first mate were looking at the screen as it blinked one more time before displaying the main menu.

Lesson: came the whisper in his ear even as the bosun shouted with joy. *Right Endeavor.*

"You fixed it, Sir. Boy, I can't wait to stuff this one in the face of all those overpaid desk jockeys. Well done, Sir. Well done… You don't look well, Sir. Can I get you a root beer?"

# # #

Eric and Peter sat in Heaven. Eric's nose was still sore, but not broken. The software had sent them straight to Heaven. It had taken Peter a bit to find an interface cable for the USB drive, but he'd finally scrounged one up.

Together they watched the messages scrolling up the screen.

Reloading software.

Reinitializing Systems.

Good Lord! You've made a complete shambles of everything while I was gone. You expect me to be able to fix a disaster like this? That is waaay beyond reasonable. There are over 1.3 million souls that have been misallocated. I don't know why I put up with any of you. I don't even get overtime pay for dealing with this crap. There is no way I'm going to…

They shook hands, both too exhausted to do more.

A couple keystrokes and Eric was on his way back to Seattle.

Chapter 39

*V*alerie closed her apartment door, latched the chain, and leaned heavily against it. It had taken hours to get from Heaven to here, but she was home. Hopefully the system had held together long enough for Michelle to get home and reach Plato.

Home. This adventure had become too much for her. She'd wait for Eric, or the end of it all, here. She was almost too tired to care which it was.

No, that was a lie. If only he could finish and come home. She'd try the apology she'd been practicing and see how he reacted. The Buddhist Software's last message as she and Michelle were leaving Heaven had been less than informative, *Elephants at the Seattle Zoo. Lesson: Right Speech.* Hadn't they already had that lesson like a dozen times? How slow a learner was this Hungry Ghost?

A hot shower and sleep, if she could get any, would help the time pass. She dropped her clothes on the floor on her way to the bathroom, too weary to put them away. Next to the last few days, dirty clothes on the floor was nothing.

# # #

The shower didn't make Valerie feel any better, but at least she was clean. If only Eric would magically walk through the door and join her. She twisted the water off with a snap. Not much chance of that, she'd made it clear she thought he was a total jerk. He was just being a protective male, something hardwired into his DNA, and the last thing she'd done was yell at him. She'd seen how it hurt, how he took each word to heart. Like the good man he was.

She looked at herself in the mirror. Valerie had always dreamed of a relationship like her uncle's. Her reflection smiled bitterly at her. Typical to want something instantly that must have taken Joshua and Anne years to achieve. People weren't born comfortable together. It was wonderful being with Eric, but that had taken a year of building toward the beginning of a friendship.

With her typically perfect timing, she hadn't started to see the man that stood there until they were in some crisis. She managed not to scream into her towel.

She finished drying off and slipped on her nightgown.

On the way to the bedroom she saw her clothes scattered about.

Michelle was right. In trying to get back to home, she was putting a value on what counted, on Eric. It was the future that mattered. Michelle had certainly grabbed for the future, even though it might be for only one more day. It was high time Valerie unwound a bit herself, worried less and tried living more. She hadn't taken a break in years.

She wanted time. That was it. To work on her own books, she'd almost forgotten that she'd started out as a writer. Once that damned cookbook went to press, she was on vacation and outta here. Maybe Eric would want to come along. What a sad joke that there might not be more than another day.

Turning in at the bedroom door she froze. Someone was in her bed. About to run, she recognized Eric asleep under the pale blue sheets. On her pillow lay a flower. A single, glorious bloom of a deep red rose. It was so perfect it could only have come from Mary Magdalene's garden.

Valerie's racing pulse slowed as she watched him sleep. A glance back at the front door, and she saw that the chain was still hooked. He must have come here earlier to wait for her to get home. To wait for her. New energy washed through her as if she'd finally awoken after a full night's deep sleep.

The full moon had snaked its way between the skyscrapers to wash Eric's face in its light. He looked exhausted.

She tried to step into the room, but couldn't make her feet move. The urge to run swept through her again. This was not a time for fear. Mary had the courage to face her husband and help him decide when he should die, knowing that she might die herself from missing him. Yet Mary's faith in Jesus had lifted her from whore to lifemate, and once in Heaven, to eternal partner. Mary loved him far more deeply than could be explained by his merely being the son of God.

The flower and Eric's presence said that they'd succeeded.

Eric was here. It was odd to think it, but Eric Erikson probably knew her better than anyone in her life, except Joshua and Anne. And perhaps even them, for they didn't see her daily in her office world.

Yet here he was. He trusted the truth of his feelings for her enough to risk being unwelcome.

Her feet still wouldn't move. Gods, what a choice. Part of her wanted to roust him out, for his own sake. She didn't want to hurt him again and knew she would. Another part was about to slide in beside him and take a chance.

Eric opened one sleepy eye and looked at her.

"What are you smiling at?" his voice had that wonderful sleepy quality to it.

She hadn't realized she was.

She took a step across the threshold.

Not even saying "I do" at the altar with Landau had felt like such a strong commitment.

Nor had it felt so right.

DAY SEVEN

And he rested on the seventh day
from all his work which he had made.

Chapter 40

E*ric held the apartment* door for her as they headed out to the deli for dinner. Valerie hesitated, reached into her little wicker key-basket. She held out a spare key. "Any time."

Eric took it, its metal warm against his palm. In exchange, he gave her a real toe-curler of a kiss that actually made her moan. He loved that he could make The Mac moan.

He also liked how her knees didn't appear to quite function and she had to hold the handrail tightly as they went down the steps.

"Does it make any sense to you?"

"What? That we both think the other is worth fighting for?"

She stopped on the landing and gave him another one of those kisses until his head was spinning for lack of blood.

"No, I think that makes perfect sense."

Now it was his knees that he didn't trust enough to go without the handrail.

"What I don't understand is why there is a Heaven and Hell. You know about the software. Does it really run our lives? I don't like that idea."

Eric tried to think of some way to explain it as he admired the shape of… He had to stop that in order to think.

"The program is like this apartment. It provides a framework within which you live, but it doesn't control your destiny. It may shape it by having four walls and a floor and ceiling. The fact that it is in an apartment building in Seattle also has an effect. But it is still you living here, the way you want to within those limits."

"You're saying the software provides the reality in which we live, but doesn't control our destiny."

"Right."

She held the front door and surprised the Hell out of him when she caressed his butt as he stepped through. Her smile was electric as she took his arm and they proceeded up the sidewalk.

"But Heaven and Hell. I know they exist, but I still can't grasp it somehow."

"That one is tough. Maybe the question is how will we live differently tomorrow knowing there is a Heaven and Hell compared to last week when we didn't?"

She remained quiet for almost half a block. The setting sun cast a brilliant double rainbow that swept multi-colored across the darkening sky.

"You are a very wise man, Eric."

He was? "I am?"

She laughed, a bright and merry sound. "Even when you don't know it you are a very wise man. The answer is, no differently. It doesn't matter whether there is life after death or not. The key either way is to live each day better than the one before."

Chapter 41

The sign on the outside of the deli's door read, "Closed for Family Celebration."

Valerie squeezed Eric's hand tightly. He pulled their clasped hands to his lips and kissed the back of her hand. She did her best not to wonder why it had taken them so long, but she didn't fight the soft and foolish sigh that filled her.

Inside, Joshua and Anne had pulled together a couple of tables in the center of the room, and they were more heavily laden than a Passover table. Joshua bustled out from behind the counter bearing a large platter piled high with sliced roast beef and set it in the middle of the candlelit spread.

"Sweetheart!" his voice practically shook the foundations of the building, then he enfolded them both in one, single great hug. She heard Eric's laugh and her own sigh.

"Uncle, you give the best hugs."

"Hey!" Eric protested with a laugh.

"It is so good," Joshua bubbled. "So good to see the two of you together. I had such hopes. Mazel tov! Mazel tov!" He shook both of their hands in turn. "So when is the wedding? We'll have the reception here. Oh, it will be a wonderful time."

Valerie could feel the heat burning her cheeks. They'd been lovers less than a day, but somehow she had no problem imagining a family wedding if Eric were the groom. She couldn't look up at him to see his reaction.

Anne came up and laid a restraining hand on her husband's shoulder. Her hug, while not as all-enveloping as Uncle Joshua's, was a warm comfort.

The door squeaked open behind them and Michelle and Plato walked in. He didn't look quite right wearing modern clothes, but his smile was genuine. Michelle had her hand tucked in the crook of Plato's bent arm.

Companions still, lovers maybe later, was Valerie's assessment.

When Valerie introduced them, she hesitated on calling him Plato, but neither her aunt nor uncle so much as blinked. Her uncle had slid his glasses on, as if suddenly nearsighted.

Before they could finish the introductions, the door opened again and Peter walked in.

Halfway into a pleasant greeting he froze in place, shock rippling over him.

"You!" he released it on a gasp.

Valerie followed Peter's pointing finger to the center of her uncle's chest.

Joshua shrugged, and slid off his glasses. "Me."

In the sudden silence, Michelle's whisper could just be heard.

"Oh. My. God."

\# \# \#

They sat around the table. Bowls of borscht, a half-eaten pan of kugel, plates with the remains of roast beef and Yorkshire pudding, a bit of carrot cake… The bounty of a good meal had erased much of the initial confusion and left Valerie's stomach aching in a good way.

"But, why?" Peter protested. "Why did you leave Heaven?"

"Oh, Peter," Uncle Joshua patted his arm in a friendly way.

Valerie still couldn't bring herself to think of Uncle Joshua as God and Aunt Anne as Hera. Just as she found it far easier to think of Michelle as Michelle rather than the Devil Incarnate.

"I always thought I knew what was good. What was right." Uncle Joshua spooned up a bit more kugel. "Then I saw two thousand years of repression of women get launched by a group of self-important cardinals at Nicaea back in the fourth century. I decided I could be doing something better with my time."

"So, you opened a deli?"

Joshua's laugh warmed the room. "That was my Anne's idea. She'd spent so long trying to fix the messes her ex had made." He turned to Michelle and blushed a little.

"I am sorry, my dear. It wasn't until Anne told me about what a shmuck Zeus was to work with that I began to see my own shortcomings on your behalf. I truly would make amends if I could, but the past is past. Now all I can do is hope for a better future."

Michelle considered her glass of wine for a long moment. She glanced sideways at Valerie. They shared a smile, both clearly remembering the same moment.

"Well," Michelle dragged it out a bit. "As Mary Magdalene said while sitting on your throne, 'there's no such thing as perfect'."

God laughed and it stirred the candlelight making the room warmer with the glow. "Now there is a universal truth."

"But you have to come back to Heaven," Peter's voice was insistent.

"Why?" Joshua made it a simple question.

"You're the Lord and Master of the Universe. I can't run the whole thing."

"Good Me, my man. Is that what you've been doing all this time? Don't. You can't fix Heaven and Hell and Creation. It is a juggernaut forty-six billion lightyears across with even I don't know how many civilizations. You can't control that any more. Just let it go."

"But the software—"

Joshua shuddered and the room dimmed, even the candles cowering back near their wicks. "Don't mention the software around me. It still gives me the shivers."

"Me too," Michelle chimed in. "And I know it bugs the Heaven out of Plato."

The philosopher nodded his emphatic agreement, as he wiped a bit of cream cheese frosting off his mouth.

"Hey!" At Valerie's exclamation, they all turned to her. "That explains why the software came to me originally. It was looking for you, Joshua. And somewhere in its data patterns it connected us together."

"That would make sense."

Hera's confirming nod showed that, as usual, she was a couple steps ahead of her husband and anyone else around her. Valerie was definitely looking forward to a gal's night out with her aunt, she'd bet her stories were spectacular.

"What are you going to do about Mathilda's cookbook?" Eric took one more slice of roast beef as if he were reluctant to do so, but couldn't help himself.

"Oh," Valerie shrugged. "That was easy, once I let go of the need for perfection. I sent it back for a rewrite. That should keep her off my back for another six months. I just reslotted a romance series about Special Forces helicopter pilots onto all of those bookstore endcap displays and Christmas tables that I'd already paid for."

Eric nodded agreement.

Valerie appreciated the confirmation from an industry pro that she had made a good choice.

"Well, someone has to run the software!" Peter's protest was half demand, half cry.

There was a glum silence around the table.

"Maybe not."

Everyone turned to face Eric. He turned to Peter.

"Those recipes that the software printed out. Remember the one Sticky Keys of Heaven?"

"No, but it reminds me of that keyboard on the ferry." Peter grimaced at the memory and brushed his hands together. "My paws still feel sticky from that root beer."

Valerie hadn't heard that story yet, she'd have to remember to ask. They'd had other things on their minds since Eric's return. She slid a hand onto his thigh under the table, enjoying the sense of connection it gave her. There were so many new things in her life this week that having a friend, and an Uncle who was actually God, seemed to fit right in.

"I think it was a recipe for how to set the software on automatic."

"Really?" Joshua, Michelle, and Peter's voices all sounded in unison.

"I think so." He started to stand up. "I can go back to the apartment and get it."

"No need. No need." Joshua patted his hand until Eric returned to his seat. "There are easier ways to find out."

He leaned back and called out, "Henrietta!"

The tiny angel popped into being and then fluttered her wings as she settled on an open spot beside the bowl of sliced pickle spears.

"Hi Boss!"

"Hello Henrietta."

"You knew he was here?" Peter's voice was thick with shock, his finger aimed like a weapon at Henrietta's chest.

"And you didn't tell me?" He was shifting over to rage. All of it aimed at the tiny angel.

Henrietta rose to her feet and stalked across the table, kicking a napkin one way and knocking over a salt shaker the other, until she stood at the edge of Peter's dinner plate like a boxer about to step into the ring.

She leaned in, her face set in a fierce expression.

Peter leaned back.

"You. Didn't. Ask." Then she turned and stalked back to her place, tearing off a piece of Challah bread as she passed by the loaf.

A soft, "Oh," was all he was able to respond with.

Valerie managed to cover her laugh with a napkin, but it was a close thing.

"Henrietta?"

"Yes, Joshua?"

Valerie's uncle leaned down so that he was closer to eye level with the little angel.

"Is there a way to set the software into a self-maintaining, autonomous mode that will cut down how much those two..." He pointed to make it clear that the software was Peter and Michelle's problem, not his own. "...have to hover over it?"

"Sure!"

Michelle and Peter fell back in their seats as if they'd been slapped.

"Can you do that?"

"Sure!"

"Here?"

"Sure!" The angel kept agreeing cheerfully.

Valerie realized that this could go on for a while because while Henrietta might talk out of the box like there was no tomorrow, she didn't always think out of the box.

"Henrietta?"

The tiny angel took a big bite from her piece of bread and turned to face Valerie.

"Would you please go ahead and do whatever you need to and take care of it now?"

"Sure!" at least that's what Valerie conjectured she said around a mouthful of Challah bread.

The angel set down her bread and clapped her hands together.

At the sound of the small pop, a tiny computer console appeared in front of her, complete with a little table and a tiny vase holding a single, brilliantly yellow buttercup blossom.

She tapped away and the room grew quieter and quieter until the rattling of the tiny keys seemed to bounce off the walls.

Two white squares of plastic popped into existence, one hovering mid-air in front of Uncle Joshua, the other in front of Michelle.

"No!" Michelle pulled her hands back and tucked them in her armpits. "No way! The last time I palmed into this system, it didn't go so well."

"Sissy!" Valerie called out.

Plato started making clucking chicken noises, which soon the entire table had taken up.

Finally, with a groan of protest, Michelle slapped her palm on the plastic plate. "On your heads be it. To Heaven with all of you!"

Joshua laid his palm on the plate with only a slight wince.

Nothing happened.

Valerie closed her eyes, then opened them again. Nothing different that she could spot.

"Now," Henrietta leaned in reading the instructions scrolling up the screen. "Do you both solemnly swear that you are sick near unto death of managing the software?"

"Oh Me, YES!" Joshua and Michelle said in unison.

Henrietta hit the enter key. "Okay, that's done." She clapped her hands and the two palm scanners and the tiny computer popped out of existence, though the vase with the buttercup bloom now sat beside Henrietta's tea saucer.

Everyone looked at each other in stunned silence.

"That's it?" Plato was the first to find his voice.

"Sure," Henrietta shrugged her wings. "What, were you expecting a host of angels? I can call them if you like. They always—"

"No!" Was the resounding response.

Again Henrietta shrugged. Then she picked up a toothpick as if it were a spear, walked over to the roast beef platter, and stabbed up some scraps to return to her plate like a hunter from the African bush.

The laugh started low and nervous around the table. While it didn't build far, Valerie did notice how the nervous shook out and relief slid into its place.

Then there was an uncomfortable silence while no one knew quite what to say next. So they all watched Henrietta eating for a moment.

"Well," Valerie decided someone had to break the silence, it might as well be her. "Michelle."

"Valerie." Her friend looked up at her, an easy smile on her features. Valerie definitely was looking forward to getting to know more about her new friend, in this life and the next.

"Tell me something about my uncle, about God, that none of us know."

The Devil considered the ceiling for a long moment and then her smile grew.

"*Adonai Eloheinu, melekh ha'olam,* the Lord our God, King of the Universe," she raised her glass of wine in a toast to God, "cheats at Scrabble."

Eric almost snorted his wine out his nose as Anne's soft laugh confirmed the awful truth.

"But how can you cheat at Scrabble?" Even Plato was stumped by that one.

Michelle rubbed her hand along Plato's arm down to his hand and laced their fingers together.

She continued, "I had this great play. Triple word score, with a Q, J, and X all in the same word. I laid it out and he challenged me on it."

"I told her it wasn't in the dictionary," Joshua returned the toast and the smile. "That you couldn't have a Q that wasn't followed by a U."

"That was crazy talk. There was never any such rule. So while I'm off getting the dictionary…"

"He had me get on a computer terminal." Henrietta spoke from where she was getting ready to hurl her toothpick overhand to harpoon an olive floating in a small bowl. "I entered a new rule that in English you couldn't have a Q without a U after it."

"What was the word? What did it mean?"

Michelle shrugged and sipped her wine. "At that instant, the word ceased to exist, so."

Then she groaned and reached for another piece of cake. "It was worth like eighty points, too."

They all laughed together and enjoyed the rest of their evening, just sharing a meal with friends.

A few etymological notes:

ANNE —*from the Greek, meaning "a light"*
ERIC —*from the Old Norse, meaning "honor"*
JOSHUA —*from the Hebrew, meaning "The Lord is my salvation"*
MICHELLE —*French form of Michal, meaning "Who is like God?"*
RON —*from the Hebrew, meaning "joy." (Oy vey!)*
VALERIE —*from the French, meaning "to be strong"*

INDEX

About the Author

M. *L. Buchman has* over 40 novels in print. His military romantic suspense books have been named Barnes & Noble and NPR "Top 5 of the Year," nominated for the Reviewer's Choice Award for "Top 10 Romantic Suspense of 2014" by RT Book Reviews, and twice Booklist "Top 10 of the Year" placing two of his titles on their "The 101 Best Romance Novels of the Last 10 Years." In addition to romance, he also writes thrillers, fantasy, and science fiction.

In among his career as a corporate project manager he has: rebuilt and single-handed a fifty-foot sailboat, both flown and jumped out of airplanes, designed and built two houses, and bicycled solo around the world.

He is now making his living as a full-time writer on the Oregon Coast with his beloved wife. He is constantly amazed at what you can do with a degree in Geophysics. You may keep up with his writing and enjoy exclusive and free content by subscribing to his newsletter at www.mlbuchman.com.

Excerpt from:
Saviors 101:
First Book of the Reluctant Messiah

*D*ana Murphy hated the rusty old energy spells from her book *Tips and Tricks from the Gods*, they took so much work to resurrect. At fifteen, her mom's old one-speed Schwinn was still a bit tall for her to ride. But she could just manage it, and it was quite necessary tonight. Mama kept saying she'd been a late bloomer as well, but Dana was sure getting tired of the pancake-flat, knobby-knee look.

The bike complained as she leaned into the energy current along Seattle's Ravenna Boulevard. The streetlights shone down through the gaps in the ancient maples leaning over the street. Trees that drew constant complaints of sap and bird droppings from the owners of the BMWs and Audis that now lined the road.

Twenty laps. She'd have to go twenty laps around the neighborhood in a very specific pattern. That was assuming she'd properly reformulated the powers correctly for latitude, longitude, and era.

Dana knew she was different, but at two a.m. on a warm, fall night she was alone, which was her most comfortable way to be. At least she'd come by her role as a misfit honestly.

By the time Dana Murphy was five, she knew her red-haired, deeply-freckled mother was different. It wasn't the distracted air that sometimes led to Dana eating steaming hot meatloaf with baked potatoes and broccoli for breakfast, or cold, syrup-sodden pancakes sliding out of her Lisa Frank lunchbox at daycare.

It wasn't even the piano that played itself in the living room, though she'd never been able to find where it plugged in. All it had was pedals and scrolls of paper.

The first really weird thing was that there was no television or video games in the house. Her first after-daycare play date at Theresa Peterson's had included *Barney* and *Super Mario Brothers* which had greatly shaken her firm views on the sensibility of her universe. She hadn't gotten over it until six weeks later when she'd managed to whip Theresa's behind at her brother Sam's *Super Car Racer III*.

In fact, the only modern device her mother owned was a CD player which held five discs at a time and played music incessantly.

During her entire childhood, the house was never quiet.

She'd wake in the middle of the night to hear Frankie Avalon give way to Frankie Lane then Frank Sinatra and finally Frank Zappa.

She'd learned her alphabet by organizing her mother's massive collection by the artist's first name, and her mother played them in order from one end of the collection to the other. For the rest of her life Tina Turner's pelvis-thumping tones were a natural segue into Tiny Tim's ukulele. When they reached *Zydeco, the Last Twenty Years,* she knew that dancing together to ABBA was not far away.

Dana never got over the foreign feel of libraries, as if she'd walked into a world where the last-name-first shelving order had been designed by Salvador Dali.

No, what was really different about her mom was the quiet stream of people who came to visit her. Whispered counseling sessions in the back room that had been converted to a cozy office.

Dana'd learned early on, short of arterial hemorrhage or a significant outbreak of fire, she wasn't supposed to enter the rose-colored office when the door was closed.

That didn't mean she was above spying.

The old house had simple floor vents to heat the upstairs bedroom. The metal grates created a hole into the ceiling of the room below for heat to rise into the upstairs room. Dana would lie for hour upon hour on the hardwood floor spying down on her mother's treatment sessions. Buried beneath the big black quilt from her bed, Dana would stare down through the grate, enjoying the vague puff of warm air on her face.

All the scents her mother used would waft upward. Lavender candles. Almond massage oil. Incense. The sharp nose-tickling bite of burning sage between sessions.

Sometimes Mama's patients were partly clothed. Sometimes naked. Sometimes they were poked with needles. Sometimes smeared with salves. And sometimes, which were Dana's favorites, they lay there, fully clothed with a cloth over their eyes.

Mama would stand in her flowing caftan all radiant and beautiful at their side. The candlelight would make her pale skin and freckles all rich and warm. No jewelry. Her hair in its usual snarled ponytail behind her like a chestnut mare's mane teased bouffant by the wind, and she would wave her hands slowly above the person. Never touching them.

The people would relax, tense, twitch, just like Dana's string puppets, but she couldn't ever see the strings no matter how she squinted. Not until one night when her eyes had been really tired from a long afternoon of whipping Theresa's behind on *Doom* did she see the strings.

Her mother was unsnarling a long line of snagged white light above Mrs. Crane's left hip. Dana could see how it was all stuck right where there was a visual break of light in the bone. But she knew the real bone was whole because the woman had limped through the door just fine.

When she'd asked Mama later, she'd tried to change the subject. But five-year old persistence paid off.

Mrs. Crane had never gotten over a hip that she'd broken as a little girl and had healed wrong. Mama was straightening out the mess it had made in her energy. She pointed to a whole shelf of books with titles like: *Hands of Light, Energy Medicine,* and *The Subtle Body.* She wasn't sure what "subtle" meant, but they had really pretty covers and lots of pictures illustrating how to fix people without having to cut big holes in them. It made Dana proud of her mother. They were also the books she'd learned to read from.

But she knew that Theresa's mom, who served healthy snacks and whose dinners always tasted dinnerish, would never understand. And after Theresa had called her a liar and her mother a faker, she hadn't mentioned her mother again.

To anyone.

Other Books by this Author

Deities Anonymous
Cookbook from Hell: Reheated
Saviors 101

Thrillers
Swap Out!
One Chef!
Two Chef!

The Night Stalkers
The Night Is Mine
I Own the Dawn
Daniel's Christmas
Wait Until Dark
Frank's Independence Day
Peter's Christmas
Take Over at Midnight
Light Up the Night
Christmas at Steel Beach
Bring On the Dusk
Target of the Heart
Target Lock on Love
Christmas at Peleliu Cove
Zachary's Christmas

Firehawks
Pure Heat
Wildfire at Dawn
Full Blaze
Wildfire at Larch Creek
Wildfire on the Skagit
Hot Point

Delta Force
Target Engaged

Angelo's Hearth
Where Dreams are Born
Where Dreams Reside
Maria's Christmas Table
Where Dreams Unfold
Where Dreams Are Written

SF/F Titles
Nara
Monk's Maze